*For Virgin
In an
friend*

DAY OF THE DEMON

RANDY MCCHARLES

Day of the Demon

Copyright © 2016 Randy McCharles

First edition. All rights reserved. No part of this book may be reproduced or transmitted in any form or by any means, electronic or mechanical, including photocopying, recording or by any information storage & retrieval system, without written permission from the copyright holder, except for the inclusion of brief quotations in a review.

This is a work of fiction. Names, characters, places, and incidents are the products of the author's imagination or are used fictitiously and are not to be construed as real. Any resemblance to actual events, locales, organizations, or persons, living or dead, is entirely coincidental.

Cover art by Stephanie Tkach

ISBN: 1530366313
ISBN-13:978-1530366316

DEDICATION

This work is dedicated to my friend Rick Morrison, whose unpublished manuscript served as an inspiration for this novel.

ACKNOWLEDGMENTS

A special thanks to those writers and readers who provided feedback on various drafts, making this a much stronger work than it would be otherwise. Any errors or omissions are entirely the author's own.

DAY OF THE DEMON

The Dreams of a Child

Alethea came alert to the sound of laughter, shrill and hollow in the cool night air. With eyes closed, she shuddered, wishing the sounds away. When they persisted, she cracked open her eyes to see shadows swaying against the tent's canvas wall. The images were angular, showing no sharp edges, the pattern of two animals struggling together. More shrill laughter. They were not fighting.

The girl was her sister, Ilsa. The man could be any of the traders; they were all the same. Providence and little else kept them from her side of the tent, drunkenly demanding of her that which Ilsa gave so freely.

Knowing rest would not return, Alethea drew her blanket about her shoulders and crept outside. A dozen small fires illuminated the night, lighting her steps through a scattering of tents toward a stream that babbled a short distance from the camp. She had not taken ten steps when a rough hand caught her shoulder. A full, deep-throated voice accompanied the hand.

"Just where do you think you're going, missy? What's wrong? Can't bear to watch the others enjoy themselves?"

Alethea turned beneath the trader's grip. He was tall, wearing an open shirt without sleeves despite the chill spring air; a massive chest and thick-muscled arms glistened in the firelight. His head was shaved, with heavy brows the only hair on a brutish face pockmarked from excessive use of sageroot. Behind a broad, hooked nose, dark eyes leered at her.

"N—No, Lathan. I was going to the stream. To wash. That's all."

The trader glared at her. "I don't trust you, girl. You're too slippery."

Alethea struggled to free herself from the trader's grip, but his hand was too large, too strong. "Let me go, Lathan! I was just going to the stream."

Lathan laughed. "You can wash after we play. It's time you earned your keep around here. Your sister can't pay for the both of you forever."

Again she struggled. The trader's grip was like steel. In desperation, she kicked him in the shin.

Lathan stopped laughing and slapped Alethea hard across the face. Her head snapped to one side, her cheek burning from the blow.

"You'll pay dearly for that, girl!" He drew close and bore into her with his eyes, his sweating body potent with the stink of sage wine and sagcryl. His breath came in short, heavy gasps, as though his body were weighed down by the drug.

Alethea felt his mind reach toward her. Fury. Malice. Lust. An urgent need for satisfaction, for dominance. But her mental barriers were strong. Even with the drug, Lathan failed to break through. She felt him grow weak with the effort.

Finally, he spat into her face and pushed her away. "You think you're good, don't you? We'll see soon enough how you do with a man in your bed."

The moment the trader turned to storm off toward the tents, Alethea darted to the stream. Even as she ran, she felt his mind following, pushing at her barriers, reluctant to admit defeat. Then she heard him curse, and the probing was gone.

The night was quiet near the water's edge. Three of Sindarin's seven moons drifted like watchful gods across a sky bright with pinprick stars while the shallow stream near her feet babbled of peace and assurance, bringing to Alethea memories of a distant life, a time when she, Ilsa, and their mother had lived among those faithful to the Path of Arwyth.

It was there she had learned of the Elsian world and of the other way of Speaking True, the way without the drug. She had learned other things as well, good and wonderful things. Most wonderful of all was the knowledge that somewhere in the World of Spirits, a True-Friend waited, a being whose fondest wish was to speak with her and share its wisdom and confidence.

Then their mother died of fever and she and Ilsa sent south to live with a distant uncle who despised the Path and its restrictive precepts.

A shout from the camp distracted Alethea from her thoughts. Ilsa had run from their tent, her clothes left behind, auburn hair streaming in the night, laughing in the joy of her escape. Alethea knew that laugh well, a drug-induced cackle that deepened in the throat; a strained, husky sound that bore witness to the bondage of sagcryl. A man stumbled out behind her, swearing and cursing, his own mind ravaged by the drug. Chasing after his victim, he cast waves of pain before him in hopes of bringing her again into submission.

Ilsa grunted and stumbled, her mental barriers having never been strong even with the benefit of the drug.

The man seized her by the wrist and dragged her back to the tent. Ilsa laughed again.

They had been with Lathan for what seemed years but was only two months, their virtuous uncle having sold them to the first trader who would meet his price. Ostensibly, they were servants, to cook, clean, and fetch water and the like. Lathan and his men had more familiar duties in mind. But Alethea had learned much from the people of the Path. Her barriers were strong. As yet, none of the men had broken her. Ilsa, two years her senior, had not been so fortunate.

Twice, Alethea had run from the camp. The first time Lathan caught her, he beat her so severely that she lay in the tent she shared with Ilsa for five days, unmoving. The second time he poured sagcryl down her throat, the dose so strong that the drug-induced frenzy nearly killed her. Her sense of

True-Speech became so heightened and the chaos in her mind so intense, that she had pounded her head against the ground until consciousness left her. Alethea had not run away again. She did not like to think what Lathan might do for a third attempt.

She had always escaped the lusts of the men, though. When they could not dominate her mind through True-Speech, they were too humiliated to force her body. Yet they never gave up trying. Especially Lathan. Ilsa protected her too, by complying with their wishes when they let her younger sister be. Alethea agonized over Ilsa's circumstance, but knew there was little she could do. If she interfered, the men would have their way with them both. Each evening brought renewed dread that tonight she would be taken.

Alethea shuddered as a wave of malice brushed against her awareness; her barriers instinctively snapped into place. It had happened before, always when the men were drunk and more daring. But then she stumbled, almost falling. The wave's magnitude was too strong, and growing stronger, like water rising too high against a dam. Alethea braced herself and tried to clear her head, but her ears began ringing. It was as if her skull were being crushed. No man was this strong! Someone had taken an overdose of sagcryl and was directing his own agony against her. It was a deliberate attack.

Fighting the pain, Alethea reached out through True-Speech, seeking the source. Lathan! The tall trader lurched toward her from his tent, eyes wild, face feverish, his mouth a hellish grin.

"You're mine now, girly!" Lathan rasped, his voice so low it was little more than a grating sound. The trader's exposed skin folded and mottled from the drug. White sagcryl bled from his pores. He had torn his shirt in frenzy and cut his lip, but there was no blood; the drug prevented the wound from bleeding. Lathan's sagcryl-crazed mind pressed outward, stabbing with furious lust against her weakening barriers.

Alethea stumbled to her knees, crying out as the pressure against her skull became more than she could bear. Her thoughts grew jumbled, pieces of memory bubbling up to distract her from the pain. Her mother, unmoving and peaceful on her deathbed. Her uncle's cruel smile. Lathan pouring sagcryl down her throat. Ilsa crying in the night. A white-clad Circle Elder speaking: Through a True-Friend, strength might be drawn from the Elsian world. Alethea groaned. She had never found her True-Friend.

The trader's hands, red and rough from the drug that ate at his skin, touched her shoulders, knocking away the blanket and clutching Alethea's shift. An overpowering stench, stronger than tannery acid, ate at the soft tissues of her nose and mouth. She reached up to beat at his arms, the meager pain she inflicted lost amid the agony of the drug.

Then everything stopped. The pain. The nausea. The horror inside her mind. The fumbling grip on her flesh. Lathan lay on the ground, his eyes closed in forced sleep.

Ilsa stood over him, a large stone in her hand. Her eyes were hazy with sagcryl, perhaps a hundredth of what Lathan had taken. She crouched beside the trader and felt his wrist. "Demon's Blood! He's still alive. And the mottling on his face! He's no better than a Skin-Runner."

"Ilsa, I..." Confusion infused Alethea's mind; words would not come.

"You'll have to go now," Ilsa said. "Leave the camp. Lathan won't be satisfied until you're his slave."

"Go?" Alethea dragged herself to her feet and stared at her sister. "Go where? What about you?"

Ilsa also stood, tossing the rock into the bushes. "I'll be all right. I have an alibi in the tent. Lathan will never know who hit him. With that much sagcryl in him, he may never know he was hit. But it is no longer safe for you here. The men have lost patience with you."

As hard as her sister's words were, Alethea knew them for truth. If not Lathan again tomorrow, it would be one of the others. They'd taken to using stronger doses of sagcryl in recent days. Only now, with Lathan lying unconscious at her feet, his skin mottled like a snake's, did Alethea realize she was the cause. The men meant to break her. She could no longer stay with the traders. Despite earlier failed attempts at flight, she would have to try again.

Alethea's eyes sought those of her sister in the frail light. "You have to come with me. You refused before, and I couldn't make it on my own. Together, I know we can do it."

Ilsa shook her head; long auburn hair swirled about her face, hiding her eyes. "There is nothing for me out there. I'd only hook up with another band of traders. No, I'll stay. Maybe I can convince Lathan not to chase after you, or I can mislead him. But both of us gone? He'd follow us to the Demons' Pit, just to kill us."

They'd had this argument before, always with the same outcome. On most things, Alethea understood her sister, but not this resolve to stay with Lathan. "Where will I go?" Alethea demanded. "How will I live?"

"Go to Toroth and the Circle of Elders," Ilsa suggested. "The Path is a kinder prison than Lathan's tents. Or find that True-Friend you so desperately believe in. Or seek out the Circle's Black Sheep, Minesh. He can give you better advice than I."

And here it was, the familiar impasse. Ilsa insisting that Alethea go but refusing go with her. And when Alethea responded that she needed guidance, Ilsa steered her on the one course she herself had rejected all her life— the Path of Arwyth.

And once again, Alethea reached her own impasse. No matter how she hated and feared Lathan and his men, she did not want to leave Ilsa. Yes, she wanted her freedom. To leave the traders. To follow the Path and find her True-Friend. But not at the cost of her sister. Ilsa was all she had. And, Alethea forced herself to admit, she did not want to be alone. She had never been alone. Alethea's eyes wandered down to Lathan's prone body. *Am I strong enough to submit to these men, so that I can stay with Ilsa?*

Her sister seemed to know Alethea's thoughts. "The price is too high, sister. I was a fool to pay it. Now I live with the pain, the compromise, the hunger for the drug. You are wiser, Alethea. Go and be free."

"Come with me then!" Alethea cried. "We can be free

together."

Ilsa laughed, her voice still deep from the drug. "It is too late for that. I have made myself into what I am. There is no going back."

Alethea shook her head. "You're wrong! You're lying!"

"Am I? Do you wish to see what I am?" Ilsa dropped her barriers and leered at her, an unwholesome animal grin.

Alethea held her breath. They had not shared minds since they were children, and she feared to see what her sister had become. But how could she leave? How could she think of leaving, without knowing? Tentatively, she reached out through True-Speech. What she saw tore at her heart.

First, there were men— scores of greedy eyes, drooling lips, and groping hands. The stink of sagcryl fouled the air, with deep, rasping groans too close to the ear, the noise of a lover in frenzy. Alethea grew ill as the volume rose inside her head. She had been with a man before, but not like this. Never like this.

Then came the loneliness, and ugliness, the constant search for something or someone to relieve the self-loathing, and the sure knowledge that there was no hope, no release. That she was a tool for those disgusting enough to use her, those who knew what she was and relished in it, cheapening her all the more. Violating not just her body, but her soul. Reaching into her very being and stealing away the fondest memories, the most precious dreams, the most fervent hopes, until nothing remained but emptiness. Enough so that she often cried out for death, but had not the strength to embrace it.

Alethea turned away. She could look no more. Tears spilled from her eyes. Ilsa touched her arm, her own cheeks wet. They embraced, each sharing the other's grief. Alethea, the horror of her sister's life and the pain of leaving her. Ilsa, the sorrow of letting go. Through True-Speech, Alethea could feel her sister's pain, could almost understand her need to stay.

"You must go now," Ilsa whispered.

Alethea nodded and wiped at her eyes with the back of her hand. "Will the Circle take me in? Will Minesh teach a girl? I don't even know where to find him."

"All men know the manea sits at Herlen's council, but he is also rumored to roam the Cambre Hills. You will never pass the Tower Guard at Toroth. Better to try the wilderness."

"But how will I live? What of tree-lynxes? And snakes?"

"Wait here," Ilsa told her, then crept back to the tents. She returned carrying a shoulder pack of field clothing and a slender, cloth-wrapped bundle.

Alethea dressed while her sister opened the bundle.

"It's a plasteel knife from one of the men," Ilsa told her. "How that Demon's son got hold of a relic from the Settling is a question likely answered by murder."

The sheathed blade felt light in Alethea's hands, lighter than an ordinary knife. As sharp as steel and unbreakable, if the stories were true.

"Tie it close to your side," Ilsa instructed, "concealed beneath your clothes. Don't let anyone see it. The knife is valuable and men will take it from you. And put mud on your face. You're too pretty."

Alethea strapped the blade beneath her tunic, cinching the leather buckle tight. The belt was much too big and looped twice around her narrow waist. "Whose knife is this?"

Ilsa scowled. "Lathan's. He owes it for the trouble he's caused you."

"What about your troubles?" Alethea demanded.

"He could never repay me for that."

"He'll hurt you for taking the knife, Ilsa. Why are you doing this?"

Ilsa dropped her eyes. "You are the purest thing I have. The only thing. I—I'll take pride in knowing you are safe."

Alethea clutched her sister's wrists. "You can still come with me."

"No," Ilsa shook her head. "I can never do that. There's nothing for me out there."

"Why?" Alethea demanded. "Do you desire the camps so much?"

"Yes!" The wildness in Ilsa's eyes made Alethea step back. Her sister's hand flew to a pocket, retrieved four round pellets of sagcryl.

Alethea shook her head, knowing what her sister planned. "No!"

Ilsa swallowed, and it was too late to turn back. "You will have to go alone now," Ilsa told her. "I've taken a strong dose and will reach frenzy quickly. I—I wouldn't be good company."

Alethea's eyes welled with tears even as her fingers balled into fists. She wanted to scream at what her sister had done.

"Will you hate me now?" Ilsa asked. "Even as we say goodbye?"

Alethea dropped her eyes and leaned forward to embrace her sister. Ilsa's response was awkward. Already the drug was taking hold. By the light of the three moons, Alethea could see the skin on Ilsa's neck grow rough and mottled. Ilsa Spoke to her True, using the faculty that, for her, came only when she used the drug. Alethea knew she would not speak with her voice; already it would be deepening.

Words echoed in Alethea's mind. "Don't look upon me now, sister. Remember what it is you seek, not what you leave behind. My heart will be alive in yours. Don't fail us both."

"Please," Alethea insisted, Speaking directly to her sister's mind, knowing it was no use. "Come with me."

Ilsa took in a deep breath and the shook her head. "I am not like you. If I leave the camps, I'll have nothing. The camps are all I have left. Now go."

Releasing her sister, Alethea fled, crossing the small stream into the forest beyond. After a few steps, she stopped and turned to watch Ilsa stumble back to the camp. Already she was half-animal.

Alethea reached out with her mind for one last touch, but the overdose of sagcryl had so sensitized Ilsa's mental barriers that Alethea almost cried out. Ilsa turned, snarling in a voice more like a beast's than a young woman's. Without warning, she dropped her barriers and Alethea saw her sister's emotions warped out of control by the drug.

Alethea gasped and fled, running almost blind through the trees. She ran from the animal her sister had become, from the animal circumstance would make of her own wretched life if she stayed. She ran from Lathan and his men, who were animals even without sagcryl. Most of all, she ran from the pain, the twisted, insatiable passions that were the legacy of the drug.

$$\Omega$$

Ilsa stopped outside the tent she had shared with her sister and turned in the direction Alethea had gone. That way led to freedom, she hoped. A freedom of mind and body that she herself could never know. A freedom she prayed to the spirits — spirits she had never prayed to before — that Alethea would find. Almost, she wished she had had the courage to follow her.

And in the world of Elsian beings, a single soul gazed down upon Ilsa's shaking body as in tears the ill-fated young woman sank to the ground and howled like a tormented beast. How she longed to reach out and touch that troubled mind with the message that all is not sorrow, all is not lost. For as Alethea ran, so ran the dreams of a child. And in that dream, despite all other sorrows, there remained hope.

Teacher of the Rites

Atop the high escarpment known as Land's End, the manea of Sindarin stood, considering. Though icy winds buffeted against him, Minesh scarce noticed. The cold was nothing. The wind, a constant companion. The dizzying heights held no terror. He had stood at this place through more winters than he could remember and his surroundings were as familiar to him as his thoughts. And yet...

At the manea's feet sat the object of his consideration. His pupil comported himself cross-legged on the cold stone of the cliff, arms resting on his thighs, back straight, head held ridged. His gaze stared unseeing into the late winter haze of the distant horizon. The youth's bearing carried a haughtiness that challenged even the weather.

Minesh frowned and shook his head. At sixteen winters,

Prince Corin was as able-bodied as any boy his age. He had spent a good portion of his youth ahorse or afoot and bore a mended bone or two. His father, King Herlen, had seen to that. And yet, by all that was worst in a prince, Corin still held himself above other men, as if by consequence of birth he was somehow better than his fellows. A scion of privilege rather than leadership. His father had failed to remedy this defect. The Circle, Minesh noted with distaste, had likewise failed.

"You strain, Corin." Minesh strove to keep his voice dispassionate despite his growing disappointment. "You try too hard."

A burst of air rushed from Corin's lungs and he snapped his head around. Thick locks of coal-black hair whipped about his neck and shoulders. From between clenched teeth, his breath surged in frosted puffs. Gray-blue eyes, cold as winter, glared with choler. "Can you read me so exactly, Minesh? Can you truly gauge my efforts?"

"And you question too quickly," Minesh added. "You have too much pride."

"Who are you to tell me—?"

The boy cut off his complaint as Minesh moved away, passing his gaze to an ice-frosted webwood bush that sparkled like silver lace in the fading sunlight. "You will never master True-Speech, Corin. Not until you learn to control your passions. I begin to think myself a fool for even listening to the Circle. Perhaps they were wrong about you."

The Prince was on his feet in an instant, thrusting himself between Minesh and the fragile plant, uncaring that several of the delicate branches shattered as his soft, lamb's wool cloak brushed against them.

"Perhaps it is you who are at fault, manea. You followers of Arwyth seem to think yours is the only path." The boy's eyes took on a hint of smugness, the impudent student educating the teacher. "There are many ways to rule among men, and there are other means by which to master True-Speech."

"Dolt." Minesh frowned at the icy fragments of webwood at Corin's feet, no longer glittering, some crushed to dust beneath the Prince's calfskin boots. Corin's was an argument he had heard all too often. The manea's answer came without effort, words he had used a thousand times. "Only by Arwyth's Path may one master the vigors of both mind and body. By any other path, you become the servant of those you touch."

Corin's face flushed red. "I am no one's servant!" He ground his teeth, his lips curling into a snarl; a loathsome trait Minesh noted was common among Herlen's line. "And I have gained many skills without adhering to your rules."

Minesh leaned forward, pressing Corin against the webwood, its shattered branches sharp as knives where they jabbed into the Prince's back. "Why then, do you shrink from the Hest? You delay too long, Corin. Perhaps you are less prepared than you claim."

The boy fidgeted where the webwood dug into his coat, and his voice lost much of its bluster. "A prince of Sindarin shrinks from nothing. My father would not have sent me were I not capable. I am ready to take your rites."

Minesh backed away, leaving Corin to untangle himself from the broken webbing of the tree. He was tired of the games these young ones played, tired of their arrogance. Why do the young feel they know so much? They who have barely tasted life! He again regarded Herlen's eldest son. Too many years he had administered the rites. Too many years and too many kings' sons!

Dismayed, Minesh reached out in True-Speech, seeking the world beyond the Shroud. Contact with his True-Friend came smooth and quick, restoring his inner peace. "He is so young, Galin. Sometimes I think I'm just wasting my time."

A familiar voice whispered within the manea's mind, calm, full, and at once intimate yet impossibly distant. "You must not despair, Minesh. Even should his mastery come not by your hand, still you must be patient. He is trying."

"But with such pride!" objected Minesh. "Even should he succeed, he may misuse his gift. And pride is but one of his failings. His attempts at True-Speech are awkward, clumsy."

Galin's laughter echoed hollowly. "I recall your manea saying the same of you."

Minesh let that pass. "Suppose the Hest rejects him?"

"That has happened before."

"I wish an end to this," Minesh grumbled. "The strain is beginning to tell on me."

"Give him the rites, Minesh. Give him the Hest. Let him find his own path."

"Haven't you shown off enough?"

The interruption came from outside Minesh's thoughts. Corin had untangling himself from the webwood and now stood glaring at him.

"You see, Galin. He taunts me even now."

"The deer will change that," answered Galin. "Pride, when mastered, engenders strength. Give him the rites."

Minesh broke from True-Speech to stare into the cold, steel-gray eyes of the young Prince of Sindarin. Corin's was a proud family with a proud history, each heir having mastered True-Speech without submitting to the drug, each having learned wisdom and the value of the soul. All but this one. By his outward appearance, Corin was an admirable young man: determined, confident, a born leader. But when Minesh looked past Corin's barriers, what he saw was the heart and soul of a wanderer, a man not fit to rule anything.

It was at times like these that Minesh wished he had chosen another profession. Or that another profession had chosen him. Without giving answer to his charge, the manea turned and began picking his way among the pines and detritus of the plateau.

A Prince of Sindarin

Corin made no move to follow, but stood, numb hands balled into fists. Angry thoughts screamed through his mind.

Such insolence is intolerable! Not even the Circle in Toroth dares treat me so. Does the manea not know who I am? Father would never permit such mistreatment. Hest rites! What has any of the Circle's mysticism to do with the Square? Strong laws and strong law-keepers are what maintain order. Why does the Square tolerate it?

He'd have words to that effect with his father when he returned to Toroth. Two weeks with Minesh at the end of civilization and what had it bought him besides frostbitten toes? How much longer would the old man keep him?

A gust of wind rose, slamming into Corin and shrieking through the tumbled rock of the escarpment with a mocking cry. Corin froze and peered about the empty landscape, half expecting to see a ghost or a shade of the spirit with whom Minesh had spoken. It was said that spirits beyond the Shroud could penetrate a man's barriers and read his thoughts. Superstition. Still, what if Minesh's True-Friend had heard his disrespect and shared that knowledge with the manea? It was one thing to crow and bluster. That is expected of a prince. But to divulge his innermost thoughts? And if the spirits could penetrate his barriers...?

Finding nothing with his eyes, Corin reached out with his mind, awkwardly employing his undisciplined faculty of True-Speech. The wind responded with another mocking cry.

Demons! If a man's own thoughts can echo from the mountaintops, what privacy do any of us have?

Head down, Corin left the ridge and trudged back among the broken scree, following the narrow track the manea had taken. Again he listened with True-Speech, but heard only the wind. *Is my talent so deficient that none will hear me? Or is mine the greater test, because I am the son of a king?*

Not even the wind answered.

He found Minesh waiting outside the shelter, a small metal hutch so lichen-encrusted that a casual glance passed it off as a weathered boulder. The hutch was one of two surviving shelters not made of stone or wood, shelters brought to Sindarin on the colony ship.

Corin swelled with pride as he compared the Circle's tiny hutch to the magnificent Dome of the Ancients in Toroth's Sanctuary Park. The Dome, a hulking repository of pre-settlement artifacts, belonged to the Square, Sindarin's governing body. And who was the Square, if not Corin's father?

The manea's hutch was a decrepit shed in comparison,

hidden away in the wilderness, forgotten by all save the Circle and those few outside the Circle who took the rites, either by choice or by the demands of custom.

Legend claimed the hutch had stood in the Cambre wilderness since the time of The Settling, two thousand years ago. Legend also claimed that Minesh had lived there just as long, though Corin's father believed Minesh was two hundred years old, not two thousand, and his father was no fool. No, there had been maneas before Minesh. The hutch was merely the refuge of the Circle's Final Teaching.

How Corin wished an end to his Final Teaching. In not many years, his father would step down from the Square, and there was much Corin would do before taking his father's place. Freezing in the emptiness of Cambre was not one of them. His sole consolation was his decision to end this useless tradition of sending heirs to the Circle. It would be his first act when he became king. For now, however, the Circle's Final Teacher stood waiting for him, the manea's ancient face set in a frown as cold and bitter as the wind.

"And whose creed do you follow, young prince?" the manea demanded, his voice hard and unfeeling. "That you would seek beyond the Shroud without aid of sageroot and crysalis? Who are you to invoke the Elsan to your petition while turning a deaf ear to those who would instruct you?"

Corin's first impulse was to lash out, remind the old fool to whom he spoke, but the manea was an enigma. Like the Circle Elders, Minesh had lived the life of many lifetimes. Unlike the Elders, he held himself above the law. No command would stay his tongue. No assertion of rank would bend his knee. Instead, Corin tried a different tack. "Am I to shame my father? And the Elders? Do you wish to be the one who reports to them my failure?"

The manea made no answer, but turned and walked the last few yards to the shelter. Corin watched his hand dart out to brush the hidden lock. Solar motors whirred to life and, with a soft flushing of air, a narrow doorway opened. Inside, a small cot filled one side of the hutch while two chairs and a fog table, its flat, rounded surface gleaming with translucence, took up the remaining space.

Corin sat in one of the chairs as the door slid shut with a soft thud. Silence filled the hutch and the fog table cast a greenish glow, the windowless chamber's only light. The manea's ancient face appeared lined and craggy in the gloom, otherwordly. Corin always felt uncomfortable when Minesh brought him here.

To Corin's knowledge, the manea's hutch held the only solar motors on Sindarin, though he assumed the Dome of the Ancients must also have them, unused in two thousand years. Minesh had described their workings with a certain pride, smiling foxlike when he explained that the Hunters could not detect them. Minesh's True-Friend had told him so. Corin was tired of hearing about Minesh's True-Friend.

The manea lowered himself into the remaining chair and scowled at Corin, a hard expression that few apart from Corin's father dared. The old man's hand disappeared from view and the fog table misted from green to blue as from its center a gleaming blade of polished crystal emerged. The shard was long and thin, blunt at the bottom and rising to a single sharp point, like an inverted icicle with its sides filed flat. And, like an icicle in intense sunlight, it seemed to glow with a peculiar brightness all its own. Corin had never seen anything like it.

The manea smiled, the worn lines of his face curling around taunt lips as he took the shard into his hands and turned it slowly, as one might a prized jewel.

Corin failed to suppress the awe in his voice. "Is that the Hest?"

The manea did not take his eyes from the blade. "Had you worked at your studies you would have no need to ask."

Indignation replaced awe. "Don't rouse my anger, old man. If you know my mind, you know also that I don't believe the old tales. Even women laugh at them."

Minesh's voice remained cold. "Do not mock the sisters of Sindarin, Corin. Among them are many who have followed Arwyth's Path to discover their True-Friend. They could teach you much of the truthfulness of the Legends."

Corin snorted. "Truth! Your precious Path is nothing but a children's story; rules to control my life. What about what I want?"

Minesh stopped turning the blade and his expression darkened, yet his voice remained steady, irritating Corin further. "You have not listened, Corin. You must listen to hear the truth."

"Listen?" Corin had done nothing but listen for two full weeks. "To who? These spirits you speak with don't see fit to speak with me. Am I to spend my entire life chasing spectral voices and mythic fables?"

The old man shook his head. "You must exercise faith to earn knowledge."

"I do have faith." Corin hammered a finger against his own chest. "I believe in myself. And what I know to be real."

Minesh set the blade back on the fog table, his hands seeming reluctant to release the crystal. "You believe in nothing, Corin. And you know nothing."

Corin choked on the words. No one spoke to him this way. No one. Not even his father. He searched for a scathing retort, and came up short. "This?" he demanded. "From you? A manea who can't even teach the King's son the skills that are rightfully his."

The attack came without warning, a wave of brutal force far stronger than any of the earlier exercises. Corin threw up his barriers as Minesh had taught him, yet the mental shield shattered like brittle glass before the old man's onslaught. Pain exploded behind Corin's eyes, reaching through his entire being. The manea's wrath gripped his soul. For one brief moment, existence was agony.

Then Minesh released his grip and Corin sagged sideways, sliding onto the hutch's floor. Through muddled senses he felt the old man haul him to his feet and pull his face in close. The manea's eyes were frosty daggers as he renewed his attack, this time, thankfully, with words.

"Fool! Stronger men than you have died for thoughts like yours. Herlen has spoiled you. He's raised a puppy, not a prince!" The old man released Corin and turned away.

Corin steadied himself and straightened his clothes. Anger pulsed in his veins, competing now with fear, an emotion Corin had little familiarity with. Minesh's attack had toppled him like dry grass. He swallowed blood, having bitten his lip during the attack, and glared at the manea. Nails cut into palms as he clenched his fists. "I will be your king!"

"Not if I reject you," the old man murmured. "If you would be king, you must earn the right."

Corin stood speechless, his mind reeling with Minesh's words. His father's family had governed Sindarin since the Time of the Settling, the leadership of the Square passing unchallenged from generation to generation. The Circle had no power to dictate law. His father heard their counsel as a courtesy and, admittedly, rarely heeded it. Still, Corin sensed truth in the manea's words, and recalled his father's insistence that shirking the Circle's rites was not an option. Looking back, there had been worry in his father's voice. Could the manea's words be more than empty threat?

Slumping back into his chair, Corin lowered his face to hide his anger. "I'm sorry," he said. "I had no right."

"No, you did not," the manea agreed, turning toward him. "Always remember that. You have no rights in either world until you find your place within yourself."

"Will you still administer the rites?" It took every effort to speak the words.

"Would your father expect any less?"

Corin flinched. "I don't need his permission. I am my own man."

The manea snorted and sat down. "That is still a subject of debate, Corin. You are no one's man until you learn to conquer your passions. Only when you command the halls of your own mind will you become a man. And even that is just a beginning."

Keeping his eyes lowered, Corin gritted his teeth. "I was wrong."

"The three most important words you will ever learn. Listen to them. Repeat them often."

Composing his face into a stone mask, Corin looked up at

the manea, and saw instead the shard resting on the table between them. The fog table glowed red now, but the light surrounding the crystal remained white and pure. This was really going to happen. "Will the touch of the Hest sting?"

"Will you shrink from it if it does?"

Beneath the table, Corin tightened his hands into fists. "I wish to prepare."

The manea's voice dulled to a whisper. "Then begin by believing those foolish legends and all that study you took without thought. Search your memory for the stories, Corin. Listen to the truths they contain."

Corin felt anger return to his face. "You are telling me to have the faith of a child. I am a man now."

The manea sighed. "Is it such a terrible thing to be a child?"

Corin's gaze swept past the blade to find the old man rolling up his sleeve. The manea's arm was thin and pale. A wide pucker two inches long scared his wrist— the mark of the Hest.

"Bare your arm," Minesh said.

Corin found he couldn't move. He looked from the manea's scar to the blade then back again.

"Are you afraid?" the manea asked.

Corin gave no answer.

"You must bear the mark if you would bear the Hest. Do not fear it, Corin. When you have sought and found your True-Friend, he will help you carry the burden."

"How?" Corin demanded. "How will I find him?" For two weeks he had sat in the bitter wind, peering through a shroud he couldn't see for a spirit he couldn't find.

"He will reveal himself at the appointed time, after you have proven your worth."

"When is that? Don't you know? If the time is appointed?"

"You mock me, Corin. If you persist with this attitude the surge of the Hest will strike deep; perhaps so deep you cannot bear it. Clear your mind of doubt, Corin. Open yourself to the blade."

It was too late to back down. Corin's father had sent him on this fool's errand, and if he came back a failure he would shame not only himself but his father as well. Corin ground his teeth and rolled back his sleeve, then watched as the manea reached forward and took up the Hest. The old man's fingers gripped the blunt end, turning the sharp point toward Corin.

"You will learn humility now, Herlen's son. Take hold of the blade!"

Corin found his hand moving forward almost of its own accord. As though in response, the crystal shard flared with a brilliant white light. Instinctively, Corin pulled back his hand.

The manea's voice fell to a whisper. "Where is your courage now, young fool? Is the Prince of Sindarin a coward?"

Corin thrust out his hand, answering the challenge. But as his fingers wrapped around the crystal shard, pride twisted into pain. "I—I can't let go. It burns!"

"As it should," the manea murmured. "As it should."

The Beast

Minesh maintained his grip on the blunt base of the blade as Corin struggled. He could read frustration in the boy's face. Recalled that same expression in the face of the Prince's father and in his father before him, and in all the others he had trained. He remembered also his own first touch, so many, many years ago, when it was he who sat in Corin's chair. Almost, he felt again the power of that first encounter with the Hest, the sheer helplessness it had engendered. Yet he felt no pity for the Prince. He had warned and Corin had scoffed, refusing to believe.

Will your disbelief help you now, Corin? What secret passions and unacknowledged frailties will the Hest reveal to you? Can you doubt, behind the pain, the overwhelming pain, that your very soul is being laid bare before the Elsan beyond the Shroud? And after that, after even that, the Hest may still reject you.

Abruptly, the Hest surged forward in Minesh's hand. The

manea watched Corin's eyes widen as the sharp crystal slid through his fingers, up past the heel of his palm, and then buried itself in the Prince's forearm just above the wrist. The boy cried out and memory recognized the agony young Corin must now be experiencing.

"Yield to the Hest!" Minesh rasped. "Let the shard take you!"

Corin cried out. "The pain... Take it away!"

Anger flared through the manea. "You stupid boy! Do you wish the blade to take your mind or your life? Decide quickly or the Hest will decide for you!"

The Prince's arm throbbed with light where the shard had entered. Though the incision gaped open, no blood flowed from the wound. The crystal hummed with power from within Corin's flesh, filling the hutch with its presence.

Reaching out through True-Speech, Minesh found the Prince's thoughts scattered. If Corin did not find his center soon, Herlen would have one fewer son. "Submit to the shard!" Minesh shouted, hammering his thoughts into the youth's mind. "Relent, or the Hest will destroy you!"

Corin's reply came as a scream. "I can't! The burning!"

"You fight it. Give in or it will be too late!"

Corin opened his mouth but no sound came. Even as the fire of the Hest threatened to overwhelm him, a wave of bitter cold washed through the hutch, and a stench like a thousand rotting corpses infused the air. Dark shadows shifted about the room, eclipsing the light of the fog table. Minesh sensed an alien malevolence within the shadows, an entity that sought to destroy not just the light but the Prince as well.

The manea swore and flung a warning through the Shroud. "No! The Beast cannot prevail! Galin, you must stop him!" Then he launched his mind toward Corin, pitting his will against the dark force that sought to overwhelm the boy.

The malevolence he found in Corin's mind was at once familiar and abhorrent. It had been years since Minesh had last encountered the Beast, at which time his friends in the Elsian world had overpowered and confined it. Since then he had administered the rites without challenge. Minesh had not prepared for the possibility of a confrontation. That the Beast returned now was misfortune on a deadly scale.

In the few moments that had passed, the small shelter had grown dark with shadow. Ice sheeted the walls and the still air reeked with corruption. In Corin's untrained mind, the Beast prevailed. If aid did not arrive soon, Minesh and the Prince both would die.

"I cannot find him," Galin answered from beyond the Shroud. "The Beast is no longer contained in the pit."

"Never mind that!" Minesh shouted. "Link quickly! The boy is being taken!"

As his True-Friend reached out from the Elsian world, Minesh sucked in great mouthfuls of air. The instant their minds touched, strength surged into him from beyond the Shroud. How many Galin had helping him, Minesh couldn't even guess; they were not few. As darkness fled, the shard within Corin's arm flared like an exploding sun and the Prince jerked in his seat, crying out as the Hest's touch surged with renewed life. Minesh observed the Prince's mind through True-Speech and saw that he was now too exhausted to fight. Corin had no choice but to give himself over to the Hest. It was enough. The Prince was out of danger.

Minesh left him and again reached out to his True-Friend. "Can it be another?"

"I think not, Minesh. I recognize his manner. Arazmud is free."

"And you did not foresee this? The Prince could have been taken!"

Galin's answer was hesitant. "We have known that Arazmud would escape eventually. We did not expect it so soon."

"Then we have all been ill prepared," Minesh admitted.

The manea passed his gaze about the hutch and found the Hest resting once again on the table. Corin sat crumpled in his chair, exhausted but alive. A quick examination found the Prince's mind undamaged. A little worse for wear, perhaps, but finer for the experience. Furthermore, Corin knew nothing of the Beast that had threatened him. From what little he did remember, the Demon attack had seemed a facet of the rites. That was probably just as well.

"Will he come again?" Minesh asked.

"I think not," replied Galin. "Many now watch over the rites. No one will interfere."

"I hope not. I no longer have the strength for these surprises."

"You grow old, Minesh, but you cannot rest yet. You know as well as I what the Beast may portend."

"What? The Mastren? It is too soon."

"Perhaps. Perhaps not."

Minesh returned his gaze to the slumped form of the Prince. The Legend of the Mastren was quite specific; he would come when the Beast was free. Of course, the Beast had been free many times. Twice now in Minesh's own lifetime. The Mastren had not come then. Why should he come now?

And yet...

Legends

With excruciating slowness, Corin pieced together that he was still alive. At least, he assumed death could never hurt this much. His entire being consisted of darkness and pain surging in icy waves across a storm-ravaged sea. Thin bands of red streaked through the darkness, spectral lightning in the night sky. Waves of agony crashing against an unseen shore.

Boom.

Boom.

Boom.

A calm, inner voice told him the waves were a heartbeat. His heartbeat.

"Corin? Are you well?"

The words came from within yet outside himself, from somewhere beyond the pain. *My True-Friend?* The brief hope died with the realization that the True-Spoken words were Minesh's. Doubt returned. Did the Elsian world even exist?

Darkness gave way to the pale cloudy light of the fog table

and Corin raised his head, wincing as the rhythmic pain intensified with the movement. "I—I was wrong about the Legends," he whispered, reluctant to admit that the Hest, if nothing else, was very real. "I'm sorry." This time he meant it.

"Don't be sorry." The manea sounded amused. "Be glad. The Hest has accepted you."

"Then... it's over?" Corin remembered the shard entering his arm, then ice that burned. Pain like he had never experienced, even when he had sliced open his hand in the practice yard. He would accept a hundred sword cuts before experiencing the Hest again.

Minesh pursed his lips. "It's a beginning. The Hest has accepted you. Now you must accept the Hest."

"Not again!" Corin cringed as the old man picked up the crystal blade and caressed its gently glowing edges with his fingers. "I—I couldn't stand it."

"The Hest takes you but once," the manea said, his gruff voice gentle with assurance. "Have no fear. You will feel it link with your mind as you would reading another man." Minesh again offered the crystal, this time blunt end first.

Corin hesitated, and then reached out with his fingers. The Hest answered by extending its glow to envelop his hand. Corin winced in expectation, but no pain came. Then his fingers touched the blade.

The power of the shard entered Corin, not a burning now but a light and an energy that filled his mind, illuminating every avenue of his thoughts. It was as Minesh said, True-Speech with another mind, a mind without barriers. Corin had never felt so clear a connection.

Only it was himself he was reading, something he had never thought possible. And for the first time in his sixteen years of life, Corin knew himself. He could see the inner workings of his mind, how ideas and responses percolated through the clutter of his memory and inherent biases to become finished thoughts that were truly and uniquely his own. Corin frowned as he gazed into soiled corners of his mind that he had never suspected and would prefer not to have seen. *Am I really so cold and arrogant?* But he saw other parts of himself as well that afforded greater pride.

The presence of a second mind nudged his awareness; Minesh had joined him. Not an attack this time, but a sharing. And not just with him but with the shard. Still, Corin's mental barriers snapped into place of their own accord and his private thoughts remained his own. Minesh, too, had barriers in place, far stronger and more abiding.

Gazing outward, Corin saw the fog table mist to yellow. But a second light illuminated the room; the shard in his hand burned with a pure white flame. Across the table, the scar on Minesh's arm opened up and a specter of light escaped his flesh, merging with that of the Hest. Fear gripped Corin as he noticed for the first time the wide gash across his own arm, fresh and clean in the radiant light. Then heat, not an icy burning but a glowing warmth, flushed his arm and the gash opened, yielding its own arrow of light to join with the Hest.

Corin's thoughts reeled. Wounds let blood not light. He glanced at Minesh, but the manea's stolid expression offered no explanation. In Corin's hand the crystal shard glowed, and in that glow he sensed an intelligence.

He was still trying to fathom what that might mean when he noticed two men and a woman standing in the cramped space of the hutch, each bearing the mark of the Hest. Their faces were grim but the set of their jaw and the depth of their eyes bore a confidence and a wisdom that alluded to a high purpose. Corin stared as bands of light reached out from their forearms to join with the crystal.

Minesh gasped and Corin turned to see the manea's eyes widened. He tried to read the old man, to find some answer to what was happening, but the manea's barriers prevented him. With controlled urgency, Minesh took the crystal blade and set it back on the table. His hand darted out of view and the shard descended into its hidden compartment. The fog table misted back to green and Corin realized that the lights and the three visitors were gone.

"Who—?" he began.

"Not with your mouth, Prince. Use your mind." The manea leaned back in his chair, his face expressionless in the gloom.

Corin hesitated. He didn't know where to start. So many questions. Would his True-Speech be different? Better? Had the Hest changed him in some profound way? He extended his mind and easily found the manea; he sat two feet away, after all. The awkwardness of the contact was familiar, however; Corin's ability seemed in no way improved. "Those people. Spirits? Who were they?" Corin had never thought you could see spirits.

The manea was slow to answer. "One of the Legends you refuse to believe. Perhaps I'll remind you of it after you complete the test that lies before you."

"Test!" Corin reverted back to regular speech. "I thought I just passed the test."

Minesh grinned. "As did I when I first came here. If all the trials were known beforehand, no one would come. But you already know that you must seek your True-Friend in isolation."

"We're in the Cambre wilderness," Corin said. "You can't get more isolated than that."

The manea reached into an alcove and withdrew an earthen flask and two iron mugs.

Corin watched him pour wine into the wide cups. Its vapors were dark and rich, smelling of apples and forest herbs, and also of sage. He shifted back in his chair and raised a brow at the unexpected aroma.

"Don't be alarmed," Minesh said. "We both know there is no escaping the herb. Just thank Arwyth that you and I are not addicted to it like so many on Sindarin. You are too shielded in your father's tower in Toroth; is the herb so foreign to your senses?"

"It's..." Corin watched as Minesh retrieved a glass jar from a high shelf. The jar was sealed with wax and contained something gray-green and coiled like old rope. "It's just that the Circle is so adamant in its teachings. I didn't expect it here."

"Sageroot," the manea grunted, turning the jar in his hand. "How could you not expect it? Its traces are everywhere. It isn't like the plants native to Sindarin, or the others our ancestors sent ahead to help terraform before the Settling." He peered into the glass. "It is a root that grows in damp places above ground, sometimes clinging to rocks or other plants. It feeds off water and sunlight and has neither leaf nor flower, but releases spores into the air and water."

The manea turned his gaze to Corin. "It is the spores that are euphoric, addictive, that enhance True-Speech. And the spores are everywhere. Even the purest cannot escape their presence in food and drink. And yet, taken in small quantity, one builds tolerance rather than addiction."

"I know all that," Corin said. *How many times have I heard it? Every day of my life?* "But what of the crysalis mineral? Is that also inescapable?"

Minesh replaced the jar on the shelf. "Crysalis. Now there is something even the Elsan won't talk about. No, Corin. Crysalis is hard to find and must be mined. You will find none in this brew. Besides, the blending of sageroot and crysalis into sagcryl is a secret jealously guarded by Skin Runner priests. Simply mixing the ingredients into your wine will not produce the drug."

"That's reassuring," Corin said, accepting one of the mugs. *Or is it?* After two weeks in the Cambre wilderness enduring the manea's dry repetition of the Circle's same old tales, he was still unsure how much he should believe. His gaze roamed back to the clean scar on his arm. Though freshly made, it felt long healed. *Even the Hest may not be all the manea claimed.*

"As for your True-Friend," Minesh continued, "what we have done so far is merely practice, exercising your faculty of True-Speech. You had no real hope of finding your True-Friend. That may come only in isolation."

"But—" Corin clenched his fist and barely restrained himself from hammering the table. *No real hope!*

Minesh went on. "You have followed the lessons and been accepted by the Hest. Your faculty of True-Speech is enough to commune with men."

"And animals," Corin asserted. *Or so the Circle taught.*

"Animals, perhaps." Minesh nodded his head uncertainly. "There is also one who stands beyond the Shroud, awaiting your call. You must go into the wilderness and seek him out. You must find your True-Friend, Corin. You will begin at dawn."

Corin took a large swallow of wine. Two weeks wasted. What else should he have expected of the Circle? Still, he saw no benefit in complaining. "And you?" he asked.

Minesh sipped from his cup. "I have other tasks to attend."

"You mean I'm to go alone?"

"That is the meaning of isolation."

Corin calmed his speeding heart by rolling the mug between his palms. "How did you talk my father into that? There are dangers in these hills. He must have protested."

Minesh shrugged. "He did. But Herlen knows the requisites as well as anyone. Still, I would have been disappointed had he not objected. He is a wise ruler, your father. Not one to send men running to their deaths. Some of his predecessors wouldn't have batted an eye at the needless death of even their own children."

"What about weapons?" Corin asked, ignoring the old man's pontificating. "And provisions?"

The manea reached into a cupboard and retrieved a large knife that he placed on the fog table. "You may also take a water skin. You are to wander the wilderness alone, Corin, until you find your True-Friend."

"But..." Corin stared at the knife. Alone? With just a knife? "What if I never find him?"

Minesh shrugged. "Then, my Prince, you shall become very proficient at living off the land. Or very dead."

Corin stared at the manea's ancient face. *Is he joking? He doesn't look like he's joking.*

"You will take my bed here for the night," Minesh said. "It will be some time before you enjoy the comfort of another."

"What about you?" Corin asked, suddenly more afraid of spending a night alone in Minesh's hutch than of wandering in the wilderness, and hating himself for it.

The manea rose from his seat. "I will see to your horse. To ensure the test is true, he will be your sole companion. And your witness."

The hutch's door opened to a black, star-filled sky and then slid shut behind the old man, leaving Corin alone and afraid.

Escape to the Moon

Unable to continue without sleep, Alethea collapsed atop a small hillock shrouded by bushes. She didn't recognize the wide leaves, not in the enveloping darkness. A night and a day had passed since she had fled Lathan's camp, and as she lay in an oval of new grass gazing up at a star-filled sky, she worried over the aftermath of her leaving.

Had Lathan blamed Ilsa? Was Ilsa all right? Were the traders following? What would happen if Lathan found her?

Unlike her previous two attempts at escape, Alethea had avoided the populated areas along the coast. Towns and villages dotted that path with food and clothing easy to steal if left unguarded. Not that Alethea considered herself a thief, but desperation made people do things they would otherwise never consider. Hiding among other people as she worked her way north had seemed a wise idea.

But it turned out that Lathan had contacts in all those places, places where he traded goods and information. Many of those contacts were more than willing to admit they had seen a girl matching Alethea's description: early teens, slim, straight auburn hair with mahogany undertones uncommon among the people of Sindarin, bangs cut just above the eyes. Alethea had tried to hide her hair, stuffing it beneath her coat or sweeping it back from her face. But the traders had Ilsa with them, a slightly older version of the girl they were looking for, with hair several inches longer. Anyone who had seen Alethea would mark the resemblance.

Alethea knew she had to try something different if she hoped to escape this time. So she had fled north, entering the first village she came to. With morning an hour or more off, few people were about, but she had walked up and down each street, making sure to pass near anyone who looked out a window or work outdoors by lantern or moonlight. Then she left, continuing north until she came to a stream that ran west toward the sea.

Though spring had arrived, ice melt in the mountainous country to the east fed the stream. After removing her shoes and rolling up her pant legs, Alethea clenched her teeth even before stepping into the ice-cold current. Sharp rocks and slippery weeds threaten to send Alethea flying face first into the water, but she persevered and followed the stream inland, leaving no trail to follow. When the sun glowed faintly on the horizon, she stepped back onto land and continued north, certain that no one had seen her. When her feet warmed to where she could again feel her toes, she turned east and worked her way further inland.

By midmorning, Alethea could not be more lost. She knew she was somewhere in the Sethnin Plains, a mix of grasslands and scattered stands of trees that covered much of the known south. People rarely ventured this far east, however, except to hunt game, though richer hunting could be found in the rich forestlands further south.

It made sense that Lathan would have more difficulty finding her if she didn't know herself where she was. And Alethea didn't need villages to survive. Her mother had been an herbalist and frequently took her and Ilsa into the countryside east of Toroth to gather herbs and plant medicines. Not only could she recognize many edible plants, but she had grown proficient at snaring rabbits and ground birds and knew how to start cook fires.

Alethea had yet to snare a rabbit, however. Putting distance between herself and Lathan held greater urgency.

As she lay in the grass, Alethea set aside her hunger and allowed her gaze to drift across the heavens. Rhea, Sindarin's largest moon, crept above a nearby stand of trees and Alethea focused her eyes on the lines and curves of its continents. Scattered mountains covered the north while most of the south held no land at all, but consisted of a sea of deepest blue. Unlike the six smaller moons, Rhea was like Sindarin and had an atmosphere, a warm glow that surrounded the slow moving orb. Would Rhea be far enough? *If I could get* there, would Lathan find me?

She laughed, knowing that no one had ever been to Rhea. Humankind had come to Sindarin from somewhere, somewhere much further than Rhea, she was sure. But leaving again wasn't an option. Not even to a moon she could almost reach out and touch.

Would any place be far enough? Sleep took her as images of Rhea, Lathan, and Ilsa chased each other through her thoughts.

Isolation

Corin came awake to confining darkness and unfamiliar shadows. What! Where am I? Then, as the close walls and prominent fog table registered against his memory, the events of the previous night came flooding back. Only a few hours had passed since he had taken the Hest rites and Minesh had left him.

He lay on the manea's cot for several long minutes replaying in his mind the agony and light of the shard and the words Minesh had spoken, and found himself doubting. Much of what had happened seemed impossible, and all of it left him confused. Perhaps he had dreamed the whole thing. Then he stared at his arm. The mark was there. By the red glow of the fog table he made out a two-inch incision, precise as a razor-cut. Raw and unhealed, but letting no blood. It had not been a dream.

Throwing back the blanket, Corin sat on the edge of the bed. The crispness of the chill air suggesting the hour was early. On the fog table, a sparse meal of dried meat and thick-crusted bread waited accompanied by a heavy mug that perfumed the small hutch with the sweet fragrance of last night's wine. Minesh must have returned while he slept.

No eating utensils were in evidence, just a heavy hunting blade better suited to skinning rabbits than buttering bread. Beside the knife lay a stoppered water skin. Nothing else. No garments. No pack. No provisions. Lifting the wine to his lips,

Corin wondered when and how his next meal would come.

Outside the hutch, Corin's breath frosted before his face. The sky was purple with morning, the sun not yet risen above the Cambre Hills. Frosted earth crunched where he stepped and ice needles clung to hawthorn branches, painting the landscape white. To the north, a heavy gray haze threatened to prevent the day from becoming much warmer. Corin shivered and pulled his wool coat more tightly about his shoulders.

There was no sign of Minesh or the manea's horse. The improvised stall the old man had built from tree branches stood empty.

The canvas shelter where Corin had slept the past two weeks was likewise empty. His blankets, spare clothes, everything, were gone. He felt certain Minesh had left the canvas sheeting as a test; taking the flimsy material, or even the thin ropes that secured it, would count as failure. He wouldn't be surprised if the manea lurked nearby, watching.

Focusing his thoughts, Corin cast out his mind, clumsily he knew, and found only the waiting patience of his own massive black stallion, Serl, tied to a tree near the stall. Dropping his barriers allowed Corin to search a little further, but he found only silence. Isolation.

With nothing else to do, he saddled Serl and set out toward the Ilden Plain. It would be warmer in the lowlands. Since he had no set destination, west was as good a direction as any.

It took an hour to descend the escarpment using Minesh's winding trail, and almost that long to navigate the wide jumble of broken rock that littered the lower slope. The endless grass and scrub of the plain stretched west and south.

Perhaps fifty miles to the north, the snow-capped Aenlaen Mountains stood like a wall across the horizon. To Corin's knowledge, no one had ever found a path to the other side, if there was an *other side*. On his father's maps, the Aenlaen marked the end of the world.

A day's ride west would bring him to the Serpent's Tail, a southern branch of the Aenlaen that was passable to one who knew the ways. On the other side lay Toroth, his father's city, on the coast of the Sunfall Sea. If Corin had found his True-Friend during his stay with Minesh, that would be his route. But he had not found his True-Friend. If he returned now, it would be in disgrace.

Instead he turned Serl southwest toward the wilderness of Rune. Forests, vales, warmer climes, better shelter, roots, berries, and wild game. And Isolation. Rune was too close to Karlac for most men's liking. Though the Sagan Priests had been put down generations ago, men still avoided the site of their blood rituals. Superstition. Corin was above that. Even Minesh had agreed that Karlac was probably no more dangerous than other wilderness regions.

On the banks of the Elki River, Corin reined in and gazed back at the sharp rise of the Cambre Hills, a lumpy mix of hawthorn, scree, and snow. A pang of regret clenched his chest and it took him several moments to realize why.

Before leaving Toroth with Minesh, Corin had never been alone. Not truly alone. His station as prince kept him surrounded by servants and yes-men. Minesh had treated him — not as an equal, certainly — but as someone of whom something was expected. For the first time in his life, Corin had been forced to stand on his own merit rather than on his father's. It was a good feeling and it brought a smile to his lips. He might not have learned what Minesh had wanted him to, but neither was he leaving those lonely hills as empty-handed as he had at first thought. He had taken the Rites of the Hest, an experience unlike anything he had expected. And the Hest had accepted him as was required by the Circle. He would be king after his father.

Serl stamped a hoof against the ground as if to say it was time to move on. Corin nodded. With a toss of the reins, he urged Serl forward across the icy water.

Hours dragged by, marked only by the lazy progress of the sun as it marched across the sky, shortening and then lengthening the shadows cast by man and horse. Corin saw no people and few animals, even birds, as the low peaks of the Serpent's Tail grew taller. Summer would see more game, as well as hunting parties, but otherwise there was little reason for anyone to venture this far east. Most towns and villages lay close to the sea, where fish was plentiful and the weather more accommodating.

Corin passed the time by casting out his mind, seeking his True-Friend. Minesh had said that he must be alone in order to succeed. For the first time in his life, Corin was alone. Truly alone. When he grew tired of finding nothing, he sought instead to touch the Shroud, the veil that Minesh claimed separated Sindarin from the Elsian world.

"The dwelling place of the Elsan is not like Sindarin," the manea had said, speaking more clearly than the Circle Elders in Toroth. "It is not a world up in the heavens circling a star. It is here, all around us, and around all the other worlds in the heavens. It is a place of spirit, intangible to grasping fingers. Through True-Speech, we may sometimes reach through the Shroud and speak with those who dwell there."

Intangible to grasping fingers. Corin didn't know if it was possible to see or become aware of the Shroud, but it only made sense to find that barrier first before attempting to reach beyond it. It would give him a direction, at least.

When he grew tired of reaching for the unreachable, Corin found himself doubting. *How can I not doubt? I've never seen the Shroud or a spirit. Just because Minesh and my father and the Circle Elders claim to speak to spirits doesn't make it so.*

Corin had seen men lie before, and for worse reasons than avoiding humiliation. More than once in the past two weeks he had contemplated deceit, simply telling Minesh that he had contacted a spirit, that he had found his True-Friend. How would the manea know otherwise? A True-Friend was supposed to be a private thing. And if he could lie about it, so could others. Perhaps everyone who went to the wilderness returned a failure, some admitting defeat while others feigned success. It was not impossible that there was no Elsian world.

And yet... he *had* seen spirits. Three of them in the hutch after the Rites. Or had he imagined it? Minesh had responded oddly. What had the manea seen? Anything?

Even so, some of it must be true. Before the Rites, Corin had believed the Hest nothing more than a piece of crystal, an altar for the Path of Arwyth. Then it had touched him. Corin's thoughts traced back through that first touch, pain far greater than a mere slash to his arm could account. And then the second touch, where he had read himself, something he had never thought possible.

Exercising True-Speech once again, he reached inward, attempting to read himself as he had done in the manea's hutch. Nothing. Perhaps it only worked when touching the Hest.

Corin did, however, have a good memory, and recalled much of what he had seen.

Arrogance. That was a surprise. As a prince, he had been raised to command. To show no weakness. To be strong and bold. How had boldness become arrogance?

And anger. Less surprising. He often let anger get the best of him, or used it as a tool to get what he wanted. No wonder the manea had been annoyed with him most of the time they were together. His own impatience and lack of progress had spawned much anger.

But he had seen kindness as well. Corin had never been one for material things, and often gave what he had to those with greater need. His father only laughed at the number of coats, cloaks, and knives he went through.

As the hours passed, Corin reflected on how others perceived his actions. Alone in the wilderness, he made a vow to do better, to become the leader he strived to be and not the highhanded princeling he sometimes achieved.

The Deer

By day's end, Corin had traversed the southern portion of the Ilden Plain into a lightly forested area watered by runoff from the tip of the Serpent's Tail. With the sun low in the western sky just south of the mountains, he came across the region of the Singing Stones, a tumble of rocky meadows shadowed by the menacing peak of Karlac's Bane. The southern edge of the tall mountain's face gleamed silver in the pearl-white light of evening, a stark contrast to the shadowed remainder that appeared almost black as night.

Corin spent several minutes taking in the view. While his father's maps offered a detailed rendering of the known regions of Sindarin, studying them was not the same as riding through mountain passes or across the wide plain, or standing beneath Karlac's Bane. It was as different as living a story rather than reading about it. Before leaving Toroth with Minesh, Corin had never travelled further than twenty miles from the room where he had been born. And now the world was at his fingertips.

The ground became uneven as he rode further west, and he remembered that there had been mines here once—sandstone, limestone, a little iron, and yes, crysalis. All before the days of the Sagan Priests. No one had bothered to resettle. The open pits and excavated quarries were all that remained of Man's past interest in this place.

Several angel-flies flitted among the bare rock and tumbled boulders, their luminous wings of gold, red, and blue offering the only color. Having never seen one before, Corin paused to bask in their rapturous song, which was like a small child singing in a high clear voice, only the notes echoed and went on forever.

Most people could not hear them, for they made no noise. Corin recalled Minesh's words: "The angel-fly is the only creature on Sindarin that communicates instinctively through True-Speech. Its song reverberates unchallenged along the corridors of the Shroud, a glorious, resounding hymn!" Minesh attributed the distinction to a *selective adaptation to a strong diet of sage spore*. Corin was reluctant to accept so simple an explanation. Why had no other creatures on Sindarin *adapted*?

The Singing Stones of Karlac were famous for harboring the moth-like insects. Why they swarmed among the broken rock was another question never adequately explained. Corin watched the hypnotic flutter of wings for several minutes before pressing on.

He took refuge that night in a large fissure that had been

burned in years past by lightning into an ancient, twisted oak. His feeble attempts to start a fire were fruitless so he resigned himself to sleeping in the cold dark. Snaring game in the sunset hours using a thin green branch also proved futile, so he spent the night hungry and cold. He woke the next morning feeling irritable, much hungrier, and no less cold despite the approaching dawn.

When he emerged from his tree-hole at first light, it seemed to Corin that his luck had turned. Not a hundred yards away, in a field of common mallow dotted throughout with jonquil and guelder rose, grazed a mottled brown deer. Corin smiled, the prospect of quelling his hunger filling him with confidence. Slipping his knife from its sheath, he set about stalking the deer.

As the son of a king, Corin had never learned a true huntsman's skill. Throughout his youth, hunting had consisted of horse and bow and a squadron of mounted men, the killing of beasts little more than a cruel game, nothing to do with food or survival. Now Corin had no bow, no squadron of riders. And the business he was about was no game.

The lengths of his trousers grew heavy with dew as Corin crawled through the tall grass, knife in hand. The sharp, green-yellow blades concealed thorns that pricked and tore at his skin, even as small, jagged rocks bit into knees and palms. Corin silently cursed Minesh for sending him on this absurd quest, and cursed again as the sky overhead revealed a dew of its own. Icy rain pummeled his back as he crawled, streaming in tiny rivulets through his hair and into his eyes. Every few yards he stopped and wiped the water from his face. His wool coat and trousers were soon soaked through, his fingers so numb he could scarce hold the knife.

When he came within thirty yards of the doe, she raised her head. The deer stood motionless, as though listening to the soft fall of every raindrop. Her head never moved yet her eyes caught every turning of a leaf in the breeze. Corin lay still in the grass, not breathing, struggling to silence the pounding of his heart. The doe stared straight at him, her large brown eyes calm yet piercing, as though seeing right through to his soul. Corin swallowed and shifted his grip on the knife.

Like a coiled spring suddenly released, the doe leapt away.

Corin was on his feet in an instant, sprinting in the opposite direction. He vaulted onto Serl's unsaddled back and dug in his heels. The great horse snorted and sprang forward, horse and rider thundering across the sodden fields.

The big black was fast but the deer led them into a wooded area where she knew the ways and turns. Even so, despite the tangle of branches and the hazard of hidden gullies, Corin urged Serl on. Around close stands of fox-willow, through thick hedges of gorse, over melt-fed streams and hidden mud holes, they tracked the deer.

In a wooded dell of aspen they lost her. Corin reined Serl in. The big black stood in a small clearing, sweating and rain-slicked, snorting his thanks that the chase had ended.

Corin was not so thankful. Climbing down from Serl's unsaddled back, he stood beneath the inadequate shelter of the trees, his thighs raw and sore from riding bareback in the rain. His hair was plastered to his skin, his clothes soaked and heavy, his breath labored, and his stomach empty. Angrily admitting defeat, Corin collapsed to the earth and let the cold drizzle of rain wash the bitterness and exhaustion from his upturned face.

Surprisingly, he found the cool rainfall refreshing, the patter of raindrops against his closed eyelids a comfort. Fresh, clean air coursed through his lungs. Pungent forest scents — clover, grass, earth, and leaf mold, rife with vitality — filled his nostrils. The damp ground made a mattress for his back, the thick grass a pillow for his head. Never had Corin felt so much at one with the wilds. It was as though his soul had found a new home, a place where he belonged and was welcomed.

A grumbling in his stomach interrupted Corin's reflections. Happiness became hunger pangs. The sweet taste in his mouth, bile. Death by starvation seemed ever more likely. He wondered what his father would say should he be found dead in the forest. Corin's lips formed a grim smile. It would almost be worth dying just to see the expression on the King's face.

Corin sobered with the realization that just one day of his isolation had passed and already he was willing to surrender to failure. At this rate, he would never find his True-Friend. In desperation, he dropped his barriers and cast his mind about at random. Perhaps at this bleak moment, this nadir of his despair, Corin's True-Friend would comfort him.

What he found was something else entirely.

Corin sat up in the wet grass, lost in a turmoil of conflicting emotions. Life, new and struggling to be free. Death, the reluctant realization of a necessary sacrifice. Happiness and despair. A paradox of emotion flooded Corin's being. It came so quickly and so forcefully that he could neither name nor measure it. A complete trusting, caring, hoping, instinctive attachment. It stunned Corin with its gentleness.

He sought to link with it, to contact the source of these foreign thoughts, to heighten his True-Speech and know who or what he had touched. But even as Corin fumbled with his awkward abilities, attempting to lock onto what he hoped were thoughts and feelings from the Elsian world, the sensations fell away. Once again he was alone, with Serl, the trees, and the rain.

Walking Serl, Corin circled the area hoping to rediscover the mind he had touched. Perhaps another person wandered nearby, lost and alone as he was, possibly hurt. Repeatedly, he attempted to push beyond the Shroud, clinging to the hope that the contact had been his True-Friend. He met only silence.

He found a bed of breadroot in his searching, and some wild asparagus growing between two rocks. He ate them greedily but it was hardly enough to quell his hunger. Toward evening the rain abated and then stopped, but the oak in which Corin had spent the previous night was soaked inside from the rainfall. He shivered inside his wet clothing, knowing that he would have to start a fire. If he failed this time, he could die.

Searching beneath rocks and fallen branches, he managed to collect sufficient dry tinder. He used his knife to cut or peel away damp portions from larger twigs. Among the shattered rocks he searched for flint with which to strike a spark, but found only limestone, malachite, and other minerals he did not know.

He had once seen a woodsman start a fire by rapidly rubbing two dry sticks together. As he scraped away the damp, outer bark from a pair of likely twigs, he wished that he had paid closer attention. His first attempt failed miserably, as did his second and third. He gave up after nearly an hour, his hands raw and his fingers stiff and bruised. He went hunting for more roots to curb his hunger and his frustration. As the last gray light of evening fell, he tried once more and was successful.

The spark came at the very crest of his anger, just as his temper boiled to the point of utmost rage and overwhelming despair. The single wisp of thin, white smoke that rose unexpectedly from the worn twigs sent his bitter thoughts fleeing and renewed Corin's slight hope that perhaps all was not against him. He almost blew out the spark as he tried to fan it higher. Calming himself, he protected the twigs by making windbreaks with his hands. Corin's patience was rewarded as the small point of warmth blossomed into golden flame.

He tended the tiny fire like a lover, coaxing it higher, careful not to be too anxious, allowing the small flames to spread on their own. For the first time in two days, Corin found himself grinning. Twenty minutes later he warmed his hands before a roaring blaze. Night fell, bringing darkness, but Corin didn't care. He went about throwing more branches onto the fire, building it higher until the blaze grew to a towering column of flame.

It was only when Serl stomped the earth with his hooves and nickered, his eyes rolling white in the firelight, that Corin realized his madness. He took a dozen deep breaths, calming his heartbeat. Then he stacked the remaining wood in an accessible heap. Dragging an old stump out of the trees, he set it close to the fire and sat down. Within moments, Corin recalled his hunger and, in remembering, the hunger consumed him. He tried to occupy his thoughts by again seeking his True-Friend.

The mind touched his quickly. Too quickly. Corin nearly fell off his stump chair from the impact. It was the same mind he had felt earlier, the one in opposition, where life and death seemed to embrace each other in a struggle of love. His eyes searched the darkness, finding nothing, yet the presence grew nearer. Rising, Corin stared into the night, senses rushing, hoping against hope at last to identify this strange mind from the wilderness.

She stepped out from the darkness so silently that Corin almost missed it. From across the fire her deep, brown eyes returned the reflected flames in a steady gaze that told of fortitude, intelligence, and courage. Having made her presence known, she made no move to come closer.

Corin hesitated before reaching for his knife. It had to be the same doe he had chased earlier. Only now she did not run, but stood regarding him. It worried him that she did not run; it was unnatural. Could this be the mind in turmoil? He pushed the thought aside, smiling as his fingers tightened around the hilt of his knife. Food!

He considered the distance, the prospect of leaping the fire or creeping around it. Perhaps if he threw the knife, rather than attempt moving closer?

Moments slid by.

Why didn't she run? Why didn't he make his move?

Corin thought then of his purpose in being there, his task of finding his True-Friend and his eventual succession to the Square. His stomach reminded him that he must not perish in this quest. He took courage in the thought that the deer was here to sustain him. Sent by — whom? — the Elsan? Why not? It was right. Fitting. He would take her.

As he shifted his weight in preparation to leap, the doe stepped closer to the fire and turned. Corin stopped short, his fingers slipping on the knife. Dark blood caked the doe's hindquarters. She turned further and he saw the broken shaft of an arrow lodged deep in her flank, five inches of thin wood extending. The wound went deep, gashed open even further by the doe's apparent attempts to dislodge the arrow.

Then he saw the rest.

There was a bulge in her belly, a bulge that kicked and shook with a violence all its own. She was ready to give birth. The broken arrow interfered somehow, therefore the conflict in her mind, and possibly the unborn fawn's mind as well. Corin now knew why she had returned to him. Why she chose, this time, not to run. What he did not know was why she would trust him.

The doe hobbled around the fire and touched his hand with her nose. She nuzzled the fist that held the knife and then lay down by the fire, her movements awkward as she sank to the earth. The fawn inside kicked so fiercely, it surprised Corin that she could endure it. She gazed up at him, those full, innocent brown eyes reaching out, touching his very being, trusting him with her life and the life inside her.

Corin frowned. This is all wrong. Impossible. Animals don't behave this way. Yet despite his insistent hunger, his urgent need for meat, he somehow felt obliged to help. Insanity. If the doe weren't with child, he wouldn't hesitate in killing it. But this...? He shook his head and knelt beside the deer.

The animal shook in quiet spasms when he touched the arrow. It went deep, very deep, the unborn life within straining against it.

Sheathing his knife, Corin took hold of the broken shaft with both hands. He pulled as gently as he might but the arrow remained firm. He pulled harder, but it was no good. He would have to use the knife after all, though not as he had originally intended. Time was short, but he took a few moments to warm the blade in the fire, to cleanse the steel in flame. When he could delay no longer, he took the knife and cut into the doe's flank around the base of the arrow.

The animal shuddered as the blade went in, the heated steel searing flesh. Corin paused to peer into her eyes, eyes that silently watched him, brown orbs glittering in the light from the fire. A soft hiss broke the evening stillness as the blade found its way deeper. When the blade was fully inside, the large belly jerked and Corin's hand fumbled on the hilt.

The blade was too short. There was nothing he could do except to press the knife's hilt into the wound after the blade.

The deer writhed beneath him and Corin felt the pressure of the fawn pushing upward against his hand. The doe's severed muscles opened further and he pulled back the sleeve of his shirt, probing deeper until his hand and wrist became lost inside the wound. Warm blood bathed his fingers, weakening his grip on the knife, its sweet scent reminding him of his hunger. The warmth of imminent birth touched him as he pulled at the exposed shaft with his free hand while cautiously cutting around the arrow with the knife. He could feel the shaft loosen.

Abruptly, the belly kicked again, this time with more violence than Corin thought possible. He cursed as contracting muscle plucked the knife from his fingers. Corin grappled for the base of the arrow with his blood-slicked hand, but it too was lost, swallowed by layers of muscle.

Corin had no choice but to withdraw his hand from the wound. From fingertip to elbow his arm dripped hot blood, steaming in the chill air. Wiping his arm against the damp wool of his coat, he saw the scar of the Hest stark against his pale skin.

Beneath him, the deer moved and a small, stick-like leg protruded from beneath the doe's flank. But it stopped there; the fawn lay trapped behind the arrow.

Corin looked again into the doe's eyes. Amber orbs fraught with desperation and pain returned his gaze. No doubts clouded his mind; the emotions in the aspens that had moved him so were those of the deer, the first animal he had read through True-Speech. Hers was the mind he had felt in opposition. Life; Death. Love; Sacrifice. Corin knew then what the deer wanted — what she had wanted all along — to sacrifice her own life that her young might live.

Corin's gaze moved back to her exposed flank— the arrow shaft, the gaping wound, the flowing blood. Revulsion seared his soul. Must it be this way? The fawn would live, but the mother would die.

He would have his meat.

Corin lifted his gray eyes skyward, staring into the darkness without seeing. Tears burned his cheeks. *It's only a deer, an animal. I've eaten venison all my life. Why should I care?* And yet... he had gazed into the doe's eyes, touched her mind, read her thoughts, encountered her soul.

Lowering his barriers, Corin shouted in True-Speech, begging for help, from anyone, anywhere. No answer came. Just the unborn fawn crying for life; the mother offering up her life in exchange.

Corin shouted louder. In his mind's eye he saw three personages with scars, two men and a woman. The same he had seen in Minesh's hutch. Three beings with determination in their eyes and light shooting from their forearms.

The pain came without warning, beginning in his wrist and advancing swiftly to his brain. Corin stared at the scar on his arm. The wound had parted, emitting light into the darkness. Pain rose with it, the agony of the Hest rites. Corin opened his mouth and screamed into the night. Then the Hest emerged from the wound in his arm, glittering in the night like a thousand fiery diamonds. Corin wanted to faint, but the Hest wouldn't let him. His lungs gulped in air as he fought to marshal his thoughts, to will away the pain, to deny the Hest's existence.

And it worked! The light dimmed. The shard receded. The agony grew less. Beneath him the doe moved. Or rather, the fawn moved within its mother; the doe had lost consciousness.

"No!" Corin cried again, this time willing the Hest to return, accepting the agony.

The shard answered, a blade of light shooting from his arm, growing longer than it had appeared in the manea's hutch, becoming a sword. Pain exploded in Corin's mind, enveloping his thoughts, swallowing his soul. He never knew for certain what happened after that.

Apart from the pain and the light, he seemed to recall blood. He remembered the arrow falling free somehow and his knife lying wet and bloody in the grass. He remembered new life spilling out onto its knees in one quick gush of blood and water, warm and slippery, an awkward gangling confusion of legs that flailed against him, a small brown face sucking in air and turning its head to its mother. He remembered the pain leaving, the light receding, and then blackness.

The Bear

Corin opened his eyes to daylight. In the east, a bright sun nested within the spreading branches of a grove of aspens. New spring leaves flickered and trembled in the breeze beneath a crisp, azure sky. Above him, the face of Karlac's Bane towered like an unfriendly giant, rough and silver-gray in the sharp sunlight.

Was it morning? Or had days passed? Corin knew without looking that he was covered in blood. It felt dry and itchy against his skin. His clothes were stiff. He was hungry.

With sudden alarm, he sat up and examined his forearm. Beneath a layer of crusted blood the scar appeared no different than it had in Minesh's hutch, a thin clean line about two inches long. Dried blood caked his hands and clothes. The grass around him looked as though it had seen a war.

Something wet and cold touched his ear and Corin dove for his knife, plucking it from the stained grass and rolling to face the danger. The fawn tilted its head and stared at him with innocent brown eyes. Corin put down the knife.

The fawn's mother lay in the grass nibbling at the tender blades within reach; new spring grass, green shoots sprouting up among last season's yellow. As Corin rose to his feet, the fawn danced around him. The doe looked up but otherwise did not move. Her flank where the arrow had pierced was a bloody mess, but seemed to be healing. The Hest had closed and cauterized the wound.

A memory of pain came back in a rush. How? Why? Corin cast aside those questions. His hunger was more urgent.

After rebuilding the fire from last night's embers, he searched the glades for roots, spring berries, and edible bulbs.

He never strayed far from the wounded deer, afraid to leave her lying defenseless in the camp. At a stream he washed his face and arms; the blood on his clothes would have to wait until he could rinse them thoroughly and dry them by the fire.

Throughout his efforts, the question of the Hest continued to haunt him. Minesh had said nothing of summoning the Hest, of using it as a tool. In fact, he had suggested just the opposite, that the Hest would take him only once; there would be no more pain. The pain. The excruciating pain. Again and again he found himself standing in a glade staring at his arm, remembering and wondering, until hunger snapped him out of his stupor.

Each time he returned to the fire, the deer watched him, her eyes filled with calm, thanks, and a dozen other emotions Corin could not begin to understand. Each sight of her reminded him of the opportunity he let slip by, the venison he could be roasting over the fire. And of the impossibility of what had happened. Then the fawn would frolic near him and a regretful smile would pass his lips. He collected grass for the doe to eat, soaking it first in the stream to provide moisture to restore her lost blood.

The day passed quickly as Corin's search for edible plants took him further and further afield. His efforts were pathetic; he knew he was no woodsman. Always, when he returned to check on the doe, he was hungrier than before.

Night approached and the air grew chill. Dark and cold surrounded Corin's fire like enemies. The fawn lay close to its mother for warmth.

Despite his foraging, hunger ate at Corin, occupying his every thought as he sat on his stump chair warming his hands over the flames. His stomach growled like a cornered tree-lynx. Corin startled himself when he realized that a part of that hunger came from outside, perceived by his sense of True-Speech. He cast his eyes to the doe and saw that the fawn was asleep. Something was wrong, though; the mother seemed more afraid than hungry. Still clumsy in True-Speech, Corin reached out to find what he feared would be waiting.

The beast came barreling out of the trees. A sten-bear, half again as tall as Corin and five times as heavy. It had claws the length of Corin's fingers and jaws that could crush rock. The sten-bear headed straight for the wounded deer, instinctively knowing which prey would be most easily won.

Serl reared and kicked the air with his hooves, whinnying a warning. The sten-bear ignored the stallion, rushing straight for the doe.

Corin could have run. He could have leapt on Serl's back and vanished into the night. Instead, he jumped between the deer and the charging beast. It was an act of instinct, made without thought.

The sten-bear hesitated only a moment before roaring a challenge at its new target. To Corin's knowledge there was nothing a sten-bear feared, neither man nor beast. Terror welled up within him as the animal approached, slowed perhaps by curiosity at this food that didn't run.

Corin ignored the knife at his hip, useless against so massive a beast. Instead, he braced his feet shoulder-width apart and gripped his right forearm with his free hand. Silence ran thick in his ears as he clamped his teeth together and summoned the Hest. The deer behind him touched Corin's mind once, sending emotions of thanks and need. Then the Hest came and the pain enveloped him.

It was worse than anything the sten-bear's jaws could do. His left hand steadied the blade as the giant creature rose up on its hind legs to tower over him, its hook-clawed paws poised to strike. Corin struck first.

The creature screamed from the depth of its chest as the Hest cut deep, entering just below the ribs and angling upward. The sten-bear surged forward, eager to eradicate the source of its pain, crushing Corin beneath its weight. Thick paws groped at him, sharp claws raking his clothing, tearing through to pierce frail skin beneath. Putrid breath steamed into Corin's face and growls of anger and pain howled in his ears. But even as their bodies met, Corin thrust the Hest upward, turning it inside the creature's chest, probing. It was some moments after the howling ceased that Corin realized the beast was dead and the Hest was gone.

The animal's gaping jaws rested just inches from Corin's throat, its nostrils still filled with the warm breath of life, that lingering presence that remains after the spirit has gone but the flesh still wishes to remember. Corin lay pinned beneath a thousand pounds of fur, fat, muscle, and bone. He knew without trying that his starved, battered body lacked the strength to free itself.

It was the doe that freed him. After hobbling to where Corin lay trapped beneath the bear, she lay on her side and pushed against the carcass with her strong hind legs, bearing up enough weight so that Corin could pull himself free. He fought bruised muscles as he climbed to his feet. His scratches were mostly surface, though some of them would scar. He gave his injuries little thought as he found his knife and went to work.

After piling more wood onto the fire, he broke five green limbs off a nearby tree and sharpened the narrow end of each. At opposite sides of the fire, using a rock for a hammer, he pounded pairs of stakes into the ground so that they crossed at chest height. Then, using sten-bear intestine for rope, he bound the crosses together so that they would not slip. Next he skinned the animal with his inadequate knife, once again covering himself with blood and gore. When he finished, he hammered the remaining stake into the mouth and through the torso, and used the last of his strength to lever the heavy carcass up and across the frame. Then he collapsed onto his stump chair and waited.

The meat spat and sizzled as fat dripped into the flames. Time seemed to slow and then stand still as Corin's hunger and exhaustion worked to defeat him. The meat had not finished roasting when he began stuffing seared pieces of flesh into his mouth; in his hunger, he did not notice the bitterness. He ate until he could eat no more.

All the while, the deer watched him.

His hunger at last sated and longing for sleep, Corin knew he had not the luxury. Again using his knife, he scraped fat and flesh from the animal's hide, removing as much as he could. Then, using his makeshift spit, he dried the sten-bear hide over the coals, taking care not to allow the fur to catch fire. Some of the remaining meat he finished roasting over the coals and wrapped in small scraps of hide.

With his knife, he cut a round hole through the largest section of hide and pulled it over his head so that it hung from his shoulders like a heavy poncho, covering his back and chest and hanging down past his knees. Most of the fine wool he had worn from Minesh's hutch, now bloodied by deer and bear and clawed to shreds, he burned. Of the remaining hide, he kept what he could for blankets.

What he could not use from the sten-bear, Corin threw onto the coals and watched it burn until weariness overtook him. The last thing he saw before sleep took him was the steady gaze of the deer from across the fire. When he awakened to sunlight several hours later, both doe and fawn were gone.

The Karlac Tombs

It took Alethea two additional days of walking before the sweeping grasslands of the Sethnin Plains gave way to wooded hills. With little to occupy her thoughts, her heart pounded with worry for Ilsa as well as the fear that Lathan would find her. He would be looking; of that she was certain. Not because Alethea was of any value, but because of wounded pride. Lathan claimed that no slave of his had ever succeeded in running away. And he had come after her twice before.

Cresting a broad hummock, Alethea looked down into a wide river valley dominated by slow moving water that could only be the western arm of the Elki River. She knew from a map she had once studied in Toroth that the Elki flowed from headwaters in the Aenlaen Mountains south along the Cambre Hills before turning east to the Sunfall Sea, essentially dividing the inhabited region of Sindarin into north and south. She knew that north of the river this far inland lay the wilderness of Rune.

With no desire to swim through icy water, Alethea made

her way down to the riverbank and then travelled upstream until she came upon a small island that divided the river creating a fast moving narrow. A dead poplar leaned from the bank and she was able to push the tree until it fell, making a natural bridge.

After stepping nimbly across, Alethea paused to heave the end of the tree into the river, where the swift current grabbed the few remaining branches and pulled it away from the island. The roots on the bank wouldn't let go however, so the tree lay there in the current, half submerged. Not fully erasing how she had crossed, but a good disguise nonetheless.

Breathing hard and wiping sweat from her face, she briefly considered attempting to fish the river. But if Lathan had found her trail, Alethea would rather be lost in Rune than sitting on the banks of Sindarin's second largest river.

It took mere minutes to cross the island, which was lightly treed and held no evidence of wild game.

The river on the far side was broad yet shallow enough to wade across. Alethea gasped when she stepped barefoot into the river, the water of the Elki seeming much colder than the stream she had followed two days earlier. Perhaps it was just that the water was deeper. Despite loose pebbles, slime, and ooze that threatened to pull her legs out from under her, Alethea made it across without mishap.

Rolling down her pants and pulling on her boots, she quickly scooted up the bank and into the trees, hidden from any eyes that might be watching.

As night fell, the poplar and evergreens gave way to wide, twisted oaks and Alethea suddenly knew where she was. Kemplar Steeple, where in times past Sagan Priests had communed with Demons. A stony mountain peak rising above the trees to the north was all the confirmation she needed. Karlac's Bane. The area had been well marked on the map she'd seen as a child. Not so that people could find it, but so they could avoid it. Long abandoned and shunned by all, it was perhaps the last place Lathan would think to look for her. With that realization, the exhaustion that came with receding stress hit her. Even so, she set several snares before collapsing into sleep within a dry shallow in the lee of a fallen oak.

Waking with the sun, Alethea found a wild chicken caught in one of her snares, pecking at the wire. Plucked and roasted over hot coals, the scrawny bird tasted like heaven. She ate every last scrap of meat and crisp skin and still her empty stomach complained for more. But hunting for more wasn't an option. She didn't want to risk Lathan following her, so she erased any sign of her camp and moved on.

Karlac's Bane grew tall to the north and the ground rougher, with outcroppings of rock making it difficult for anything other than grass and sturdy shrubs to grow. Alethea knew she was nearing the Karlac Tombs. Memory dug up tales of Man's long ago arrival on Sindarin, tales she had learned from the people of the Path. Some deep disaster had transpired in this place, but try as she might, no details would come. There had been many deaths, she remembered. Enough to include *Tombs* in the region's name. Alethea peered about, searching for anything that resembled a grave marker among the jagged rock. All she found was desolation.

Steep ravines and deep fissures in the stony earth grew more pronounced as the sun neared the western horizon. Alethea found herself stepping cautiously while searching for a sheltered place to sleep.

As twilight descended toward darkness, she neared the edge of an abandoned pit, an old open quarry just off a water-filled gorge. Unnatural noises, sharp and guttural, echoed from the shadows below. Even muddied by the rush of water, she could tell the sounds were human. The discovery came as something of a revelation; it had been three days she had last seen another living soul.

The Karlac Tombs was the last place on Sindarin she expected to find anyone. Even hunting parties avoided the area, superstition being what it was. There were always other places to hunt. That was why she had come this way; Lathan would have no reason to come here. No one would. And yet there were voices. Could it be Minesh? *Here and not in Cambre? Doing whatever it is a manea does in the wild?*

The illogic of the idea was insufficient to prevent Alethea

from peering into the pit. She reached out with her mind as well, employing True-Speech to taste the emotions of whomever was below. She told herself that if the pit's occupants were hostile, she would move on. If not, perhaps she could inquire after Minesh.

True-Speech warned her an instant before her eyes. Deep in the pit, roughly a dozen men moved like animals, leaping from rock to rock. Most were half-naked, even in the chill evening air, their skin mottled in the deepening gloom, pale flesh surging with dark, swollen blotches, as though a thousand insects sought escape from beneath. The warning, however, came too late. A dozen minds, all in various stages of frenzy, reached out and found her, told her she was dead. A scream escaped her lips, yet failed to drown out the voices.

Alethea had never seen such people before, but knew what they were— Skin-Runners! Tales told to children to keep them indoors at night. Stories shared by adults in quiet voices describing the loss of parents or cousins.

Heart hammering in her chest, Alethea turned and fled.

A cry came up from the pit, an outpouring of evil that jarred her bones, turning her legs into useless sticks. Vile emotions assaulted Alethea's barriers, pounding like sharp rocks against thin glass. Her heart pumped pain, not blood. The cries grew louder and she fell, spilling into loose sand. Her lungs refused to take in air. Her gaze strained for a place to hide. There was none.

Spinning on her heels, Alethea ran blindly into the dusk. Gasps of pain escaped her lips as she stumbled against jagged outcroppings of blasted rock. Spine-fingered branches of a dead chaparro bush stung her arms and face. Behind her, the cries grew closer. The Skin-Runners had cleared the pit.

"Spread out!" commanded a husky voice, its pitch lowered by the drug. "I want her alive!"

"I hope she's young," a voice answered.

"No matter. It's the meat I want."

Alethea broke left as heavy footfalls grew louder. Shouts rang out in all directions. The Skin-Runners were closer now; they would soon have her. With nowhere else to turn, she reached out to the Elsian world. "Help! Oh please, help me!"

Nothing. The footfalls grew nearer.

And then a voice echoed in her mind. "Where are you? What must I do?"

The reply so startled Alethea that she missed her footing and fell crashing to the earth. The ground came up hard, but her momentum kept her moving. She rolled over and down into a small ravine, coming to rest in a narrow tangle of brambles.

"There she is!" A man stood at the top of the ravine, a hulking shadow outlined against a purple sky. He waved an arm. "Go left and head her off. I'll climb down here."

"She must be young," someone called. "She runs well."

"Good. Strong legs. I like that."

"I hope she's clean. The drug takes them more deeply when they're not used to it."

"Just catch her! Go!"

Alethea rose and ran, ignoring the exhaustion in her legs and the horrors that pounded against her barriers. Brambles caught and tore at her clothes. Tiny prickles from claw-flowers clung to her hands and face.

The ravine ended, opening into a box canyon. Moonlight shone like silver, illuminating black rock that rose on all sides. Booted feet pounding against rock echoed all around her. In the wall ahead, a deeper shadow marked an opening. Alethea ran toward it, her feet kicking up sand from the canyon floor. Men's voices, clamoring like animal cries, rang through the night.

She had almost reached the opening when a near-naked man stepped in front of her. Alethea's scream brought a laugh to his lips. Then everything went dark.

The Gorging

"Not too tight, Roman. I don't want her blood cut off."

"As you say, Bruenor. The legs as well?"

"For now. I relish the fear in their eyes when I cut the

cords."

"What about her clothes?"

"Leave them. It builds excitement in the Gorging. There is something profoundly satisfying in the way prey flinches when I rip them off."

Roman looked carefully at the priest. "I thought you'd like to have her first."

Bruenor shook his head. "No, the drug is wearing off and there isn't time to go through frenzy again before the rites. I'll take my pleasure with the rest of you in the Gorging, when I cut the skin." He paused and glared at Roman. "If she is marked before the rites, I'll cut out your heart."

An involuntary knot tightened in Roman's throat. "I'll watch her myself, Bruenor."

"You! You're not even a phyte-runner. How can I trust you?"

Roman showed his empty palms. "I have never failed you, Bruenor. You know that!"

"Watch well, then, Roman. If in the heat of frenzy I find this morsel touched, I swear I'll cut you myself and stretch your skin through the fires of Hell. Clear?"

"On my life, Bruenor!"

"Your life! Until you accept the Demon, your life is worthless." Bruenor shook his head again and walked away, his hand slapping the blade at his side. It was a rare plasteel knife, taken from the girl.

Roman watched in silence as the priest lifted the door to the tent and walk out into the night. Then he and the girl were alone. He wasted no time in crouching beside her, his ears sharp for footsteps; the stirring sounds of night were all that greeted him.

Breath hissed through Roman's teeth as he explored the girl with his eyes. In sleep she looked like a child, younger than her years. And her skin, so clean! He touched her cheek with a finger. No makeup to conceal enlarged pores. She wore no makeup at all! He moved his fingers to caress her hair. Not dyed, yet the red hue was so unusual, almost brown. Not fiery, like so many other women. And soft. So soft.

It isn't fair. It was I who caught the child in the canyon. And when she screamed, it was I who brought the butt of my knife crashing down upon her skull, causing her to collapse like a straw doll. True, others helped carry her to the grotto and Bruenor's tent, but it was I who caught her. This should be my tent, not Bruenor's. I should be having her now, not keeping her safe for the priest while he prepares for the Demon's bloody Gorging. Keep her? I should have taken her when I had the chance!

Roman's anger subsided as he studied the girl on Bruenor's sleeping mat— legs straight, arms tied above her head, body stretched as far as possible, laid out like a sacrifice. Roman grinned at her unconscious form, thin and supple, like a reed. Just the way he liked them. Almost without thought, his knife was in his hand. Ordinary steel, it flashed silver in the light of the small fire inside the tent.

The girl's tunic was of rough wool. Coarse wooden buttons held the worn cloth together, two at the breast with four more running down the front. Roman brushed his blade beneath the top button and it tumbled away, allowing the tunic freedom to move against the soft rise of warm flesh beneath it.

He knew that if he touched her and Bruenor found out, he would be killed. The danger just excited him more. The knife was his favorite part. That and the terror in his preys' eyes when they watched him use it.

Hooking the knife into a rip in her pant leg, Roman widened the tear to reveal a lean, muscled thigh, tanned brown from many summers of Sindarin's harsh sun. Ripping the cloth further, he ran the flat of the steel against soft skin, back and forth, as though sharpening the knife's edge with the moisture from her body, imagining as he did the myriad ways in which he could abuse her young flesh. He liked doing that first. The body could endure only so much before it gave out, but in his mind he could cut her over and over and over again.

Saliva collected in Roman mouth and he began to sweat. Thin streams of perspiration beaded on his forehead and dribbled down his face to collect at his chin and fall in glistening drops onto her warm flesh. Bruenor would know if he cut her, but there were still things he could do. Things that didn't leave scars. Well, not visible ones.

He drew his knife back to her tunic, found the second button. It fell away as easily as the first. White flesh — flesh that had rarely seen the sun — peered out from the parted tunic. Roman nudged the cloth further with his knife, drawing the blade across exposed flesh that flushed pink where steel passed. The breath of life within made the skin rise and fall, caressing the blade.

It was too much. Licking his lips, Roman set the knife down and began pulling his shirt above his head. When he could see again past the cloth, he found Bruenor standing at the tent's flap, glaring at him with wide, cold eyes.

"You filthy Maggot! I should kill you right now!"

Roman leapt to his feet and backed away, hastily pulling his shirt back on. "I—I didn't touch her. I swear!"

Bruenor's hand went to his side and returned clutching a whip that he snapped before him with an expert flick of the wrist. Thin leather cut the air. "Swear, Roman? You should have done that before, to the Demon!"

The whip cracked again and the knotted tip found Roman's neck. He screamed as fire flared from the touch. His hand darted to his throat and came away again. He stared at fingers that glistened with scarlet blood.

Again Bruenor's arm rose and fell. This time the lash struck Roman's chest, near the heart. Pain lanced from chest to head and he collapsed to the floor of the tent and writhed in the dirt. He heard the whip crack a fourth time and his shoulder blossomed with fire. A wounded, animal howl filled his ears and Roman knew it was his own. He felt his body jerk with spasms. Blood flowed from his throat and chest and shoulder, but it was the fire burning his torso that was his undoing. Why had he risked the girl?

The shuddering slowed and Roman waited for the next stroke with clenched teeth. When it didn't come, he allowed himself to breathe again and opened his eyes.

Bruenor stood over him. "I hope you enjoyed your sport, Roman. I told you not to touch her. In that pleasure, I shall lead."

"I—I never touched. She is still yours."

"You had better not be lying, Roman. For your sake."

"B—By my life, Bruenor, I did—"

"Your life again! You're too concerned for it. Give it to the Demon, Roman. Become a phyte-runner. Then a niac. Then you will know life. Become one of us. Humph. One more act like this and you'll be prey instead. Clear?"

"A—At the Gorging, priest. Tonight! I—I will. At the Gorging. P—Please. Send for the healer. I'll not break trust again."

"You are right, Roman. You will not. This was the last time. Once more and I'll cut out your heart and feed it to the pack. Clear?"

Roman jerked his head in assent and curled into himself, lying in a growing pool of his own blood. He heard Bruenor turn and leave the tent. Outside, the priest's voice barked orders.

$$\Omega$$

Alethea regained consciousness slowly, her head pounding in time with her heart, reminding her of what had happened. She opened her eyes and saw that it was still night. She was inside a tent, larger than the one she had shared with Ilsa, but old and of poor quality. The ceiling was coarse linen. Uneven patches of animal dye streaked the edges and drew vague images across its length.

She tried to move and discovered her arms stretched above her head and her hands bound. Her tunic felt wrong at the throat. All she could manage was to turn her head.

When she did, she saw a man being treated by a healer. A male healer rather than a woman; odd. Then she remembered the man's evil face leering at her in the moonlight. The one who had struck her. Why he was being cared for, she didn't know, but Alethea hoped the beating had been painful. Seeing him there lying battered on the floor offered hope that someone here might help her.

Ignoring the pain in her skull, she opened her mind and searched. Alethea touched several men before withdrawing.

They all had their barriers up, agitated and artificially strong, inflamed by sagcryl. When she touched them, they laughed at her. It was not a gentle laugh. Neither was it harsh; the kind reserved for men in taverns, drunk on sage wine as they watched a half-naked girl dance. It was the laughter of the damned, the mirth of madmen anticipating the fulfillment of their vilest fantasies.

Alethea shuddered with panic. Skin-Runners! They had to be. The worst nightmare of every man, woman, and child on Sindarin. People who worshiped the Demon. She reached out to the Elsian world, hoping against hope that she would at last be heard.

"It's no good, girl." A tall, muscular man strode into the tent. His hair was short and black, slicked back across an angular skull. Thick brows rose like horns above cruel eyes and a spiteful grin spread beneath a long broad nose, curved and humped from repeated breaking. At his belt he wore a coiled whip and on the other side a plasteel knife, the knife Ilsa had risked Lathan's wrath to give her. The man's brutal grin widened to an icy smile that made Alethea's skin crawl. "The dead don't hear chattel. Only priests."

Others followed the priest into the tent, all of them men. Skin-Runners. One by one they surrounded her, each worse than Lathan. She could tell by their crude smirks and the raw, savage emotion they emanated. Dear Ilsa! What have I done in leaving you!

The priest hunkered down on his knees and stared at her. It was a look that put Lathan to shame. When she turned away, long sagcryl-stained fingers seized her chin and forced her head back. His grip was a vise, but hurt less than his eyes.

"I'll take my hand away now," the priest said. "If you scream, I'll break those pretty cheekbones of yours. Clear?"

Alethea nodded. His burning eyes suggested that he hoped she would scream.

"A real find you are, child. What son of a fool let you go I wonder? Hmmm? I'll have your name."

Alethea was too scared to answer. She opened her mouth but nothing came out.

The priest frowned and lifted his hand, flexing his fingers. "Alethea!"

"Well now, Alethea. Your name matches your comeliness. You have clean skin for one your age. Why? In whose house have you trained?"

"No one's."

"Oh come, child. You must be someone's property." He fingered the plasteel knife at his belt.

"I—I was in a trader's camp. We were headed for Thadan's Market."

"Whose camp?"

"L—Lathan. The trades call him the Klep."

The priest snorted. "I know the man. A jackal. You were his property."

Alethea shook her head. "I am no one's property. I was with the camp."

"As I said, I know the man. There are no free women in Lathan's camp. Well, his loss is my gain." The priest laughed. "Before this night is through you will wish you had never left your good friend Lathan."

The breath froze in Alethea's throat. She knew he spoke truth. These were Skin-Runners, worshipers of Demons. The men surrounding her grinned and touched their knives in anticipation, sizing her up like a side of beef. Tears came, a blessing to hide those leering faces.

"You waste your tears, child," rumbled the priest. "You have no life left to mourn. Take joy in the knowledge that, before the end, you will know ecstasy like you have never imagined."

"Please," Alethea whispered. "I'll take the drug. You can have me in frenzy. Anything. Just... don't... do... this."

The men laughed.

"We will have that anyway," said the priest.

"No!" Alethea cried. "I'll become one of you! I'll swear myself to the Demon." She would do no such thing, but fear drove her to lies.

Again the priest snorted. "Not in this pack. We have but one use for a girl."

"I—I'll show you Lathan's tents. I can get you sagcryl. I—"

The priest let out a heavy laugh. "Fool girl. Lathan gets his sagcryl from me. No, our little talk has been most entertaining, but you are nothing more than Demon fodder. And when the Demon gets his, we get ours."

Alethea screamed, and found her ears ringing and white flashes shooting across her vision. The priest's hand had caught her full in the face. The bones hadn't broken, but almost. Blood trickled from her mouth, hot and salty on her tongue. When the ringing faded, she heard the priest speaking to his men.

"Take her outside. Leave her clothes as Roman cut them. Bring him as well. He'll swear his oath tonight or we'll have him after the girl. Is the drug ready?"

"There is enough, Bruenor. Enough for all."

"Good! It is almost time. Lash the girl between the posts. Bind her wrists until they bleed. Bind her ankles as well. We'll have fun with this one."

Rough hands grabbed Alethea's arms and legs and lifted her like a sack of potatoes. Cold air blasted against her as they left the tent. She managed to bring her eyes back into focus as the men righted her and lashed her between a pair of tall, standing posts. Bruenor's men grunted and laughed, shrugging off her punches and kicks as they cut her bound hands and feet and tied her spread-eagle to the posts, stretching the joints of her body to the limit. The wood felt slick and greasy where her hands touched; Alethea shuddered as she realized the posts were lacquered with old blood. Human blood.

Although she struggled, Alethea withheld her cries, somehow knowing that this was just the beginning. Later she would be unable to hold back. Skin-Runner rituals had never been described to her, but the sick looks and refusal to speak by those who knew anything at all had been enough.

Moonlight gleamed against the worn, smooth rock of the grotto entrance. She looked outward as brute shadows blocked the light. Men moved all around her, fierce-eyed and grinning. All of them fingering their knives. One man ran toward her, mouth twisting as though intending to snap at her throat. She blinked and he was gone. Three others took his place, darting past her with rapacious looks, wolves admiring the rabbit. It was more than she could take. Alethea screamed.

"Scream again, girl," suggested the priest, looming before her. Bruenor, they had called him. "No one will hear you out here."

"Please!" Alethea shouted at the sky, no longer seeking with her mind. "Where are you? Why don't you answer?"

Bruenor glanced with mock worry at the heavens, then laughed. "No one hears you, child. Just the Demon. And He will come soon enough. No need to rush things."

Alethea had thought Lathan the Devil himself. But this man. No, not a man, this monster. How could anyone...? She hadn't the words. His followers were no better. Skin-Runners! She had run from Lathan's hands straight into the arms of Hell.

A grave-faced man of medium build drew up next to the priest. His visage lacked the blind hunger of the others and his hands held a metal flask that stank of blood and sagcryl. "The drug is ready, Bruenor."

The priest peered critically into the metal cup, then waved his hand. "Very well. Let us begin."

From somewhere behind Alethea came the sound of a drum, softly beaten, its cadence pulsing through the night like a heartbeat. The stone grotto resounded with its pressure. It seemed to crawl up Alethea's body, consume her, become part of her.

A huge fire sprang to life some yards away, illuminating the grotto. By its light she saw that the men now wore nothing but flimsy wolf skins about their loins in the chill night air. The man-wolves swayed to the beat of the drum and took up a chant, the voices starting low, a deep bass that reached into the center of her brain and vibrated outward, pushing through her skin. Alethea couldn't make out the words, but the tone was evil, speaking of hunger and lust and wanting.

The two men nearest the flames scattered dust from their palms into the fire. A flash of blue-white light blinded her.

When her vision cleared, Alethea saw the priest standing before the flames, now also dressed in skins. A wolf's skull partly covered his face. He thrust one hand above his head and she saw it clutched Lathan's plasteel knife. The drum picked up its pace and the chanting grew louder. Even through her fright, Alethea found herself mesmerized.

She watched as the priest moved with the drumbeat, his motions fluid, carving the air with the knife in a well-practiced performance. Others joined him, forming a tight circle around the fire. The dancers echoed the priest's steps with ritual fervor. Bruenor swung the blade low, as though cutting a sheep, then passed it back and forth, higher, closer to his throat. Suddenly he left the circle, still swaying to the drumbeat, and approached Alethea. Using the knife, he touched her clothing and then ran the flat of the blade across the exposed flesh on her chest where Roman had removed the buttons. The blade's razor edge approached her throat and Alethea withheld a scream; she knew the ordeal would not end so soon. The priest laughed and danced back to the fire.

The solemn man with the flask approached the priest and Bruenor dipped Lathan's blade into the foul liquid, coating two inches of plasteel with darkness. Then, quickly so as not to spill a drop, he thrust the dirtied dagger into his forearm.

The priest's agonized howl split the night; but it was not the damage of the knife that caused the pain. Rather it was the burning of the sagcryl. Bruenor's eyes glazed over, grew distant, then returned, taking on a new fire. Laughing, he withdrew the knife from his flesh and licked the blade clean. No blood flowed from the wound in his arm. Then he howled again, this time in madness, his voice pitched much lower, approaching frenzy.

Alethea watched, horrified, as each man in the circle dipped a knife into the metal flask and then into his own flesh. Howls filled the night air. Some screamed when the drug took them. Others jerked like mishandled puppets. Many fell to the ground, writhing in pain, their skin mottling, a milky substance blossoming from their pores like budding flowers. The drumbeats and chants went on.

Though her barriers were up, Alethea could feel the pressure mounting. A dozen minds raging with sagcryl-enhanced True-Speech surrounded her, surging with unspeakable emotions. Bile rose in her throat as depraved thoughts bombarded her. She gasped as Skin-Runners shrieked and screamed and crawled around the grotto like loathsome were-beasts. They were nothing like Lathan's men. Enraptured in lust-filled frenzy. Pawing the earth in rage. Sagcryl bleeding from their pores. Casting out with their minds to crush and ravage and kill. They were a hundred times worse than Lathan!

Behind the screams, the drumbeat stepped up in tempo and the chanting rose, keeping time with the drum. The sounds came nearer, sliding to her left. Alethea could see them now, gathering at the edge of the firelight: drummer and chanters, the unsworn gathering at the edge of the firelight. An audience of the damned.

Please, Alethea prayed. Please let me die now, before the Skin-Runners turn their attention toward me. But death remained aloof.

The drumbeat raced. Men circled closer to the flames, leaping and kicking. Some screamed at the several moons in the sky, believing themselves the beasts they mimicked. One man jumped on another, forcing him to the ground, the blunt edge of his blade scraping across his companion's bare shoulders and back, performing by ritual the acts they would soon render for real. Alethea feared they saved the sharp edge for her.

Then the priest himself lunged at her, growling from the pit of his throat. She smelled the drug on his breath, and nausea enveloped her. Bruenor's skin folded and bled from the sagcryl surging though his veins. The cut on his arm where he had stabbed himself, however, refused to bleed. The priest's eyes were thick with haze, the redness that came with overuse of the drug. Cold light flickered within them, the eyes of a Demon.

Bruenor's mind came at her, then, his faculty of True-Speech heightened by the drug. "Not the Demon," he said.

"Not yet." He had read her. Despite her barriers!

The priest's body swayed in tempo with the drum, the plasteel knife rising and falling like a bird in a storm. His mind pushed against her barriers, tearing them down. Other minds joined his, those of his pack, howling like the wind, defeating her. The priest's blade touched her throat, teasing the skin, caressing it, but drawing no blood.

Visions exploded into Alethea's mind. She fought, but still they came. The Skin-Runners would not touch her until her barriers were gone. First, they would feed on her mind, relishing in her horror. Then they would give her an overdose of the drug and revel in her pain as frenzy took her. When she grew numb to the pain, they would cut her, but no blood would flow; the nature of the drug would see to that. Her skin would mottle and bleed from the pores. With their knives they would carve at her flesh, peeling away the skin, ever so carefully, ever so slowly, their movements steeled by the drug. The hide would be preserved, kept as a trophy, displayed to other Skin-Runners behind locked and bolted doors to advance their status.

Even with skin removed, she would not bleed. The drug would keep her alive, for a time, during which they would take her, ravage her with savage glee. Having violated her psyche with their minds, and her body with the drug and their knives, they would violate her soul with their perversions.

In the end, when frenzy faded and her flesh began to die, they would butcher her alive. Feeding from her drugged flesh, they would gorge themselves before running into the night, howling like animals, butchering every living thing they encountered. In the morning they would survey the ruin of their hunger and revel in what they had done. Then they would search for new offerings for the Demon.

The visions ceased and Alethea gasped. She had stopped breathing and now sucked in great quantities of air. Bruenor leered at her, his sick smile showing how he had reveled in her horror, her loathing, her disgust. The images he had sent still echoed in her mind. They would not go away. And somewhere... somewhere there would be a Demon.

The priest laughed, his face twisting, looking more like a wolf's skull than the bones he wore. "A Demon!" he spat, his voice so low that Alethea barely heard it. His eyes were no longer the eyes of Bruenor, but of something infinitely more hideous. A voice came at her mind in a flood, crumbling her barriers to rubble. The words were alien, harsh, and inhuman. "Yes," it growled. "There will be Demons!"

Pain seared Alethea's mind, burning until nothing remained but screeching waves of agony, a jumbled distortion of words, a confused image of beasts that came at her, hungers and hatreds that washed over her. Demons in wolf-form, vaguely man-like, touching, taking, devouring. A horrid stench assailed her, like sour milk, but stronger. She was suddenly cold. Her stomach wanted to heave, but the agony in her mind prevented her body from reacting. *I must be dead! Please, let me be dead.*

Then everything went dark. The pain remained, but sank into the background, a dull roar. Whether it was her own mind struggling to adjust, or something the Demon did, she didn't know. Without meaning to, she opened her eyes.

The thing that was no longer Bruenor stood before her, the metal flask in its hands. It pushed the drug-laced blood to her lips. "Drink!" it snarled. "Just one sip. Play with us!"

Alethea turned her head away and a claw-like hand seized her jaw, forcing her mouth open. The flask pressed against her lips, its metal like ice. The stink of blood and sagcryl constricted her throat and sent her stomach churning anew. She felt the Priest lift the flask, preparing to pour its contents down her throat.

Then a sharp cry split the night, a high-pitched wail that filled the grotto. The drumming and the chanting stopped. The flask lowered. The fingers eased. Alethea saw every face in the grotto turn to the sound, its source hidden outside the circle of firelight. At a signal from Bruenor, wolf-forms sprinted into the darkness.

The cry broke off, replaced by silence, and all eyes continued to peer into the night. While attention was diverted away from her, Alethea frantically rebuilt her barriers.

A tiny light bobbed in the darkness, a bright firefly that ducked and weaved. For an instant it was gone, replaced by an agonized scream. Then the light returned and bobbed closer. Disappeared. Another scream. Reappeared.

The priest flashed Alethea a quick glance. Blood-red eyes in a mottled face seemed to say that her reprieve would be a brief one. Then he turned away again and peered into the darkness.

Alethea watched, helpless, as the light weaved its way closer and a sten-bear shambled into the grotto on its hind legs. It was small for its kind and had a young man's face. A sword of light blazed in its right paw. Snarling manically, a werebeast leapt at it. Light flashed and the man-wolf shrieked and dropped to the ground. Howling went up all throughout the grotto as the sten-bear continued to advance. It waved its bright sword, striking down other Skin-Runners that jumped to the attack. It seemed headed toward Alethea.

The priest howled at the sten-bear like a man possessed which, Alethea realized, he was. Unlike his Skin-Runners, the Demon-Priest attacked with his mind instead of his knife. Alethea recalled how her own barriers had crumbled before what Bruenor had become. She pitied the bear. Yet somehow it managed to continue shambling toward her.

Bruenor stepped back, and Alethea saw his jaw go slack and his eyes widen. Then he roared with rage and dropped his blood-filled flask to the ground. Dark liquid poured out at Alethea's feet and was sucked up by the earth. The priest raised the plasteel knife and howled, his voice deep from the drug. The curse sounded alien to Alethea's ears, possibly in a language known only to the Demon that occupied the priest.

Then the sten-bear was upon them. White light flashed and again Bruenor screamed, this time as his right arm fell away to join the flask. The possessed priest shrieked at the sten-bear and fled into the darkness, the raw stump of his shoulder revealed briefly in the firelight.

Howling with despair, those of Bruenor's pack who could, raced after their leader. Dead and dying Skin-Runners lay scattered in the firelight. Near the abandoned flask, the priest's arm twitched like a drunken snake; animated by the drug, it still clutched the plasteel knife, seeking a target. As the maddened cries of defeated man-wolves grew distant, silence returned.

Alethea found herself alone in the grotto with the sten-bear and saw now that it was not a bear with a man's face, but a young man dressed in ragged sten-bear skins. His eyes flashed wildly, searching for enemies. Sweat matted his hair and ran from his arms. Alethea gasped as the glowing sword collapsed in on itself and seeped into his right forearm, where it disappeared. A rush of air escaped the man's lungs and he sank to his knees. Then he held his face in his hands and wept like a child.

It tore at Alethea's heart to listen to his sobs. In all her experience, she had never supposed that a man could have such emotions. He was young, surely not much older than herself. *Who is he? Why is he here? Did the Elsan send him?*

The man stood finally, sorrowful gray eyes finding hers. Even in the uneasy light of the dwindling fire, Alethea could see they were clean; the life that flickered within, though weary, burned bright as suns. His exposed skin was soft and free of signs. He was not a Skin-Runner, not even a heavy sagcryl user. He drew near and pulled a knife from beneath his bearskin coat and, with quick jerks, cut the ropes that bound her feet and hands.

Alethea's arms and legs were lead weights as she fell free from the ritual poles. The young man caught her in his arms and eased her to the ground. His eyes bore into hers as he straightened. Then he averted his gaze, as though suddenly embarrassed by what he was doing. He stepped a few paces away and stared out into the night while Alethea rubbed her wrists and ankles. Blood oozed where rope had bitten into skin, but there was no serious damage. Serious! A Demon had held a blade to her throat!

Near her feet, the priest's severed arm continued to twitch in the dusty earth. Alethea darted out her hand and retrieved the plasteel knife, sliding it quickly into Lathan's sheath beneath her tunic. She didn't believe her rescuer had noticed it, and the knife was the only thing of value she possessed. She was determined not to lose it. Alethea still couldn't believe that she had been a single breath away from being ravaged by Skin-Runners.

Her eyes shot up to her rescuer. "Why?"

The man jumped, startled, and then frowned at her. "What?"

"Why did you rescue me? Who sent you?"

The young man turned away, staring off into the night. His answer was gruff. "I heard someone calling." He tapped the side of his head. "In here. And I heard the noise of minds. I followed. I had hoped..." He fell silent.

Alethea realized that he was no less distraught then she and decided not to push him. "My name is Alethea," she said. "I don't know what you hoped, but I'm glad that you found me."

The man turned back toward her. "What were you doing? Here, I mean. How did you come to be here?" He spread his hands in disgust. "Where did you come from?"

"I was running from the camp of Lathan the Klep, a trader, an evil man. The Skin-Runners found me. Chased me through the Tombs. Caught me and brought me here. It wasn't my idea. I was on my way to..." Alethea realized she was saying too much. She didn't even know this man. "What's your name?"

"Corin," he said, frowning. "Son of... just Corin."

The man – Corin – looked miserable. His eyes darted about, seeking something. Perhaps to get away?

From the edge of the grotto came a scattering of pebbles followed by the soft nicker of a horse. An enormous black stallion trotted into the firelight. It approached the man and nuzzled his face.

Corin smiled and patted its nose. "We should get away from here." Alethea wasn't sure if he was speaking to her or the horse. "Those Skin-Runners won't come back any time soon, but I'd rather not be here when they do."

Skin-Runner Bait

Corin turned his head in the darkness, taking in the shadows of trees that blocked the starlight. Three of Sindarin's small moons raced across the eastern sky, heralding the approach of dawn. From the Skin-Runner grotto they had ridden north, skirting the western slope of Karlac's Bane and down into the wide vale beyond called Ethan's Green. From Serl's saddle he could almost see the grass and brush on the valley floor, thick with new leaves, their fresh scent rising to fill his nostrils. Even in the dead of night, the unfamiliar forest seemed friendly after the barren Tombs region.

Behind him in the saddle, the girl stirred. She had told him her name but Corin couldn't remember it. Bait is what she was, though. When a Skin-Runner pack was suspected and the Square sent out patrols, they would take young men and women along as bait. A clean young man herding goats or a fresh faced girl gathering herbs. The Skin-Runners would take anyone, of course, but they preferred those untainted by the drug. Young people or people of the Path. They often took children. The girl was perfect bait. So where was the Square's patrol?

Corin shuddered at the memory of slain bodies left unburied back in the grotto. Among the Tower Guard were those who boasted of killing a Skin-Runner or suspected Skin-Runner. It was no crime. Quite the opposite. His father encouraged the murder of Skin-Runners. He offered rewards. Corin had never killed one. Never had the opportunity. Tonight he had killed how many? Ten? A dozen? His father would reach deep into his pockets to pay for this one. That he had killed bothered Corin less than how he had killed. He had summoned the Hest — a thing unheard of — and death followed.

The bait behind him moaned in her sleep, perhaps reliving her experience among the Skin-Runners. Corin did not envy her. Whatever rites they performed with their victims had already progressed far beyond the stories he'd been told by the guard.

After leaving the grotto, she had tightened her arms about his waist and fallen silent. Exactly when she had fallen asleep, Corin didn't know. He was unused to anyone riding behind him in the saddle and was shocked to discover her able to sleep without sliding to the ground.

That she was with him was a problem. He was no longer alone; his search for his True-Friend couldn't be more fouled up. But what could he do besides take her with him to Toroth? He needed to tell his father about the Skin-Runners. A large pack in the Tombs region, though no longer quite so large. He couldn't just leave her there.

Returning to Toroth without finding his True-Friend was bad enough. Death would be preferable, or at least less embarrassing. His father would be furious. Yet it was not so much his father's disappointment that Corin dreaded as it was the manea's. And that was odd. He had never cared to please anyone but his parents.

And so the unspoken question continued to nettle him: What will Minesh say?

Behind him, the bait stirred and Corin realized she was awake.

"I need to rest," he said, pulling up on the reins. When he slid out of the saddle, his legs nearly gave way, forcing him to lean against Serl for support. He hadn't realized how exhausted he was. And weak. From using the Hest? Or hunger? Or both?

He helped the bait climb down from Serl's back and she poked her head around in the darkness, peering into the night. "Is it safe?" There was fear in her voice.

Corin left Serl free to graze then curled up into a ball in the grass, his sten-bear coat making a soft, if rancid, blanket. He really was tired. Too tired for talk. "Is any place safe?" he mumbled.

In the weariness of his mind, Corin's thoughts whirled like a windstorm. The Hest. The deer. The sten-bear. Skin-Runners. Weremen falling before him in the grotto. Blood and death. Murder. The bait, tied to the posts, frightened out of her mind. His quest for his True-Friend, ruined. The manea, stern and dagger-eyed, frowning at him in disapproval. Images whipped past him like leaves in the wind.

Then sleep took him.

$$\Omega$$

Sitting in the grass, a thin blanket she had found at the Skin-Runner camp wrapped around her shoulders, Alethea peered into the darkness, starting at every night bird's cry and tree frog's croak. Eventually Corin's horse stopped munching grass and stood still, asleep standing up. How horses did that, Alethea never could understand. She lay back in the grass and pulled the blanket tighter, willing herself to sleep. Her ears would not allow it. Was that a twig snapping? A wolf's howl off toward the mountains? A man-wolf? When she closed her eyes she saw Bruenor's face, eyes glowing red, breath like sour milk. It used to be Lathan's face she saw when sleep failed her— the animal of her nightmares. A monster had usurped that place.

The sighing of the breeze was her only solace, a gentle rhythm beneath the dissonant forest sounds. How much time passed before she realized that it wasn't a breeze at all, but Corin's low breath, she didn't know. When dawn pushed away the darkness, she was sitting up again, her elbows on her knees, her chin in her palms, and her thoughts empty, simply listening to her rescuer's breath.

Corin woke perhaps an hour later, the sun now well in the sky. The young man glanced at Alethea without speaking; he seemed irritated or angry. Retrieving a small, fur bundle from one of his saddlebags, he gave it to her and went off in search of water. What was inside must be meat because Alethea wouldn't know what else to call it. Gingerly, she stripped away a small piece and nibbled on it. It tasted worse than it smelled.

When Corin returned, she showed him the open bundle and grimaced. "How many days was this carcass dead before you threw it into the fire?"

Corin stared at her. His gray eyes seemed to expand in his skull while at the same time they darkened, becoming hard stone. She had never seen gray eyes like that. It was like staring into a lightning storm, dark clouds and quicksilver.

She expected almost any reply. What she didn't expect was for Corin to heave off his sten-bear coat and rip open the tattered shirt beneath it. His chest was a mess. Ugly red lines ran from just below his collarbone down toward his hips, four lines to each side, about an inch apart. The wounds were recent.

"I killed it!" Corin snarled. His teeth ground together as he spoke. "And roasted its flesh over the fire while its blood was still warm." He drew tight his shirt and pulled the makeshift coat back over his head. "I'm sorry if I didn't have a kitchen and chefs to prepare it for you."

Alethea studied him, sensing his anger and dismissing it. It was all a bluff. She had seen real anger before; this was not a violent man. "Does it hurt? I mean when you grind your teeth like that?"

Corin's jaw dropped and he twisted his head to one side.

"And that coat is pathetic. Where did you learn how to cure a hide? It stinks like a slaughterhouse."

The consternation on Corin's face turned back into rage, and for a moment Alethea feared she had misjudged him. Gone too far. Then, slowly, he raised his hand to his face and pinched his nose. His mouth twisted in distaste. "It does stink, doesn't it?" He let go of his nose. "I was hoping I'd get used to the smell, but I haven't." He shrugged and took the seared and undercooked bear meat from her hands. He popped a morsel into his mouth and made a sour face. "It tastes as bad as I smell."

"Give me some of that!" Alethea demanded. "I'm hungry." And together they laughed as they ate the foul meat.

After breakfast they rode on in silence. Alethea sensed that Corin's anger had returned, his body unnaturally rigid beneath her encircling arms. Her gentle probing of his barriers confirmed her suspicions that at least part of that anger was directed at her. Why that should be, she couldn't fathom. He had seemed so friendly after that initial embarrassment with the meat.

The day was warm for spring, with patches of white cloud

drifting across a blue sky. Corin removed his bearskin coat and draped it across his knees and Alethea found herself starting to drowse in the saddle.

At midday they stopped to stretch their legs and drink from a stream that spilled from a grove of olive-green pines. The Serpent's Tail wound across the eastern horizon, the low peaks lost in cloud, a sign that rain was coming. The prospect of wandering through the wilderness in the rain was not a pleasant one. "Where are we?" Alethea asked, hoping to break the silence.

Corin glanced at her with those startling gray eyes. They went well with his sharp, narrow nose and wide, full mouth. "The Tildis Dells. We'll be in Rhedan soon."

Rhedan. Alethea knew where that was. East and a little south of Toroth. She nodded and crouched beside a gooseberry bush, pretending to examine its unripe berries. In truth, she was studying Corin's face. Her rescuer stood at the water's edge, staring into the shallow current. He seemed distracted, his forehead pinched. So it wasn't just anger. Fear perhaps? *The same fear as mine?* Alethea straightened. "Do you suppose the Skin-Runners are anywhere nearby?"

A half-smile broke the tightness of Corin's lips. "The ones from the grotto? A long way from here, I imagine. Nursing their wounds in any case. That priest fellow who left his arm behind. You called him Bruenor? You need no longer fear him."

Alethea plucked a green-white berry. "I suppose you are right. It was just so horrible." Alethea thrust the memory from her mind, concentrating instead on the smooth berry between her fingers, feeling its hardness against her skin. She glanced up to see Corin staring into the distance, his gray eyes showing just a hint of blue. The anger was still there. "Where are we going after Rhedan?" she asked.

Corin frowned and looked away. "Toroth. If there are Skin-Runners at Karlac Tombs, the Square should know."

Alethea called to her mind the map she had studied. "Kelmar is closer. Or it was."

"I prefer to go to Toroth." There was an edge to his voice.

Toroth was the problem. He didn't want to go.

The unripe berry slipped from her hand and splashed unnoticed into the stream. She hated these word games. Why couldn't people, even strangers, speak directly? "Corin, why did you find me? What were you doing near the Karlac Tombs? Most people fear to go there."

Corin's back stiffened and his face became a scowl. "I think we've rested long enough." He moved away to adjust Serl's saddle.

Alethea took a deep breath and held it. *Well, it's not as though he owes me an explanation. And he did save my life. Probably plans to turn me over to the Square in Toroth when he reports the Skin-Runners. And the Square may just hand me back to Lathan. I am a runaway servant, after all.* Alethea thought about that, and decided it might be wise to part ways before that happened. She could go to the Circle in Toroth. They would hide her from men like Lathan. And help her find her True-Friend.

As dusk approached, they crested a low rise and the Vale of Rhedan opened up before them, a wide, tree-filled bowl nestled in a broad sweep of the Serpent's Tail. A slender ribbon of blue snaked among the trees— the Rhedan River, its roots in the Serpent's tail and its destination the Sunfall Sea.

Alethea had been to Rhedan once and knew the Aenlaen River joined the Rhedan at the west end of the vale. Friends of her mother had come to gather medicinal herbs that grew in the floodplain and on the mountain slopes further east. It was summer then, the weather hot, and young girls like Ilsa and herself were good workers, ferreting out the various tiny plants hidden among the rocks and tall grasses. The memory awakened a sense of hope that had been missing since the Skin-Runner camp. For the first time, she felt that Lathan and Bruenor were behind her, that she was safe.

Corin urged Serl down-slope toward the river's banks. He halted when they found a willow camp, several giant trees with bushy arms growing together to form a natural hollow that kept out the brisk Aenlaen winds. Alethea set three snares further along the riverbank – she was not going to eat that wretched sten-bear meat again unless she had to – then watched as Corin assembled kindling and used flint he had found at the Skin-Runner grotto to start a fire. Bright flames sent sparks sputtering skyward, pushing back the darkness and the chill. When there were adequate coals, Alethea checked her snares and they made a meal of fresh rabbit.

As she ate, Alethea pushed memories of the Skin-Runner grotto behind her and thought instead of Ilsa, wondering if she was all right. She also reflected upon her quest to find her True-Friend and the manea. Would the Circle in Toroth really help her? Or would she have to go east, beyond the Serpent's Tail?

"Do you know of a man?" Alethea asked, breaking the silence. "The Circle's manea? His name is Minesh. They say he sometimes dwells in Cambre."

Corin started, and the anger returned to his face. "What does a woman wish of Minesh? The Path has other guides for women."

Alethea brushed back her hair with her hand. She didn't know that. Perhaps she needn't go to Cambre. "I was taught the Path in my youth," she explained. "But never... I never... I seek my True-Friend. Minesh was my last hope."

Corin started again. Alethea could see his hands clenching and unclenching over his knees. "Minesh! Why?"

Alethea thrust out her chin. "My True-Speech is strong. I want to reach beyond the Shroud."

"All born on Sindarin may Speak True," Corin said coldly, relaxing his hands. "It comes from the sage."

"Yes, but people either let it slip away or augment it with sagcryl. I would do neither. The ways of the traders disgust me. The Skin-Runners... are worse. I seek the way without the drug."

Corin laughed, bitterly. "I know of Minesh. I doubt he can help you."

"Why?" Alethea felt hot tears in her eyes.

Corin didn't answer, but pressed his lips together as though searching for words and not finding any.

Alethea waited, then sniffed. "How much further is it to

Toroth?"

Corin shrugged. "Two days. Maybe longer. We pass through the Gardens of Nume before reaching the Victron Bridge. From there you can see the wall of the city and Haven Gate."

Alethea nodded. She would have to go with him. At Toroth she would seek out the Circle. Or ask supplies from her mother's friends and try again for Cambre.

"We should sleep now," Corin said. "The sun comes early." He passed her a length of sten-bear hide to supplement her thin blanket. He kept his coat to use as a blanket for himself.

Their hands touched when Alethea took the fur. She was surprised that Corin's fingers could be so warm when his voice was so cold. He yanked his hand away and buried himself in his coat.

Alethea smiled to herself as she arranged the smelly bearskin for warmth, but almost immediately images of the Skin-Runner grotto returned to haunt her rest. Even the security of the plasteel knife hidden beneath her tunic failed to fend off images of Bruenor's dark eyes on hers; the angry, blood red eyes of a Demon. She sought refuge in thoughts of her sister, wondering how Ilsa was, where she was. Had her plan to trick Lathan succeeded? Not for the first time, Alethea wondered if she had made the right choice in leaving her sister.

$$\Omega$$

"You worthless slut!" Lathan's voice roared with anger, presaging the hammer blow of his fist.

Ilsa cried out and fell to her knees. The blow bruised her cheek and split her lip. Hot blood welled inside her mouth as rough hands grabbed her from behind, forcing her to look up into Lathan's face.

"Where is she? Where did you send her?"

Ilsa's vision blurred and she blinked to clear it. Lathan's hand came up again. Ilsa wasn't sure where it landed, but lights danced across the tent's canvas ceiling.

"Speak! Is she worth this much to you?" Lathan struck a third time, sending shocks down her spine. Ilsa felt certain she heard bones in her face break.

"Please!" she gasped, slurring the word, each breath a battle. Her skin itched with warm blood trickling down her chin, pooling at the base of her throat and coursing between her breasts. Rough hands crushed her shoulders. Through eyes puffed half-shut, Ilsa watched Lathan's face loom closer.

"Please?" Lathan whined in mock imitation. "I've been saying please for six days. Six days she's been gone. Gone without a sign. Please! Do you think you're worth more to me than her? You are nothing! A whore! Baggage to be used and cast aside! Filth! Your sister was clean. Free from the drug. Free to be sold to the Skin-Runners. A prize for their bloody Gorgings. Bruenor would have paid a fortune in sagcryl for her." His fist struck again. "Where is the girl?"

Ilsa worked her jaw. "Gone." The word came out as barely a whisper. "You loved me once."

"Love!" Lathan spat the word. "You've never been loved. Used. Never loved."

Ilsa expected another blow. Steeled herself for it. Lathan used his mind instead, hurtling his rage against her barriers. Pain exploded through her skull, washing across her senses. Ilsa gave no reaction. She was used to it now. Long weeks of heavy sagcryl use and abuse from the traders had dulled her senses. It would take more than Lathan's weak will to elicit a response.

Suddenly cold metal pressed against her throat. With her vision clouded, Ilsa hadn't seen the knife coming. Fire burned where steel sliced a shallow line through flesh. New blood coursed down her chest.

"Can you withstand my blade, hmmm? Perhaps your flesh will relent where your mind is too foolish. Where is the girl?"

The blade dipped lower, tracing obscenities across Ilsa's collarbone. The trader seemed to know where to cut, where and how deep. How had he learned that? His artistry brought excruciating pain but failed to lure unconsciousness. Ilsa accepted the pain, knowing that was easier than fighting it. Knowing that soon the hurt would end and she would find release. That simple knowledge brought peace.

From somewhere in the back of Ilsa's being came light, comfort, assurance. A memory of her youth, of the teachers of the Path. What was it they had said? That death is not to be feared. That the spirit and mind live on beyond the Shroud, unencumbered by the wants and needs of frail flesh. That is why we must protect the mind, nourish it. That is why we must avoid the drug. The drug corrupts—

New pain brought Ilsa back to the present. Lathan had seen her escape, her thoughts hiding in the past. He had brought up the blade, was carving her left cheek. Cold air sought the fresh opening. Blood filled her mouth. Ilsa choked and swallowed.

"Tie her down!" Lathan snarled. "Pin her head between the spikes and bring me the drug!"

Released from Lathan's grip, Ilsa's head thudded against the earth. The crushed bones of her face shifted and tore, sending new agony spearing through her brain. Rough wood gashed her ears as the traders hammered hand-hewn spikes into the dirt floor of the tent, locking her skull in place. Through blurred vision, she saw Lathan sheathe his bloody knife, an ordinary blade, his prized plasteel gone missing; at least she had that. The trader accepted a cup reeking of sagcryl-laced wine from one of his men. Other hands took the cup and drank as well.

"I want a controlled search," Lathan said. "No one is to drop into frenzy. Break everything she has. When we have what we want, she's mine. The rest of you can play with what's left when I'm done."

Ilsa felt them come, gleefully chipping away her barriers as the drug enhanced their strength. Once again her thoughts raced back to her youth, to the teachings of the Path, to words she had been taught, but scoffed at.

Again the gentle light called to her, beckoning. The men were almost through. Soon her mind would be theirs to do with as they wished. "Alethea," she whispered, and ran to the light, willing her own death.

$$\Omega$$

"Damn!" Lathan shouted. "What happened?"

"You roughed her up too much," said Nagram, a skinny young man not much older than the girl.

Lathan raised a hand to strike the lad for his insolence, but restrained himself. He had taken Nagram on because he was his sister's son, and family deserved some advantage. He would have a private word with him later. Instead, he spat into the dirt. "Like Hell I did! I know what I'm doing. She took something."

"I got a name, Lathan." Eraed, a small rodent-like man, whispered with excitement. "Before she died. Minesh. Maybe it's a man. It could be a place."

"Minesh." Muttering curses, Lathan climbed to his feet and left the tent.

His men stayed behind for their sport.

$$\Omega$$

"Minesh. You are most welcome. Please, sit here beside me."

The manea tilted his head in mock respect. "Thank you, Herlen. The trip from Cambre was long."

The private study of Sindarin's king, high in the Tower of Toroth, was as large as an alehouse common room. Windows fitted with the best artisan glass lined one wall. Thick carpets covered every square inch of floor. Three fireplaces burned sweet-smelling cedar wood hauled by wagon all of the way from the Sethnin Plains. The proffered divan was wide and soft, expensive. The cushions sank deep beneath Minesh's weight. Such opulence. The insidious wellspring of Corin's arrogance.

"Have you slept, manea?" the King asked, following all the forms of protocol.

Minesh frowned. They were better friends than that. "Have you, Sire? Will you sleep before the test is done?"

Now it was Herlen's turn to frown. "You know me well enough to know the answer to that. Will you drink with me?"

The manea grinned. *He's toying with me, trying to hide his unease.* "If the drinks are pure, Herlen. I want none of that wretched garden draft this tower blends."

"Have no fear of that, my friend. I crush my own herbs. My wine is as pure as yours."

"A bold challenge from one I have bested before."

Herlen shook his head. "Still you chastise me, manea. Have I not paid enough for my position?"

Minesh laughed. "Have you anyone else to remind you of your place?"

The King grinned and handed him a silvered goblet. "I can think of many, all of them buxom and naked!"

"Ha!" roared Minesh. "At your age? You have neither the will nor the prowess for such pursuits. Confine yourself to the Path, my friend, and you will live a long and fruitful life."

"As you have," returned the King. He raised his cup in a toast and took a hearty swallow.

Minesh studied the tension in Herlen's movements. The awkward jerking of the wrist. The trembling of fingers that held the cup. Light from the nearer fire cast long shadows across the King's haggard face, a face that had ruled too long.

The manea lifted his own cup and sipped delicately, letting the rich vapors wash the dust of the road from his throat. His eyes never left Herlen's face. He lowered his cup and set it aside, then spoke the words that needed to be said. "He took the Hest, Herlen. The blade has accepted him."

The relief in the King's face was expansive. "I knew when you arrived that Corin had taken the rites. Otherwise, he would have accompanied you."

Riding beside me, or his cold flesh slung across my saddle. There were three ways to return from the rites. Accepted, rejected, or dead.

"He has yet to find his True-Friend," Minesh said. "Corin walks the wilderness."

The Prince's father shrugged. "He'll succeed. That's the easy part compared to the Hest."

Minesh watched as Herlen unconsciously rubbed his forearm, teasing an old scar. He knew only too well what his son was going through. Seconds ticked by in silence as Minesh sat unmoving, his cup ignored.

The King's brow furrowed. "What? There's more?"

"The rites were disturbed, Herlen. The Beast is loose."

Herlen took another swallow of wine and then set down his

cup. He clasped his hands. Then unclasped them and stared down at his feet. "Arazmud. Well, that happens. The Demon has been loose before. Corin is past the rites. He should be safe." Herlen looked up. "The Skin-Runners now, that's another matter. They grow bold when the Beast is loose. Arazmud has a stronger grip on them than other Demons. I may have to take steps. The garrisons we have now will not be enough—"

Minesh interrupted him. "You misunderstand me. The Beast was at Corin's rites. Arazmud tried to kill your son."

Herlen's face went pale. He lifted his hand to his lips and blinked when he realized that he no longer held his cup. "Well, it failed. We can thank our True-Friends for that. I'm sure they were watching, and helped."

Minesh sighed. "You know my meaning. I speak of the Mastren."

The King retrieved his cup and clutched it in both hands. "Again? If we ran through the streets shouting Mastren every time the Beast broke free, Sindarin would be in a state of constant panic."

"The Mastren will come when the Beast is free," Minesh pressed.

"Not in our lifetime," roared the King. "You know what the Mastren means? Everything we've built, destroyed!" Wine spilled from Herlen's cup, spattering against his fine clothes and striking the carpeted floor like a splash of blood. "There have been no signs in the heavens. No strange lights. No unfamiliar voices. The Mastren is for a future age."

Minesh's lips grew taut. "We will see no signs, Herlen. The Mastren must come before the Hunters. He will need time. Corin—"

"Corin? What? The Mastren!" Herlen drained the remainder of his cup in one quick swallow. "You should rejoin the Elders, Minesh. You're beginning to sound just like them! You people live beyond the Shroud, seeing Beasts and Demons and Mastrens behind every curtain!" He raised the cup again; frowned to discover it empty.

"It's a possibility," Minesh told him. "You know the

Legends as well as anyone. You would be a fool to ignore them."

Herlen stepped up to the wine table and refilled his cup, then offered to do the same for the manea.

Minesh shook his head. He had hardly touched his.

"Legends," muttered the King. "I have to ignore them. I'm the boy's father."

"And I am your friend, Herlen. I would do you a disservice not to warn you."

Herlen swallowed hard. Nodded. He raised his cup in an uneasy toast. "To fathers and friends," he said.

Minesh raised a rejoinder. "To your son."

Sign of the Beast

Olwen the healer bent forward and pulled back a corner of the blanket. The man on the treatment table lay unconscious, his face pale. She frowned as she took in the nature of the injury. There should be blood. Had someone already cleaned the wound? Even so, there should still be blood. The man lost his arm. And why was he under guard? She leaned in close for a better look at the injury, and gasped.

Her apprentice, sorting items at the instrument table, heard and rushed to Olwen's side. "What is it? What's wrong?"

Olwen dropped the blanket back over the wound and straightened. "Nothing. The wound is more ghastly than I had anticipated. I require a strong potion of barkwax and scabious. And an ample portion of bryony. Mix it into a quantity of strong sage wine. Hurry now!"

"As you wish, Olwen." The apprentice hesitated before leaving; Olwen knew the girl longed to examine the wound herself. Knew as well that she couldn't let that happen. When the door closed, the healer again lifted the covering and inspected her patient.

The skin at the shoulder was mottled and wrinkled, the pores twice their normal size. The man's throat was stretched and pitted, the larynx swollen. Close inspection of the face revealed skin-paint, used lightly by dancers, liberally by heavy sagcryl addicts to hide the enlarged pores. She checked the eyes. The irises were deep red. Not a crime in itself, but a strong indicator that the man was likely a Skin-Runner. A chill ran down Olwen's back.

She proceeded to examine the shoulder where the arm had been torn away. No, torn was not the right word. Severed. Cleaner than by her own knife. Already the wound was scarring over, healing itself.

The door opened and Olwen dropped the blanket back over the wound. Her apprentice entered carrying an iron flask fragrant with smells of healing. Olwen took the potion and dismissed her, watching as the girl reluctantly left the room.

Turning back to her patient, Olwen nearly dropped the flask. The injured man had opened his eyes and was watching her.

Calming herself, Olwen straightened. "My name is Olwen. I'm a Healer. I serve Peradean, Commander of the Fifth Square of Sindarin. You are in his tower at Kelmar and under his care. What is your name, sir?"

The man swallowed, not changing his expression. His gaze took in the room as he spoke. "What do you care? Your duty is to see to my well-being, nothing more. My name is my own concern."

"I see." Olwen resumed her attempt to appear clinical. "Perhaps you are still in shock from your injury."

"Don't you know?" demanded the man. "What kind of healer are you?"

Olwen raised her brows, startled by the rebuke. "I need to know something of the injury before I can properly treat it. Losing an arm may have serious repercussions. How did it happen?"

The injured man sneered. "Answering that may have serious repercussions. On your own well-being."

Olwen felt sweat sprout on her forehead and unconsciously lifted a hand to wipe it away. A Skin-Runner, even a one-armed Skin-Runner, was a danger to be reckoned with. But it was her duty to help this man. She continued delving for information. "Your injury is most curious. I can't treat you properly unless I know the nature of the wounding."

"Then don't treat me, healer. What right have you to hold me?"

"Who said you are being held?"

"Those guards standing by the door."

Olwen chuckled uneasily. "Oh. Well, as to that... this is a garrison. Commander Peradean keeps his guards posted at all times, just to keep them out of mischief."

"Hah!"

"If you're not going to tell me about your wound, you could at least drink this potion. It will speed the healing." Olwen held the flask aloft, wondering how close she could bring her hand near the Skin-Runner's teeth without risking the loss of a finger.

The man sat up using his remaining arm, wincing at the pain from his shoulder stump. He smelled the sage wine, frowned, and then drank.

Olwen watched, trying hard not to look insulted. She didn't think she could handle staying in the room with him a moment longer. "Perhaps you will feel like talking once you have rested," she said, taking back the flask.

"Yeah," grunted her patient. He eased himself back down onto the table. "And maybe I'll feel like cutting out your heart."

Olwen fled.

Ω

The messenger panted for breath as he reached the top of the stairs. The long, narrow chest he carried was heavy, as was the crested vestment upon his shoulders. The look the Tower Guards gave him was one of amusement; it was barely dawn and the King had retired late to his rooms.

Setting the chest on the floor, the messenger rapped three times against the door. He hoped the knock sounded urgent.

"What is it?" Herlen's voice growled from behind the door. "And it had better be important."

"A messenger, sire. From the outpost at Kelmar."

"What? That hole in the ground! Who sent you?"

"Peradean, milord, of the Fifth Square."

"Just a minute."

He heard a rustling of cloth as Herlen dressed, as well as low muttering. "First Minesh's fanatical ranting about the Mastren. Now messengers before dawn. How am I to get any sleep!"

The door opened and the King of Sindarin stepped into the hall. Herlen's thin, black hair was a tangled mess and deep lines marred his unshaven face. His dark eyes were heavy and cold. "And you are?"

"Liniel of Icri Haven." The messenger proffered a deep bow. "Milord."

Herlen sighed wearily. "Dispense with the formalities. Your journey has been long and my rest short. Just state your message."

Liniel reached into his tunic and produced a parchment. He unrolled it and opened his mouth. His eyes scanned the sheet and he looked up. "No formalities?"

"Get on with it." The set of the King's lips seethed with impatience.

"Well then, uh, Commander Peradean has captured a Skin-Runner. Milord."

The King's eyes glistened with amazement. "What? That's your message?"

"He sends this." Liniel reached down and opened the chest. It contained a long, clothbound bundle that he set on a side table stationed outside the King's chamber door. Taking exceptional care not to actually touch the contents, he spread opened the wrappings.

Herlen's face went white. "By the Demon, man! Peradean sent me a Skin-Runner's arm! Has he lost his mind?"

Liniel felt his face grow hot. "It belongs to the man we found. Milord. The arm, uh, wasn't attached when we found him."

Herlen frowned. "And that's supposed to make me feel better? Why send the arm at all?"

"Commander Peradean wished you to see the wound,

milord. He thought it important."

Liniel watched Herlen inspect the shoulder and knew exactly what the King was thinking. It was a clean cut. Too clean.

Herlen turned to one of his guards. "Get my healer." To Liniel he said, "Where was this found?"

"We received rumors of Skin-Runners near the Karlac Tombs. The mounted guardsmen Peradean sent to investigate found a grotto. The place was filthy with slaughtered Skin-Runners. We believe it was the site of a Gorging. Something... something must have gone wrong. Milord."

Herlen snorted. "Wrong? How can something go wrong at a Gorging? A Gorging is wrong, wrong from beginning to end!"

"Uh, yes." Liniel shifted his weight. "What I mean to say is that all of the dead Skin-Runners had wounds like this one. Peradean found the survivor wandering not far from the grotto."

"What's this ring?" Herlen reached, thought better of it, and dropped his hand to his side. The middle finger of the severed arm wore a silver ring with a red stone carved in the shape of a wolf's skull. No flesh adorned the skull, but the eyes gleamed as though alive.

"I noticed it," admitted Liniel. "I've never seen one like it before. Milord."

Herlen's healer arrived on the landing. "Oh, my!" she said upon seeing the arm.

"What do you make of it?" demanded Herlen.

The healer seemed puzzled, and slightly ill. She swallowed. "It's ah, an arm, sire."

Herlen cast her a withering look. "The wound!"

The healer peered closer. "Oh my!" she said. "Had to be quick. Had to be sharp. Very sharp. No blood. See the skin? The man was saturated with sagcryl when it happened. Is he dead?"

"No," offered Liniel.

"Oh my!"

Herlen pursed his lips. "Cut off the ring."

"Me?" squeaked the healer. Her eyes flew wide. "Oh. Oh my!"

"Then dispose of the arm in the furnace. The last thing this tower needs is a Skin-Runner's arm for a trophy."

$$\Omega$$

"It belonged to a Skin-Runner priest," Minesh said, turning the ring in his hand.

Herlen nodded. "I thought as much. Peradean is holding him at Kelmar."

"I heard about the arm." Minesh did not suggest that Herlen had burned it on purpose before either he or the Circle could examine it.

Herlen turned his gaze to the window. "Looked like a sword wound."

"But it could have been something else."

"If you're so interested," Herlen snapped, "come with me to Kelmar. Get the story from the horse's mouth, so to speak."

"I'm confident you can handle it." Minesh smiled. "I'm still resting from my last trip."

Herlen's heavy brows rose against his forehead. Minesh knew the King had expected him to insist on going.

"Then you can wait here for Corin," Herlen suggested. "He may return before I get back."

"I'll wait while I can. My duties may call me elsewhere."

The King gave him a long look before gathering his coat, then peered at him again after stepping out of his study into the hallway. "Are you certain you won't come with me?" A hint of pleading in the aging King's eyes belied the evenness of his voice.

The manea almost succumbed. He knew that he couldn't, however. His duty was to a higher power than the King of Sindarin. He let out a heavy sigh. "With the Beast loose, the Circle has its own crises to which I must attend."

Herlen gave him a peculiar look as if to say, since when did you care what the Circle wanted? But his words were politic. "Of course." Even so, he gave a mild shake of the head before turning and clomping down the hallway accompanied by two of his personal guard.

Minesh almost slapped himself. That line would work on most people outside the Circle, but not the King. Herlen knew better. *I must be getting old.*

Turning away from the still open door, Minesh reached out to the Elsian world. "I have seen the ring, Galin. And had described to me the arm that wore it. The Hest lives. Someone living has summoned it."

"Hold onto that knowledge," his True-Friend suggested. "The slower word travels, the better."

"You think so? Will the people not rise up to support him?"

"The people, I fear, will hide in their holes."

Minesh frowned. "You fear the Beast?"

"We all fear the Beast. The Beast is what we have always feared."

"What? Not the Hunters? Are the Hunters not the reason the Elsan provided the Hest and perpetrated the Legend of Four? To prevent the Hunters from destroying Sindarin?"

Galin was long in answering. "You already know that the Hunters have their True-Friends among us. It is the Beast we have fought. The Hunters and the Elsan together, each in our way, through all the eons of time. And here, now, in this place, we fight the Beast again. Sindarin is but a tiny grain of sand in the endless desert of the cosmos."

Minesh shook his head and sighed. He'd had this discussion with Galin many times. It always ended the same. While the Elsan appeared almost godlike in their ability to predict and manipulate events, they continued to insist that they were at the mercy of the players involved. And it was not an easy game they goaded Minesh into playing. "Well," he said, accepting the inevitable, "What is my task?"

"A journey."

Minesh sighed. "Of course, a journey. What crueler test could you place upon these tired bones of mine?"

"We labor out of need, Minesh, not cruelty. Never cruelty."

"I misspoke, Galin. In the name of all that is good and holy, where am I to go?"

The reply was hesitant, given grudgingly. "Karlac Tombs, to the Cavern of Stonepast."

"Karlac? If I hurry, I can travel with the King."

"Minesh... that would not be wise. The King has his business. You have yours."

The manea took in a deep breath and walked over to Herlen's wine cupboard. "I'm not wrong, am I, Galin? Corin is the Mastren? The Hunters are coming?"

Galin didn't answer for some time. When he did, his voice was soft, sorrowful. "You would do well to tread carefully, my friend."

The Circle of Sindarin

Two guards, stationed high atop Toroth's Tower, peered eastward beyond the city wall, warily eyeing movement along the wide, earthen road that led up from the Victron Bridge.

"It's the Prince's mount," said Eliard. "Of that I'm sure."

"Is that a bear riding it?" asked Vargas.

The two guards fell silent, squinting against evening's shadows.

"A man dressed in sten-bear skins," suggested Eliard. "There's someone behind him."

"A girl," said Vargas. "See how she clings to him. How do you know the skin is sten-bear?"

Eliard smiled. "I was raised at Fox Burrow where the hides are tanned. Spent my youth cleaning skins for my father. The sheen of the sten-bear is like no other."

"Tough animal, sten-bear," Vargas mused. "Come at you like a mountain. Had a cousin over Pulner way take an axe to one. Never even drew blood. Least, none of the bear's. Sten-bear tore him to pieces." His voice dropped to a whisper. "I doubt the Prince could kill one."

"Either way, it is the Prince's horse," Eliard said. "We'd best call for an escort."

$$\Omega$$

It had been a year since Alethea last visited Toroth with its high walls of pale granite, its maze of cobbled streets, its shops and markets and parks and endless throngs of citizens bustling about their business. As a child, she had refused to believe that almost half the population of Sindarin lived within its walls. It wasn't until her mother deemed her old enough to travel with her to the city's chief market that she understood.

The village where she had lived, along with many others along the shores of the Sunfall Sea, were merely satellites, collection points for goods being sent north to Toroth where any manufacturing more complex than weaving wool and tanning hides was performed. Alethea had never imagined that so many people and so much industry could exist in one place.

The sight of the city, as first the Victron Bridge and then the Toroth road rose up among the fields of spring wheat, filled Alethea with a sense of safety. The Skin-Runners were behind her now. Lathan even further behind. Soon the city walls would surround her, walls she had hoped to reach the first two times she had fled the traders' camp.

As she recalled that visit a year ago, a wave of regret washed over her. Regret and fear. Ilsa had been with her then. Their mother had been alive. They had been happy. Now Alethea had never felt so alone. With nowhere to go. No one to rely on.

Against her arms, she felt Corin stiffen. She read him briefly, probing his barriers. Was it apprehension she sensed? After coming all this way, was Corin now fearful of entering the city? He had said little as they rode through the Vale of Rhedan. Though he insisted on Toroth as their destination, she had sensed he was unhappy about going there. Alethea had pondered the seeming contradiction throughout the day.

She shifted in the saddle to get a better look past Corin's shoulder. Ahead of them, Toroth's pale wall stretched across the horizon, almost the same color as the cloudy sky. A dark gray smear marked where the road met the wall— Haven Gate. And before the gate, a contingent of guards waiting on horseback. Alethea tensed. Had Lathan reached Toroth first? And issued a warrant for a runaway servant? Had she survived the Skin-Runners only to be taken by the Toroth

Guard and handed back to Lathan?

Corin rode within five yards of the mounted guards before reining in. Alethea continued to peer around his shoulder as their Captain rode a few feet closer and stopped.

He was a large man and wore a starched white coat buttoned tightly around his thick neck. His jet-black hair was oiled and combed straight up the center of his head like a rooster. Alethea had never seen a man look more ridiculous. The Captain's nose wrinkled as the rancid fetor of uncured sten-bear hide reached him. "Welcome, my Prince." The man saluted. "Your presence has been sorely missed."

Prince?

"Tell my father I'm here." Corin's voice was low, his body rigid. The revelation that Corin was the King's son, while alarming, did little to solve the puzzle of his mood.

The Guard Captain grimaced. "Your father departed for Kelmar just this morning. I'm surprised you didn't see his party on the road.

Corin ground his teeth. Alethea could tell, even sitting behind him, as he had done it often since he had rescued her. "Minesh?" he said. "Is the manea here?"

Minesh? Corin – Prince Corin – knows the manea as well? And said nothing?

The Captain looked even more put out. "Was. Left soon after your father."

More grinding. "Then tell the Circle Elders that I wish an audience. You'll find me in my rooms."

The Circle too! Anyone who could help, and Corin said nothing.

Alethea's head jerked back as Serl stepped forward. The guards parted to make way and seemed to avoid Alethea with their eyes before drawing on the reins of their horses to follow them into the city. The Captain had not asked about her and Corin had volunteered nothing.

Prince Corin.

Realizing that an argument in the street would serve neither of them well, Alethea held her peace as Corin guided Serl through the gate into Haven plaza and along Freedom

Avenue toward the Tower.

Alethea distracted herself from her anger by taking in the city from the vantage of horseback. On past visits she had been afoot, lost in the crowds of people, most of whom were taller than she. From her perch atop Serl she saw the city from a whole new perspective, with its wide streets and siltstone buildings, casement windows and canvas awnings. Tower Street was particularly busy, with people dressed in scarlet trousers and bright blue coats. Some carried packages under their arms or balanced baskets on their heads. All made way as Serl's hooves clicked against the stonework streets, and paused to watch them pass.

What must they think? Her, a nobody, riding behind a prince followed by a contingent of Tower Guard. Then she laughed. They probably didn't even notice her. Corin was dressed in rank animal skins, the fur dirtied with blood, his face coated with dust, his hair a mess. What must they think?

A gaggle of small children ran through the street ahead of them, laughing and shouting about a bear-headed horse and horse-headed bears. Alethea should have laughed with them. She should have smiled. But she was too angry. Even Sanctuary Park, with its grassy hills and manicured trees and the great plasteel Dome of the Ancients, gleaming like a giant egg in the late afternoon sunlight, failed to make an impression.

After the park came the Sanctuary itself, a vast complex of towers and walls, gray granite shining in the sunlight like a mountain with unnaturally straight contours, the very heart of Toroth, of Sindarin. Alethea had seen the Sanctuary many times in her youth, always from the outside and usually at a distance, but still marveled at what men and women could build when they made the effort. The east wing, she knew, was the Yard, where the Toroth Guard trained and was housed. The west wing was the Circle, where the Elders held council, the heart of the Path. The central Tower was the Square, the seat from which the King's family had ruled Sindarin since the Time of the Settling. Herlen's family. Corin's father. This was where Corin took them.

There were gates and walls and then a courtyard busy with servants. Young boys came and took Serl. Corin ignored them. He ignored Alethea as well as she followed him inside a long hall with high ceilings to a broad staircase that went up and up. Finally, they left the staircase and walked down a hall of dark wooden surfaces that glistened with fresh varnish.

Corin strode into a room leaving the door open. Alethea followed, closed the door behind her, and then leaned against it.

Never had she seen so well appointed a room. It was enormous, with side rooms and closets, and an extended balcony, and a large, four-poster bed with a cloth-of-gold canopy and a thick mattress with purple blankets and fluffy pillows.

In sharp contrast to the room, Corin shrugged off his fetid sten-bear coat and sat on the bed. His shirt was torn and bloodied. His eyes seemed to stare at nothing, shining silver in the light from the balcony.

Alethea set her hands on her hips and gave him a long, dark stare. "Prince! Prince?"

Corin started and looked at her, his dirty face and tousled hair lending him an air of innocence. Alethea had to force herself to stay angry. Then he shrugged. "Would it have made a difference?"

She hadn't expected that. "I don't know. You could have told me the truth."

"I did tell you the truth. I told you my name was Corin. Well, it is."

Alethea scowled. "What about Minesh? You didn't tell me that you knew him. When I asked, you said you only knew "of" him."

Corin laughed, low and without pleasure. "No one truly knows the manea. He spends most of his time beyond the Shroud. I've been in the same room with him, but he hasn't really been there."

"You said he couldn't help me find my True-Friend. Why?"

Corin said nothing. He turned away, fumbled with the contents of a shelf without really looking at it.

"Well?" Alethea demanded. She had abandoned Ilsa to find her True-Friend, left her sister in Lathan's foul hands. That it had been for nothing was a thought too crushing to bear.

Corin threw a hand in the air and shook his head. "I don't know! Maybe he can. Maybe he can't. I just don't know. I don't know anything."

Alethea stared at Corin. He looked tired. And dirty. And dejected. Though why a prince should despair, she had no idea. Corin had everything. This room was evidence of that. Something was wrong, though. Horribly wrong. And she had no clue to what it was or what she could do about it.

A knock rescued Alethea from her thoughts. She stumbled out of the way as the wide door flew open to reveal the Captain of the Guard and his ridiculous hair. The big man huffed as though he had been running, his thick neck pink where it strained against the too-tight coat. When the Captain spoke it was halting, as though he couldn't believe what his own lips were saying.

"My Prince, Ceric himself will see you. At your convenience, he said."

Corin waved him away. "Thank you Captain Rejin." A moment later he rose from where he sat and followed the man out into the corridor. Alethea stepped immediately behind him, startled that Corin took no time to change out of his torn shirt or to wipe the dirt from his face. What they both must look like!

"Why was the Captain – Rejin? – so surprised?" Alethea asked as they retraced their path down the staircase. "You're a Prince. Why wouldn't the Circle see you?"

Corin frowned as he answered. "There's a schism between the Circle and the Square. It galls the Elders that harsh decisions are sometimes necessary in order to keep society from collapsing into chaos. They claim the cure is as bad as the malady."

"What do you mean?" Alethea demanded. "The Circle teaches the Path of Arwyth. That is our society."

Corin cast her a sideways glance. "Arwyth's Path is a Path of ethics. The Square enforces law. That's something the

Circle can never do. If the Elders were asked to deal with the Skin-Runners, they would open Haven Gate and throw wide their arms, shouting, Welcome brothers! Come share in the peace that is the Path of Arwyth." He lowered his voice. "Half the city would be slaughtered."

"I think you're exaggerating," Alethea told him.

"Whether I am or not, the Circle has always resented the Square. Always."

$$\Omega$$

Leaving the Tower, they entered a garden of short, wax-leafed trees with walks and benches and grassy areas ringed with patches of gold and blue flowers. Alethea guessed it was a private garden for Sanctuary residents, though this late in the day, with the sun setting over the western wall of the city, no one was out enjoying the spring-scented air.

A path led to a wide gate that gave entrance to the Circle complex west of the Tower. The hallways were open and clean, unadorned for the most part. Potted plants filled unused corners, the greenery adding life to the plain white walls. Corin's mood seemed to grow steadily darker as they marched up a wide stairway to an upper floor, past a startled old man in a while robe who seemed to be some kind of guard even though he couldn't possibly stop a ten year old child, and into a large chamber that appeared to be their destination.

Though broad and deep, very few chairs serviced the room. Like the corridors, the walls and ceiling were white, which was just as well as there wasn't a single window, just a few oil lamps hanging from sconces. No paintings or statues broke the monotony, though in a corner, a young woman sat on a stool playing soothing notes on a stringed instrument. The musician paid no attention to the new arrivals. The room was far from empty, however. Here and there stood pairs or trios of white-robed Elders, all of them gray-haired, many of them women, which surprised Alethea as she had assumed that all Circle Elders were men.

Few of the Elders smiled when they saw the Prince. Most raised eyebrows at his torn and bloody shirt, mussed hair, and grimy face. Though posed as if in discussion, none of them spoke.

"I wish an audience!" Corin stated loudly. The music stopped and the musician stared at them. Silence imbued the room. No one moved. No one spoke. Ancient faces pinched with righteous indignation.

Then a voice spoke in Alethea's mind. A kind voice, filled with patience and compassion. It thrilled Alethea just to hear it, even though the words were not directed at her.

"We will hear you, Corin."

Alethea peered about the room and identified the True-Speaker. It was a simple thing to do, as everyone except Corin and herself had his or her barriers down. Alethea's breath caught as that realization sank in. She had never heard of such a thing. It left all of them open for mental attack. Maybe Corin was right; the Circle was too trusting.

Focusing on the one who had Spoken True, Alethea read him. All of his thoughts and memories were there for the taking. Even Ilsa, when as children they had dropped their barriers to share thoughts between sisters, had never left herself that open. It shocked Alethea to discover that the man was none other than Ceric, Peace-Ruler of the Elders, the Head of the First Circle. In many ways, he was the most important man on Sindarin, more important even than Corin's father, the King.

The Peace-Ruler was a tall, willowy man nearing two hundred years of age. His radiant smile emanated a peace and calm that was almost palpable. Alethea read him gently, searching for pertinent facts while purposely avoiding things too personal. Somehow, everything she found touched on Corin.

Ceric had watched Corin grow up. As a youth, Corin had called him cabbage-head behind his back for the layers of short white hair that clustered about his face like cabbage leaves. Years later, when Corin learned that Ceric had read that secret from his mind, he couldn't understand why Ceric had not been offended. What did offend the Peace-Ruler was Corin's lack of that understanding. There were other thoughts as well, flooding out from the old man's mind, all of them concerning Corin.

The Peace-Ruler's kind smile twisted with a slight grin. Again he Spoke True. "But first, Corin, you must obey the rules of this Hall. Though you be Prince, none are above the sanctity of this place. You will abide by its rules or you will leave."

Alethea sensed an immediate shift in Corin's mood. What had been mere anger stiffened into hot indignation.

"You know how I feel about leaving my mind unprotected." Corin's True-Speech, though not directed at Alethea, filled the Hall as the Peace-Ruler received it.

"Even so," Sent the Peace-Ruler, still smiling. "Your disrespect will not diminish the peace of this Hall." A pause. "And who is your friend?"

"She is part of my question," Corin said. "Her name is..." Corin's Sending halted and Alethea realized that the Prince could not remember her name.

"I see," said Ceric. "Does she know to drop her barriers?"

Corin gave no answer.

The Peace-Ruler shook his head. "You have been remiss in your duties, Corin." He then turned his attention to Alethea and directed his True-Speech at her. "Have no fear, child. None will harm you here. We lower our barriers to ensure that promise."

Alethea hesitated before replying. Her True-Speech came much easier than Corin's. "But what is to prevent an attack? If someone pressed their will against me, my mind could be damaged before I raised my barriers."

The Peace-Ruler smiled with his eyes. "And who in this Hall could harbor such ill intent and not have it discovered? No, child. This is the Hall of Peace and the only threat is you and Corin. Only you could hide such thoughts. Only you have your barriers up."

Alethea watched as Corin reluctantly dropped his barriers. She read instantly that Ceric's insistence he do so was the source of Corin's anger. Yet it was the Circle's policy and not any real fear of attack that irked him. "I—I trust you," she Sent to Ceric, and dropped her barriers.

The Peace-Ruler's smile deepened. "Good. Now there will be no secrets among us, no ulterior motives."

"I know about secrets," she said, casting a sidelong glance at Corin. "Isn't that right, Prince?" Her eyes widened as Corin's unspoken response poured across the surface of his mind. Alethea didn't know what to make of it. "No! You can't blame me. I had nothing to do with bringing you to Karlac. I'm not a part of any test."

"Calmly, child," Ceric cautioned. "Now you see the blessing of this Hall. Corin has harbored an ill thought toward you, and has come to know his error. Is that not so, Corin?"

"I—I thought you were a test," Corin admitted. "Under the circumstances, how could I believe otherwise? I killed for you."

"And I thought you were a god." Alethea let out a small, nervous laugh. "Well, almost. Foolishness now, but at the time I was so scared. And the light..."

Corin turned to the Peace-Ruler, his expression hard. "The Hest came to me and I killed. What is happening to me?"

Ceric showed no surprise. No emotion whatsoever. "You have taken the rites?"

Corin pushed up his torn sleeve, displaying a small, precise scar on his forearm.

The Peace-Ruler nodded. "The Hest is yours to command. To summon at will. So it is with all who take the rites and are accepted."

Corin's eyes narrowed. "I've never heard such a thing."

"It is not common knowledge. Few are those who are accepted. Fewer still those who summon the Hest." The Elder turned back the sleeve of his robe. A thin scar similar to Corin's marked the old man's arm. "In all my years I have never summoned the Hest. Neither have any of the current Circle."

"Well I have," Corin said. "Three times now. And I don't like it."

Again, the Peace-Ruler displayed no emotion. "It is your choice to make. The deer died when I wandered the wilderness. I feasted on venison for a week."

Alethea read between them and in her mind watched Corin summon the Hest and save the deer while Ceric made the same attempt with the knife, and failed.

"You're not telling me everything," Corin said. "I saw three figures who bore the mark. They expected me to summon the Hest."

Ceric's smile tightened. "You know the Legend."

"That's what Minesh said. Which legend? There are so many."

"The Legend of Four."

"Four?" Corin's jaw dropped.

"But you said you saw three figures," Alethea interjected. She read Corin and saw the inside of a gloomy chamber, a crystal shard, and two men and a woman with light flaring from their arms.

"Four?" repeated Corin.

Ceric nodded.

Corin turned and fled.

Rule-Master of All

The stone halls of Kelmar Keep were dark with night. Near the locked door of the infirmary, a lone torch flickered in its holder. Thick shadows crossed the floor where two guards sat in wooden chairs. One was asleep, the other nodding. A wine bottle stood empty between them. All was quiet and still.

At length the second guard fell asleep. Nothing moved in the corridor. No sound breached the silence.

Then the first guard opened his eyes and grinned in the darkness.

He straightened slowly, careful not to creak the leather of his uniform. Squinting in the poor light, he marked the sleeping form of his companion and the door they guarded. Then he reached beyond the door with his mind, seeking the room's occupant. "I know what you are."

The prisoner did not answer, but he was awake. The agitation of his barriers was like the waves of a restless sea.

"I have come for you," the guard Sent. "Tonight you will be free."

"Who are you?" came the reply.

"Arnor. I run with the wolf."

"Wolf? What foolishness is this?"

"I know who you are. I saw you with the healer. Hear my mind and know me."

Keeping his barriers up, Arnor sent wave after wave of wretched thoughts hammering through the door. Cold thoughts, dark and evil. Thoughts that only a Skin-Runner would have. Murderous. Lustful. Licentious thoughts. It was safer that way. Safer than dropping his barriers to allow the prisoner to read him. Anything was safer than dropping your barriers to a Skin-Runner.

The prisoner answered. "Enough. Free me and you will be exalted."

"Exalted! Then you are a priest. Who are you?"

A pause. "Bruenor, Rule-Master of all!"

Wraithlike, Arnor rose from his seat and clamped his left hand over his companion's mouth. His right hand held a short blade, thin and sharp, which he slid from ear to ear across the throat, cutting through soft flesh and hard cartilage. The guard's eyes went wide as his body spasmed and then slumped forward, a gurgling sound escaping from the open wound. Arnor wiped his blade on the dead man's vest before unlocking the door.

Inside, the man who had named himself Bruenor stood naked at a side table, awkwardly lighting one of the candles with his single hand. "Is the other one dead?"

"Yes."

"Bring him in here. We'll cut the skin before we go."

Arnor dragged the murdered guard into the room, a man he had known and worked with for more than a year. The corpse's head thudded against the floor when Arnor turned to close the door. He felt the priest's eyes burning into the back of his skull as he stripped off the uniform, then accepted Bruenor's one-armed help to lift the naked body onto the table.

"Do you think this is wise?" Arnor asked. He gazed critically at the friend he had murdered. "Herlen has been lax in his persecution. Discovering a flayed guard in one of his towers may push him."

"Are you a coward?" Bruenor demanded. "Herlen does all he can against us. He is weak. What we this night will make him weaker."

Arnor dropped his head. "Of course. You are right."

He gave Bruenor one of his knives and watched the priest start at the feet. He made his first incision at the left heel, slicing in along the edge of the sole, loosening the thick skin so he could work it over the toes without tearing.

Arnor moved to the other end of the table and began at the man's gaping throat, slicing upward behind the right ear, lifting away the face and working the scalp from the skull. It was important that he not tear the remaining skin at the back of the neck. Bruenor would want the hide whole.

"You should have given him sagcryl first," the priest murmured as he started on the other foot. "All this blood gets in the way."

"It would have been too noisy," Arnor said. "We are not alone in this corridor. I hope no one decides to check on you before morning. Are you ready to turn him?"

Bruenor nodded. Together they rolled the man over onto his flayed chest.

Two knives were quick to find connective tissue along the back and thighs. Both men were expert at their work. Together, they lifted the last section of skin from the lower back, pulling away from muscle and bone. Arnor folded the bloodied man-hide into one of the waxed cloth sacks Olwen kept in the infirmary for storing samples. He offered it to the priest.

"No, you carry it. It was your kill."

"We'll have to stretch it soon," Arnor said, tying the sack to his belt, "before the blood dries to glue."

The priest pulled on the guard's uniform, grudgingly accepting Arnor's help. He studied the corpse a moment. "Turn it over," he suggested.

Arnor complied.

With his one arm, Bruenor used the table as leverage to dislocated the right shoulder, and then cut away at the joint, severing ligaments and tendons. Arnor helped him pop the shoulder socket and wrap the arm in waxed cloth for Bruenor to secure beneath his belt.

"They'll think it is you on the table," Arnor said.

"Until the healer tells them different. Olwen will see what we have done. That will make the revelation so much the better."

Taking one last glance around the infirmary, Arnor snuffed out the candle. When their eyes adjusted, he and the priest skulked into the corridor, locking the door behind them.

The Legend of Four

Alethea came awake to thick shadows as a hand touched her shoulder. It belonged to an elderly woman holding a dim candle.

"Peace-Ruler Ceric awaits you in the outer room," the woman whispered. She set the candle on the nightstand and departed.

Rubbing sleep from her eyes, Alethea remembered waiting in a room near the Hall of Peace and falling asleep. After Corin had abandoned her. She had not yet forgiven him for that.

By the light of the candle she found a pile of clean garments resting on a chair. They had not been there when she fell asleep. Alethea examined at the clothes she still wore: torn trousers, a dirty tunic with the top two buttons missing, and a bit of bearskin Corin had given her to rescue her virtue. She removed the soiled clothing eagerly, reflecting briefly on the nightmare that had sullied them. She expected the provided garb to be plain white robes, like those the Circle wore. Instead, they were heavy cotton outdoor wear, the kind worn by field workers. They appeared pale yellow in the dim light of the candle.

She found the Peace-Ruler in the outer room sitting in one of several cushioned chairs, a wide arrangement with jutting arms and covered top to bottom in padded cloth. Before entering the Sanctuary with Corin, Alethea had never seen a chair that was more than plain wood; she wasn't sure yet if it was a good idea for a chair to feel almost as soft as a bed.

Ceric greeted her with a smile. The old man seemed to always smile, as though nothing in his peaceful world could ever go wrong. Alethea found herself longing for a world like that.

"Please sit, child," the Peace-Ruler said in a soft, clear voice rather than using True-Speak. He gestured at the seat across from his. "I wish to speak with you."

Alethea sank into the wide chair, and had the brief sensation that she was falling when the cushion compressed beneath her weight. She compensated for the lack of support by tucking her legs beneath her. Then she folded her arms across her chest and dropped her chin into the nook they formed. She didn't think this was how one was supposed to sit in such a chair, but it suited her. Ceric sat as one would in a normal chair of hard wood, but she couldn't imagine he was at all comfortable.

"Are you frightened, child?" he asked.

"No. Yes. I feel..." Alethea couldn't decide how she felt.

"Confused," Ceric decided for her. "So is Corin. His burdens are many."

"Something troubles him," Alethea agreed. "In the Hall of Peace I learned that part of that something is me, but there's more to it. Isn't there?"

The Elder nodded. "Yes. It is good that you are aware. Good that you understand. For all our sakes."

Alethea frowned. "But I don't understand. I don't know what's troubling Corin. I only know that I wish to find—"

"—your True-Friend," Ceric finished for her. He could have read her thoughts, but they were not in the Hall of Peace now. Alethea kept her barriers raised. So did Ceric, which surprised her. The Peace-Ruler knew something that he didn't want her to learn. "Corin also seeks his True-Friend," Ceric said.

"Perhaps you shall find them together."

"In the Hall of Peace…" Alethea didn't know if she should repeat what she had read. The concept of exposing one's mind, keeping no secrets, was so new to her. So… wonderful. "In the Hall of Peace I read from Corin that he must seek his True-Friend alone, in isolation. That was part of what upset him. My being with him. His real reason for returning to Toroth was so he could leave me here. It had nothing to do with reporting the Skin-Runners at Karlac."

Ceric nodded. "You are quick. That is good. All of what you say is true. And yes, all Seekers of True-Friends must be alone." His face took on a slightly sad expression. "But I think that I have never seen two people more alone than you and Corin. He needs you, Alethea. And you need him. I think that is what led him to Karlac. From Cambre he could have gone anywhere. He set a course that led straight to you."

Alethea blushed, and then shook her head. "He disdains me. I'm just an obstacle to him. He came to Toroth to be rid of me."

The Peace-Ruler rose to his feet and gazed at the ceiling as though he were seeing the Shroud. For all Alethea knew, the gentle old man did see the Shroud. "The Elsan work in mysterious ways," Ceric said. He chuckled, then looked down at her and smiled, a warm, gracious smile. "Corin is wrong, you know. He believes he seeks his True-Friend, but first he must find himself. No man can reach through the Shroud and draw a friend to his bosom without first knowing where his bosom is. You can help him do that."

"I can?" The Peace-Ruler's assertion surprised her. She thought it should frighten her, but somehow it didn't. "How?"

Ceric's face grew grim. "The Legend of Four."

"You said that to Corin, but he ran off and I was ushered away before I could find out what it meant."

"Corin knows," Ceric said. "I believe that the three figures he saw were heroes of Sindarin's past, those who have wielded the power of the Hest before him. You know of the Hest?"

Alethea nodded. Everyone familiar with the Path of Arwyth knew of the Hest-rites some initiates took, those who desired the enhanced True-Speech the shard was reputed to bestow. When she read Corin in the Hall of Peace she had seen the shard, but Corin had perceived no such benefit.

Ceric continued. "I don't just mean that the Hest accepted them. The Hest has accepted many. The personages Corin saw actually drew upon the power of the shard in order to bring about some great event.

"Arwyth was the first, the Pastren, the Giver of the Path. In the early days of the Settling, it was she who discovered the Elsan, the world of True-Friends, who in turn led her to the crystal shard deep in the Aenlaen Mountains. Arwyth's experience with the Hest established the principles by which the inhabitants of Sindarin could bring the powers of True-Speech under control. There was no sagcryl in those day, at least not openly, but many were addicted to sageroot and took no care to restrict its use in their diet. It was Arwyth who established the First Circle of Elders and who saw the continued need for the Square, to enforce law.

"Then came Agar, the Thestren. His were the dark days of the Mind Wars, when Sagan Priests used sagcryl in their bid for absolute rule. Without Agar and the Hest, the Priests would now be sitting in Herlen's seat, his people raised as cattle for slaughter in the Gorgings.

"Jaklin was the third, the Hestren. When the Skin-Runners rose up to take the Sagan Priests' place, Jaklin used the Hest to hunt them from the Kreshin Mountains far in the east to the bitter shores of the Stillbirth Sea to the south. That was four hundred years ago. Today the Skin-Runners are still just wilderness scavengers."

"I remember now," Alethea said. "Stories from my childhood. But I don't recall names put to the heroes. Nor do I remember the Hest being involved. But that is three heroes. You said the legend speaks of four."

Ceric spread his hands wide. "The fourth is the Beast Master. The Mastren. He is also the Herald of Orion's Hunt. The Mastren's task is to bring Sindarin out of barbarity so that the Hunters do not destroy us all."

Alethea frowned. "But if these aren't just stories? If the

Four are real people? How can one man bring an entire world out of barbarity?" She thought immediately of Lathan and his traders, of Bruenor and the Skin-Runners. Her own uncle. Sindarin was rife with such brutes.

Ceric offered no answer.

Then realization struck her. "Why does this Mastren have no name? And why is Corin so upset?"

The Peace-Ruler of the Circle shook his head. "The Mastren has no name because he has not yet come. That is the true purpose of the Hest-rites; that the Hest may find the fourth hero."

"And Corin?" Alethea knew what Ceric's answer would be.

The Elder clucked his tongue. "Corin fears that the Hest-rites may no longer be needed."

Alethea climbed awkwardly out of her chair, was surprised to find her legs trembling. *Why should I care what happens to this sullen prince? No, that isn't it. Something else is happening here, something Ceric doesn't want to talk about. Is afraid to talk about? Has he raised his barriers to prevent my finding out? Whatever it is, it must be important.* Lifting her chin, she faced the old man down. "Is Corin right?"

Ceric shrugged, paused, and appeared to reach a decision. "I don't know. I hope not. That is why you must help him, be with him. If Corin is the Mastren, the Hunters will be coming, with the death of all Sindarin in their hands. Young Corin, troubled though he is, may be our only hope."

Then Ceric placed his hands on Alethea's shoulders, his eyes close to tears. "And you may be his only hope. Be his light, Alethea. Guide him. Raise him to his calling. If Corin is the Mastren, it is paramount that he recognize the goodness in Mankind. In you, he will see that goodness, and then in himself."

Remembering how she had abandoned Ilsa, Alethea dropped her face. "I'm not really all that good."

Ceric's ancient face curled into a smile, and a tear slid down his weathered cheek, a dewdrop in the candlelight. "My child, you forget that I have looked past your barriers. That I have read your soul. You... you are the best! The best that Man can be! Corin will see that in you. And will love you for it. And in loving you, he will love Mankind!"

Alethea opened her mouth to respond. Nothing came out.

The Peace-Ruler released her shoulders. "Go! Go with him, child. Your being here is the one good omen I can find. I fear for him. I fear for you as well. The Beast is free from its pit and is stirring up the Skin-Runners. Now is not a good time for Seekers to be wandering alone in the wilderness. Together... together I think you will do quite well."

Alethea bit her lip. The Elder's words overwhelmed and scared her, yet at the same time gave her hope. She wouldn't have to seek out her True-Friend alone. Corin would be with her. But... "Will he let me go with him?"

Ceric grinned, his demeanor once again calm. "Corin's words will say no, but his heart will say yes. You must not let his rough manner dissuade you."

Alethea thought hard, trying to recall the words Corin had spoken. The anger she had felt from him. The anger she'd had toward him. The fool boy hadn't even remembered her name! "Is there really anything I can do to help?"

Ceric sighed and spread his hands. "I don't know. Even so, he is for you, Alethea. And you for him. That, I do know."

A Tribe of Donkeys

Herlen reached Kelmar just as the sun rose, pale and distant on the horizon. He had pushed his party all day and on through the night, goaded by a growing sense of urgency that pressed against his soul, palpable as stone, yet unexplained. His True-Friend felt it too, but offered no cause. Herlen was used to that. "True-Friends are more tight-lipped than maneas," so the saying went. Herlen knew from experience the adage to be true. It still left him angry.

Fresh country air and the sharp, lilting song of golden-breasted starlings failed to relieve the tension. An image of that severed arm with its wolf skull ring haunted Herlen's thoughts.

Husbandmen, up collecting eggs and milking cows, watched in silence as the King's guardsmen rode into the tiny village. Kelmar bordered the wilderness; few lived there by choice.

Beyond the last small buildings rose a column of darkness: thick blocks of bituminous stone, quarried from the tombs region, dragged many miles through the wilderness, and stacked neatly atop one another, almost as high as Toroth's own tower. No one remembered why so vast a fortress had been built in so desolate a place.

"A remnant from Sindarin's dark past," Herlen's True-Friend had told him. "Its history and purpose are no longer relevant." Herlen snorted. He would be hard-pressed to come up with a more obtuse answer himself.

The King's escort drew to a halt as they rode into the marshaling yard. The stronghold's gates stood open, the guardhouse deserted. Herlen frowned.

Liniel dashed ahead, in through the gate. Moments later, a dozen guards poured out into the yard and formed a ragged line. Kelmar's guardsmen blanched at seeing the King and his escort and fell to exchanging troubled looks and harsh whispers. Herlen and his men dismounted and entered the keep as additional guards hurried past on their way outside. *Peradean will be embarrassed by this incident.*

Herlen went straight to the post commander's dayroom. He had been to Kelmar often enough to know where it was. Liniel and a half-dressed Peradean were waiting for him.

"Welcome, Sire," the Commander offered by way of greeting. Peradean hopped on one foot while attempting to pull an unwilling boot onto the other. "I trust my message didn't upset you overmuch."

Herlen's response was cold. "You know damn well it did! I'm not in the habit of breaking my fast by having a severed limb thrust under my nose. Now, where is this one-armed Skin-Runner?"

"Patience, my King," cried Peradean, still fumbling with the other boot. "First, a swallow of wine to refresh you from your journey?"

A servant entered bearing a tall flagon of wine and two large iron mugs. Herlen ordered his filled to the brim.

"Ahhhh, that's bloody good, Peradean." Herlen permitted himself a smile. "Almost as good as my own. You've taken pains to weed out the sage. I appreciate that."

Peradean beamed. "I would never insult you, Herlen. I, too, press for my own needs."

Herlen drained the mug and put away his smile. "Now, down to business. Have you broken him yet?"

Commander Peradean's face darkened. "My healer thought it unwise to attempt his barriers. When the Skin-Runner proved uncooperative, Olwen suggested we would likely kill him before he broke. That's happened before. Little can be learned before the mind goes silent."

Herlen nodded. "If that's what Olwen says, then I believe her. You have the best healer in all of Sindarin. I've tried to lure her to Toroth many times, without success. She says the city is too noisy for her studies."

"She does her job," Peradean said, dismissing the commendation. "I thought it best to wait until you arrived before questioning the Skin-Runner." He arched a brow. "There may be something special you wish to learn."

Herlen didn't oblige him; his commanders already saw Mastrens under every stone. Of all the times for that bloody Demon to escape, why did it have to happen during Corin's rites!

The king suppressed his temper. "That was thoughtful of you, Peradean. Let's hope our Skin-Runner doesn't die too soon, shall we?"

After a brief pause, marked only by Herlen's impatience, Peradean stumbled to the door and led the way down the corridor. Herlen followed with Liniel at his side. The guards in the passageway took up escort around them.

The Kelmar Commander slowed as they neared the door to Olwen's infirmary. Herlen noted the two empty chairs, the empty wine bottle, and a dark stain on the floor. "Discipline seems rather relaxed around here," he remarked. "I hope you're not going to disappoint me."

"The door is still locked," Peradean said hopefully. The Commander fumbled through his pockets. "I have a master key." He attempted a smile as he fit the key to the lock. The bolt gave a satisfying *click* as the mechanism released. Peradean pushed the door open an inch, peered inside, and then hastily closed it again.

Herlen cast him an expectant eye. "What is it?"

Peradean's face was pale. "It's not pretty," he said.

Herlen sighed. "I have a strong constitution. Open the door."

Peradean obliged and all of them, including the guards, shuffled into the infirmary. The Commander lingered just inside the doorway.

Dry, crusted blood carpeted the stone floor and a vile stink permeated the air. Pungent. Faintly metallic. On the table lay the likeness of a corpse. It was marbled brown and white— muscle, fat, bone and congealed blood, all tending toward gray. One of the guards turned and vomited against a wall.

"The, uh, right arm is missing," noted Liniel, in a seeming attempt to be helpful. His face held a noticeably green cast.

"This won't be your prisoner," Herlen predicted. "Skin-Runners wouldn't do this to one of their own. Not if he hadn't talked yet. This will be one of your two missing guards."

"But how could this happen?" Peradean demanded.

"I'm sure he had help," Herlen suggested. "Not even a man with two arms can free himself from a locked room. I'd look to your other missing guard." He turned to leave. "Are you certain the Skin-Runner said nothing?"

"Nothing," lamented Peradean, "Not even his name. I've failed you utterly."

"Yes," said Herlen. "You have."

By unspoken agreement they abandoned the infirmary and marched down the corridor to the main gate and then outside into fresh air. The Kelmar Guard stood marshaled in the yard, appearing unnaturally alert and slightly alarmed. Several positions among them were vacant.

Herlen shook his head. If Peradean had a brother or son who was less of an imbecile, he'd be tempted to have the man murdered. For the good of Sindarin. Unfortunately, the whole family was a tribe of donkeys. At least it was Kelmar they governed and not a real town.

While Commander Peradean paraded in front of his men, waving his arms and shouting reprimands, Herlen cast his gaze east toward Karlac. His gaze took in the empty Kershon fields and the groves of Aldinwood that grew beyond. Wilderness for hundreds of years. The oppression that had followed Herlen to Kelmar continued to press against him and an icy darkness chilled his soul.

Corin, my son, where are you?

Black Sheep

Corin stood in the courtyard of Toroth Keep, surveying his domain: one black horse, one hunting knife, one water skin, one ragged and stinking sten-bear skin coat, and one dwindling supply of dry, week-old sten-bear meat. Everything he needed to seek his True-Friend in the wilderness. So why did he feel so miserable?

To soothe his bitterness, he patted Serl's nose. "It can't go as badly as last time. Can it?"

A scuffle of approaching footsteps pricked Serl's ear. Corin turned to see Ceric and Alethea walking toward him, cloaked in the pearl-gray light of dawn.

"Well at least someone thought to see me off."

"I wish you well," Ceric answered, smiling mightily as always. "Both of you."

"Both?" *What is the old fool talking about now?*

"You both seek your True-Friend, do you not?" replied the Elder.

Corin clamped his jaw tight in an effort to keep any words he might regret later from escaping.

The old man stood behind Alethea, his ancient hands resting on her shoulders. "Come now, Corin. Can you bear to think of this poor child wandering alone in the wilderness? With what almost happened to her the last time?"

"Keep her here, then." Corin turned to adjust Serl's saddle. "Let the Women's Circle care for her. They can do more for Alethea than I." Corin didn't know why he spoke the girl's name. He refused to believe it was to show that he knew it now after forgetting it earlier.

"Alethea seeks her True-Friend, Corin." The Peace-Ruler's voice was as calm and patient as always. "She can stay behind no more than you can. If you do not take her, then she will be out there alone. Your thoughts will be with her constantly, worrying over what danger she might be facing."

Corin kept his back to the pair of them, pretending to work with the saddle. Gingerly, he extended his mind, employing his faculty of True-Speech. Something was going on here. Minesh had told him to seek his True-Friend in isolation; that was what Arwyth's Path demanded. The Peace-Ruler of the Circle was the last person he would expect to bend the rules of the Path. He touched Alethea first and then Ceric. Both had their barriers up. He backed away quickly, hoping they had not detected his probing. So, Ceric was hiding something; the Peace-Ruler of the First Circle, the Man of Peace, rarely had barriers in place.

The old man spoke again. "If it is Minesh you are worried about, I will deal with him. Any blame the manea may wish to lay he may lay on me."

He must be serious. Ceric and Minesh did not get on well. The First Circle viewed their Black Sheep as they viewed the Square— a distasteful necessity. If Ceric was willing to owe Minesh a favor...

Corin spun around and threw up his hands. "Oh all right. If I don't give in, you'll tell everyone what a heartless churl I am." He set his hands on his hips. "Ceric, if it will make you happy, I will gladly be a nursemaid in the wilderness. Won't that give Minesh and my father something to chortle at over their wine!"

Well. So much for words he might regret. He cursed himself for the hurt he saw on Alethea's face, and noticed her struggling beneath Ceric's grip. But the old man restrained her, had been restraining her, Corin now realized, since they had arrived. The Peace-Ruler was pushing this on Alethea as well. *What is he up to?*

Corin opened his mouth to apologize for his harshness, but before he could speak, Alethea broke free from Ceric's grip, marched up to him, and thrust out her chin. "I can take care of myself, Prince. You may even need my help."

Corin closed his mouth and suppressed a smile.

Ω

The Vale of Rhedan stood a day's ride southeast of Toroth, a wide depression in the earth where the Aenlaen River swept down from the north to join the Rhedan before turning west toward the sea. Crouched behind a jutting rock on the valley's southern edge, two men watched as an old man put out his breakfast fire and gathered up his belongings.

"He's easy. Look at him! Traveling alone. I see no weapon."

"Shhhh! Can you see beneath his robes? He may have a blade."

"He's an old man. What harm can he do?"

"Quiet, fool! No wonder I lead. You have the brains of an ass!"

"And you the tongue—"

"Shut up! Do you want him to hear us?"

"I don't give a damn, Lathan! Are we going to take him or not?"

"I said to shut up, Nagram! I think I recognize him."

The two men fell silent, squinting in the harsh morning light. Lathan reached into his coat and drew out a cheval crystal, a short glass shard that expanded the range of vision. Lifting it to his eye, he peered more closely at the stranger.

The burgundy-blue of the old man's vestments represented the vaulted towers of Toroth. No surprise this close to the city. Lathan's gaze fell to the frayed crest on the arm. He stared at the image a long time, thinking he should know it. A dark bird of some kind. A raven perhaps. With a leaf in its beak? That had to be wrong. Memory gnawed at him.

The old man turned and the crest twisted out of view. He began tying his things to the saddle of a mangy-looking horse.

"Which way is he headed, Lathan?"

"How should I know? And I won't risk finding out, either. I'm not going to touch his mind. Not until I know who he is."

"Does it matter who he is?" Nagram demanded. "He wears the tower's colors. He must carry a purse, or something valuable. Perhaps he's from the Circle."

The crest and vestments fell suddenly into place. "That's it. Look how old he is, you dolt! How clean his skin!"

"I can't see his skin," Nagram said.

Lathan passed his nephew the cheval crystal. "That's the manea, idiot. Minesh. The Black Sheep of the First Circle."

Nagram peered out through the crystal. "The one from Ilsa's thoughts? The one Hyrmus told us about? What makes him special?"

"He's the trainer, you ignorant fool! The Elder who lives in the wilderness and beats True-Speech into young minds without using the drug."

"So?" Nagram put down the cheval crystal. "The Circle does all sorts of crazy things in the name of Arwin's Path."

Not for the first time, Lathan restrained the urge to hit his nephew. "That's Arwyth's Path, you idiot. And not everything the Circle does is crazy. According to Hyrmus, Minesh's mind could crush yours, and he wouldn't even need the drug! That's why the girl went looking for him."

Nagram returned the cheval to his eye and squinted. "Humph! He's a scrawny old thing. I bet in frenzy we could take him."

Lathan crunched his hand into a fist. "Nagram, one day your stupidity is going to get you killed."

"Maybe I'm just not a cow—"

That was it. Nephew or no nephew, Lathan drew his knife and pressed the blade against Nagram's throat. "Perhaps that day has come."

Nagram swallowed, his Adam's apple caressing the razor-sharp steel, reminding Lathan that the girl had stolen his plasteel knife when she had run. Another reason to get her back. He put the knife away. "Come on. Let's get the others."

Ω

Minesh walked his horse at an easy pace. He was in no hurry

to get to Karlac. If there was urgency, Galin would let him know. It was one of the few privileges of having a True-Friend that, in Minesh's mind at least, was more blessing than curse.

He had always avoided the Tombs region. There was nothing there. In history, it was the location of Man's first arrival on Sindarin and the unmarked mass graves of those who had not survived that arrival. In Legend, it was the location of Stonepast. Only Stonepast had not yet happened. And the Legend itself held little more than a name. That Galin was sending him there did not bode well. With the Demon loose—

Minesh heard the flight of feathers a heartbeat before the arrow took him in the chest. A heavy weight in his chest forced the breath from his lungs. Then he toppled backward from the saddle. He hit the ground easily, doing no damage, but the arrow jarred in his chest with the impact. Minesh clamped his eyes shut. The pain was excruciating, but he had dealt with pain before.

He felt the minds before hearing the sound of boots. Opening his eyes, he saw a band of men come to gloat over him.

"I know who you are," the tall one said, their leader from his stance. Muscles bulged beneath his thin coat, and his head was shaved. "Don't try anything. My friend here has a second bolt aimed at your heart."

"Who are you?" Minesh croaked. He thought perhaps the arrow had punctured a lung.

"That's not important," the man told him. "I'm looking for a girl."

"A girl?" Minesh was amazed. "I know of no girls."

"He's lying, Lathan," said one of the others.

Lathan flicked the man a cruel glance that commanded silence. Minesh had seen this type before. All full of themselves.

"I think you know this one," Lathan said. "She ran from me to come looking for you. She's a pretty little thing. Long auburn hair. Clean skin. Calls herself Alethea."

Minesh wagged his head. "She never found me."

"In that case I've no reason not to kill you."

"Wait!" Minesh's thoughts raced. *Time. I need time.* "You have a healer?"

"Of course I have a healer." Lathan grinned. "I'm not going to waste her on you."

"Remove the arrow," Minesh told him. "Tend my wounds. There may be a way."

Lathan snorted. "Only an idiot would fall for that trick."

"No tricks. You said you know who I am. Then you know I have a True-Friend beyond the Shroud. If this girl—"

"Alethea," Lathan provided.

"Right. If this Alethea is seeking me, my True-Friend may know where she is."

Lathan rubbed his chin with a thick-fingered hand.

"Let's finish it, Lathan," said the younger, weasel-faced man next to him. "You can't take any of this seriously."

Lathan smacked his knuckles across the man's face and then scowled at Minesh. "The girl first," he said. "Tell me where she is. Then I'll see about saving your worthless hide."

Minesh closed his eyes and reached out with his mind. Galin was there.

"I am sorry, my friend. I arrived too late to warn you. Your pain—."

"Damn the pain! My journey! Stonepast. You said it was important."

"It is. Corin will have to get by without you."

"Do you know of this girl? The one this Lathan is so interested in?"

Galin hesitated. "She is with Corin. They both seek their True-Friend."

"With the Prince?" Minesh was horrified.

"There is no harm," Galin said. "She too is required."

Minesh didn't want to even hazard a guess at what that could mean. "Should I tell this man? I can make a deal. His healer may spare my life. I can be there to help Corin."

"You are too trusting, Minesh. This one is nearly of the Demon. His kind makes promises only to break them."

Minesh sagged. "Yes, you're right. I am a fool. I have lived a long life. I should welcome death."

A loud, animal laugh forced Minesh to open his eyes. Lathan stood over him, his skin mottling from the drug, his eyes sparkling red in the morning sun.

"Too late, old man," Lathan rasped. "It took more sagcryl than it should have, but I heard your little conversation. Enough of it, anyway. How that little tart wound up with the Prince is no concern of mine, but I'll have her back."

Minesh struggled to marshal his thoughts. If he was to die this day, he would take this animal with him.

But Lathan was ready for him. "A promise is a promise," the large man rumbled.

Minesh watched as the trader leaned forward and yank out the arrow. A screamed erupted from his throat as the barbs tore backward, ripping new flesh. Stars exploded against the back of his eyes. And new blood bubbled from the wound in his chest, seeping into his shirt. When he could see again, Lathan loomed over him with a small leather pouch. By smell alone Minesh knew its contents.

Lathan laughed as he pinched silvery powder between his fingers. "Healing herbs, as promised." Grinning, he pushed the undiluted drug deep into the wound.

The pain of a thousand arrows pierced Minesh's chest. His arms and legs, of their own volition, thrashed against the ground, his head hammering against the grassy trail. His throat howled, shattering the clear morning air with anguished cries that deepened in pitch, one after the next. Sagcryl burned in his blood like fire. The skin on his chest began to crawl and mottle with a life all its own, the itch of ants infesting his skin. His heart pumped sagcryl through his veins, outward from his chest and up into his brain. He lay helpless as his emotions struggled free of his lifelong control, heightened beyond human reason.

The memory of Lathan's diabolic face hung before him, the sound of distant laughter echoing in his ears. Then came silence as his murderers left him to die. The sky spun blue, fading to black as his body writhed and twitched. He called out to Galin, but his inexperience with the drug hindered rather than helped his mastery of True-Speech. Minesh thought he heard a faraway, "I am sorry," but he could have imagined it. He could have imagined anything. His mind was exploding.

Faster and faster his blood pulsed, like fire spread to dry tinder, burning to a fevered pitch. His sole release was one final tormented scream. It came out a low, animal groan, the sound of terror rasping in his drug-deepened throat.

Then terror faded to relief as a creeping silence defeated him, imparting its mind-deadening release, unconsciousness' promise. Blackness took him, and the manea knew peace.

The Night of the Demon

It was night when Bruenor and his pack crept into the city. He didn't lead them to Haven Gate where the Tower Guard was certain to discover them, but to the southwest quarter, where the city wall extended out into the sea. A smaller gate service serviced the docks area, manned not by the Tower Guard but by regular City Guard, one of whom knew Bruenor's face and passed coin to each of his fellows to secure passage.

"Your arm!" one of the men was foolish enough to say.

Bruenor struck with his remaining fist, knocking the man to the ground. The Skin-Runner then glared at the other guards, who dropped their gaze. No one spoke as they allowed unchallenged passage into the city to Bruenor, Arnor, and three others who had joined them during their journey.

Bruenor hid his injury beneath a heavy cloak as they made their way to a warehouse district a dozen streets north and several streets west of where they had entered the city. Few people were abroad in the night, but all carried the same rumor on their lips, whispering or laughing together over the mysterious severed arm that had arrived morning before last to disturb the King from his sleep.

"They'll pay!" Bruenor rasped. "They'll all pay! After tonight, no one in Toroth will be laughing."

Arnor cast him puzzled look and Bruenor grimaced. "After

tonight no one in Toroth will ever laugh again!"

They left the streets, ducking into a narrow alley that wound its way to the back door of a small warehouse near the wharf. The rank odors of ocean salt and rotting fish scented the night air, and the harsh slap of waves buffeting sand and rock echoed hollowly beneath the nearby docks.

Bruenor pounded on the door: two thumps, a pause, three thumps, a longer pause, and a final thump. He felt someone try to read him from inside, and then the door cracked open. A wary face looked out into the night, then eyes widened in surprised recognition, and finally shock. Bruenor pushed the door all the way open and he and his men marched inside.

There were nine men present, all from Bruenor's original pack dispersed at Karlac. They carried the aspect of whipped dogs, haggard and defeated.

"By the Demon!" Keliel whistled when he saw Bruenor. "We feared you were dead! Word from the Tower—"

Bruenor pulled from his belt his trophy from Kelmar and tossed it onto the table. It rolled, leaving the waxed cloth wrapping behind. All the men stared. Dried blood coated raw flesh where the skin had been removed. Obscenities littered the arm's surface where Bruenor had played with his knife.

"Send this to the Tower!" he snarled. "They'll soon have more arms than they know what to do with."

One of the men jumped, rewrapped the arm, and fled through the door. The night swallowed him.

"B—Bruenor. What does this mean?" It was Roman. He had probably been the first to run when they were attacked at the grotto.

Bruenor stared at the cowardly neophyte. Good niacs had died at Karlac, and here was Roman, safe in Toroth. He wondered if he shouldn't just kill him now. "It means," he said, casting his dark gaze slowly about the room, "that the Day of the Demon is upon us! The Great Feeding!"

His words were met with gasps and muttering, but the eyes of his followers burned with red fire.

Using his single arm, Bruenor threw off his cloak. Underneath he still wore the uniform Arnor had stripped from the bloody arm's owner. A dark stain covered much of the collar and chest. Bruenor ripped off the garment and threw it in the fire. His raw shoulder gleamed in the light of the lamps. The flesh that grew over the wound was puckered and red.

"We have seen the Hest!" he cried. "The Mastren has come! The Day of Stealth is ended! Tonight we shall run wild in the streets and prey upon the city. Tonight, the Demon shall be revealed in all his glory!"

Startled looks flashed from man to man, a mix of dread and hunger.

Bruenor spun about the room. "The Phyte must be gathered. A sacred Pae-thn held at the first rising of the eye of Hergo's moon. Send word to the Pack Leaders. All must be present."

Roman sputtered, "B—But what does it mean?"

Bruenor glowered at him and dropped his voice to a snarl. "You have not yet accepted the Demon. Tonight, Roman. Tonight. Afterward there will be no new oaths. No neophytes. There will be phyte-runners only. And niacs. And... there will be meat!"

Groans of hunger rose from the men. Roman swallowed and backed away.

"With the Pae-thn begins the Day of Murder," Bruenor told them. "We shall hold our rites each night, in the open. No longer in secret. No longer shall there be a single sacrifice, but meat for every Runner. All shall become niacs. All shall kill and feed. All shall be sated!"

Wide grins passed from face to face. Except for Roman, all of the men present were niacs, Demon-sworn men who had stalked and killed their own prey.

"What of the Hest?" asked Keliel. He had been with Bruenor at Karlac, had seen what the Hest could do.

"The Hest will come." Bruenor pounded the table with his fist. "It must. And this time... this time we will be ready. I will be ready."

Anklen, one of those Bruenor had picked up along the road, stomped his foot onto a chair and leaned forward. "I swear," he cried. "By the Demon. By Arazmud himself! I shall cut the skin of this Mastren and stretch it before the Circle of Sheep—"

"No!" Bruenor kicked at the chair, toppling Anklen to the floor. "That honor is mine! The Mastren is mine! Clear?"

Anklen glared up at him, and Bruenor watched the man's eyes move to his stumped shoulder, watched the anger subside. Anklen nodded and then untangled himself from the chair.

Bruenor turned away. With his one arm he reached to a narrow cabinet and drew out a small leather pouch. The men all knew what it contained. He placed the pouch in the center of the table and gestured at Arnor to untie the string. Arnor complied quickly, dumping the sagcryl powder into a wide, metal bowl.

"Now we invite the Demon," Bruenor said. "Invoke the new day— the Day of the Demon!" He glared at Roman. "And Roman will take his oath."

Roman shuddered and took a step backward.

"Then we shall run the city!" Bruenor finished.

Each man nodded as Bruenor began the rite, trading his clothing for wolf skins retrieved from a false-bottomed chest.

An air of nervousness filled the room. Bruenor sensed it. Not since the days of the Hestren had the Wolf run openly. Then, the Hest had come and cut the Wolf down; the Demon had not been ready and the packs had not worked together. For generations since, the Wolf had hunted by stealth, waiting for the Hest to return, waiting for the time when the Wolf would confront the Hest and this time prevail. And now the time had come. The packs were ready. This time, Bruenor clenched his fist, this time the Hest would be defeated.

As there were no neophytes present, save Roman, several niacs took up the chant. Bruenor turned to find Keliel pouring sage wine and preparing to cut himself to provide blood for the elixir. Bruenor waved him away. "This is the Day of the Demon. We will take the drug raw." Keliel backed away.

The pack came forward and, one by one, pinched powdered sagcryl between their fingers. Bruenor opened his mouth and pressed the silver powder inside. It burned his tongue and razed his throat, but brought on frenzy quickly. For a moment he couldn't breathe. Around him, voices guttered low as each man succumbed to the drug. The sagcryl was pure, strong. Bruenor shook his head as he watched droplets of thick dew seep from his pores, blood tainted white with the drug.

While he'd expected frenzy to hit him hard and fast, the weight of the pain took him by surprise. He staggered back from the table and clutched at the wall to hold himself steady. It was the first time he had taken the drug since losing his arm and the place where his arm should have been throbbed and pulsed. Nerves that no longer existed burned with savage life. The drug ran through him like water, seeking his shoulder, straining against scarred skin, bubbling from the wound. Despite the presence of the wall, Bruenor found himself sinking to the floor, his cries a low moan that scarce escaped his lips.

The presence of the Demon neared and the pain grew a hundred-fold. His whole body shook. Bruenor gasped, curling into a tight ball of agony.

Through pinched eyelids he saw the pack gawking at him. Then frenzy took him completely, and from the Elsian world beyond the Shroud, the Demon came.

$$\Omega$$

Roman glanced at the door, contemplating escape. He had taken the drug and was approaching full frenzy. Knew he could run like the wolf, that no man in the city could catch him. He looked to his companions and saw the Demon. Eyes stared at him. Glowing eyes, red with hunger. Eyes that told him to run. His companions could catch him. Demon meat! Roman's mouth began spouting the oath, and he saw disappointment replace desire. Then the Demon came.

As the opening words of the oath fell from his lips, a face of alien horror appeared before him. Flesh, raw and red. Dark fur, matted and torn. Crooked, yellow teeth. A thick, blackened tongue, flicking and slavering with hunger. Eyes, bubbling red pits filled with hate, with anger, with unspeakable cruelty, insatiable lust. Desires Roman didn't understand, couldn't hope to understand. "Feed us!" they demanded.

Roman shook his head, twisting to get away. Hands held him. Rough hands. Sharp nails bit into his skin. He forced his eyes shut, refusing to see. The image laughed. It was in his mind. There was no escape.

"Be true and be one of us," it rasped. "Be false and be an eternal sacrifice."

Roman forced his tongue to move, repeating the words, knowing he was dead if he didn't. In utter helplessness, he welcomed the Demon. Then it was inside him, a part of him. Roman no longer looked into its eyes, but through them! He opened his mouth and screamed.

When the scream ended, Roman shook off the hands that held him. He flexed his arms and beat his chest, then peered about the room with eyes that glowed red. Then he screamed again, howling cries no human could make. "I am the Beast!" he roared. "I am Arazmud!"

The others howled in response. Then the entire pack leapt to the door and out into the city. Bloodcurdling cries echoed along streets and between buildings as they burst from the storage house, naked except for tattered wolf skins and fragments of wolf skull. The city was their feeding ground. It would be a run like no other.

Arazmud, through Roman, glanced back once at Bruenor, abandoned by the pack, shaking and shuddering on the warehouse floor. A weak specimen. Then Arazmud, too, took to the streets, alive once again to sate his appetite.

Ω

Across the city, in the Sanctuary's west tower, Ceric came awake with a start. Outside his window, a soul-chilling howl rent the night. At the same time, the door to his room burst open.

"By all that is holy!" yelled the guard in the doorway. "'Tis the wailing of the dead!"

Ceric bolted to the window, but could see little. Clouds hid much of the sky; few stars and only the smallest of Sindarin's moons shed their light. But for a scattering of windows still alight at this late hour, the city was a well of darkness. Perhaps a dozen streets away, a deep, baying howl split the night, followed by yet another further off. It could have been wolves or wild dogs loose in the city. Ceric knew it wasn't. A shudder passed through him as the animal howls of men in full frenzy, consumed by sagcryl, rang in his ears. Extending his mind, he felt them. Not the savage hunger of impassioned Skin-Runners, but the hateful bloodlust of actual Demons. There were many of them.

"Gracious Spirits!" he croaked. "How can this be? How can this be?"

"Milord!" cried the guard. Ceric turned to the voice. The man's eyes were wide with terror. His lips trembled. "The King is in Kelmar. The Prince left the city this morning. It is your place to lead us now. How are we to meet this menace?"

Ceric felt the blood drain from his face. "Gracious Spirits, man. I rule the Circle not the Square! Peace is all I know."

The guard's voice dropped to a near whisper. "Milord. The city is in chaos. Peace, well, peace is what we need."

Ceric wrung his hands together and tried to think. Outside his window the howling continued, stealing his thoughts. "Roust all the Guard," he said at last. "Reinforce the night watch. Instruct them to take as many of the De — the Skin-Runners — as they can. It will be dangerous. Warn them! They must protect the citizens. Go. Go! I shall be in the Circle Chamber if I am needed."

The guard fled the room, his orders giving him purpose.

Ceric turned back to the window. New screams joined the howling of the Skin-Runners, the panicked, horrified cries of the people of Toroth. "Oh Gracious Spirits save us all!"

And it was then he knew, knew beyond any doubt, that Corin was indeed the Mastren. The Elsan Legends had foretold it all. The Day of the Demon had begun.

$$\Omega$$

The guard Eliard stood hidden in shadow, not knowing what to do. He'd heard rumors of their speed and had laughed it off. How could a man run faster on hands and feet than on two legs? He would not admit this to anyone, but he had tried it once in a weapons shed where he had been alone on duty. He had fared rather poorly.

What he saw now was impossible. They were men, just men, down on all fours, with animal skins flapping about their loins. Yet they ran as fast as wolves themselves.

Eliard cringed at the raw slap of palm and bare foot against hard earth or stone as Skin-Runners sped through the streets, howling like crazed animals, striking terror into the hearts of those huddled within the dwellings they passed.

Several Runners pounded down the street right in front of Eliard. He crept further back into the shadows.

Two of the Runners slowed in front of a dwelling across the way. They seemed to sniff at it, moving closer. Then they threw themselves against the door. Voices shrieked from within, which only inspire the Runners in their efforts. Again they pitched their bodies against the door. Again and again.

Eliard felt he should do something. Now was his chance. He could rush them. Stab one with his pike. Use his knife on the other. Yes, that's what he would do. A plan. A good plan. Eliard didn't move.

With a resounding crash, the door burst into splinters. Frightened cries echoed from within, filling the night with terror. The Skin-Runners disappeared through the doorway. There was noise. Strangled cries. Heavy grunts. Victorious howling.

Eliard swallowed bile as the Skin-Runners emerged, now erect on their feet. Between them, they dragged someone. A young girl? She made no noise, but turned her head this way and that, seeking escape. Her eyes were wide with terror; Eliard could tell by the whites reflecting light from the open doorway.

He watched in horrified fascination as the Skin-Runners ripped away the girl's clothes and threw her naked into the street. One of the Runners jumped on her, howling madness. The girl screamed, continued screaming as the Runner heaved his frenzied body up and down, animal noises rasping from his throat.

A glint of metal reflecting starlight caught Eliard's eye. The other Runner held a knife. He growled in his throat, deep, like a dying animal, as he sank to his knees beside the pair and grappled one of the girl's writhing legs. The girl screamed with renewed panic as steel bit into flesh. Wailing from across the city joined her own.

Eliard ordered his legs to move, to heave himself forward. He had to do something! But his body refused. He was frozen, teeth clenched tight, his hands gripping his pike as though it were trying to get away.

The girl's screams died into moaning and sobs and Eliard saw the Runner climb off her limp body. The villain found his own knife and joined his companion in his ghastly work. The girl was, by now, too weak, too disheartened to fight. Eliard opened his mind to offer comfort, consolation, pity. He closed it again quickly. All he found was horror and pain. Total bereavement.

And then the Skin-Runners rose from the girl's ravished body, their business done. The one who had taken her held something up to the starlight. He laughed and wrapped it about his naked body.

"Spirits save me!" Eliard whispered, his tongue dry against parched lips. It was the girl's skin.

The Runners dropped to all fours again and loped down the street.

Eliard remained frozen in the shadowed alleyway, his breath coming in shallow gasps. His entire body trembled as though ready to collapse. He had never imagined… words failed.

Then he noticed a sound echoing hollowly in his ears, barely discernible against the howls and wails of the city. He listened, stupefied. It took some moments to realize what it was— rasping sobs from the girl! She was still alive.

"Spirits save me!" He turned and retched. *I'll use my pike now. I will. The least I can do is to put that poor child out of her misery.*

Eliard raised his head and opened his eyes, finally ready to take action, as three Skin-Runners sprang at him from the shadows. The pike fell from his hands. "Spirits save me!"

Ω

Dawn came to Toroth like the aftermath of a hurricane.

Wailing rose from every dwelling, excepting a few that were ominously silent. The Skin-Runners were gone, yet their handiwork remained. Warm flesh lay steaming in the streets. Corpses and near-corpses lay abandoned near broken doorways. Blood ran through gutters or pooled in shallow puddles. Scraps of dried skin slid and tumbled in the breeze.

The City Guard wandered aimlessly through the streets. Many of them, seasoned veterans, gibbered like lunatics.

Ceric, Peace-Ruler of the First Circle of Sindarin, sat in a despondent heap on a bench just outside the Sanctuary, watching it all. Pale sunlight bleached the courtyard the color of dry bones.

Why is Herlen not here? How could I have been so foolish as to send Corin away? Surely there is someone...

It was no good. With the King's younger children dwelling far down the coast in the home of their aunt, the Peace-Ruler was next in command. The children were too young anyway and the aunt... well, the aunt would have spent the night gibbering into her blankets. *No, that is uncharitable. Had I not been needed, I would have done the same.*

There was nothing for it. People looked to him for answers and there was little he could do about it. He only wished... He wished there was someone else who could ask the question.

Ceric opened his mouth and the words caught in his throat. He swallowed and tried again. "How—How many dead?" He hardly recognized the man he questioned, though they had spoken just yesterday.

Captain Rejin's distraught eyes darted about the yard, looking anywhere but at Ceric. The man's white coat hung open, unbuttoned for the first time in the Peace-Ruler's long memory, and blood stained the cuffs of the sleeves. His hair, that silly coxcomb that had always irritated Ceric, drooped to one side. The big man's voice, when he spoke, was a whisper. "It's difficult to say, Peace-Ruler. Many of the bodies... aren't intact."

"Can you guess for me?" Ceric asked, almost pleading. "I

have to know."

"The Captain swallowed. "Perhaps a hundred."

"A hundred!" Ceric dropped his face into his hands.

"Mostly children," Rejin admitted.

"Children?"

Captain Rejin sucked in a hurried breath. "I should have said young people. The Skin-Runners prefer the young, those not yet hardened to sage, or to life. They also got one of the Tower Guard. Eliard was... well, Eliard had a broken tooth. Vargas recognized it. The man is still in tears."

Ceric couldn't respond. He just stared into his hands.

"Peace-Ruler." Rejin spoke reluctantly. "The Skin-Runners, well, they've never been like this. What has happened to... What has happened?"

"It is the end," Ceric sobbed, unable to stop himself. "The end of everything. Only the Mastren can save us now."

Aftermath

It was more than a touch that awakened Minesh. More than a physical feeling. Consciousness returned slowly, his senses coming alive degree by minute degree. His eyes would not open. His chest throbbed.

His first sensation, apart from pain, was that of sound. A quiet morning, small insects buzzing around him. Then came feeling, the moisture of dew upon his face and hands. He became aware of the cold and began to shiver. He forced his eyes open. When vision came, it was clouded.

The touch came again, and he started.

Minesh's blood raced as his senses registered the hulking body that loomed over him. Animal smell tainted the air. He assumed it was a sten-bear or a mountain tree-lynx, come to investigate abandoned flesh. He forced his eyes to clear and saw the animal was a deer, chestnut brown with a small white tuft for a tail. The large, hazel eyes of a mature doe gazed down at him; he could almost feel the moisture on her nose. They stared at each other, neither of them blinking. Then she moved away a few feet and lay in the grass.

Ignoring the pain it brought, Minesh raised himself on his elbows and peered down at his chest where the arrow had pierced. The cloth of his vestments had been torn away, shredded, and his wound licked clean. Scarlet scar tissue stretched across the hole made by the arrow. Fresh blood leaked out where his movements had reopened the wound. He glanced at the deer again, then surveyed the area.

His horse had wandered off a distance and was munching grass. His belongings remained tied to the saddle. Sunlight glinted off the oiled surface of his water skin. He laughed and then winced from the pain it caused.

Lathan must have been in a great hurry to find that girl not to have robbed me. Not that I have much worth taking. And the horse eats more than it's worth.

Opening his mind, Minesh took inventory of his physical state. Everything seemed in order; the drug had inflicted no permanent damage. He was almost surprised. These old bones are stronger than I thought. The arrow wound was another story. His chest ached but at least he had been wrong about the lung; his breathing was fine. Given time, his chest would heal. But of course, that was the problem. Did he have time?

Speaking True, he called his horse to him. The animal snorted but obeyed. Minesh reached up, pulled the water skin from the saddle, and drank. Deeply. Eagerly. Washing the roughness of the drug from his throat. When the skin was empty, he let it drop to the earth.

Reluctantly, but knowing he must, he shifted his weight to get his feet under him. The world spun in a sea of color: blue, green, white, and brown. He groaned and swayed on his knees, then toppled forward. Something strong and warm stopped his fall. The deer.

Using the animal for support, he finished climbing to his feet. All of his weight was on the deer, but she remained sturdy. Minesh experimented by shuffling forward a few steps. The deer moved with him, a living crutch. When he could stand on his own, the deer moved away again, watching.

Slowly, painfully, he hobbled about the glade. Blood dribbled down his chest, and he tore the hem of his vestments to bandage the wound. Searching behind rocks and beneath the larger bushes, he found black bryony, a creeping vine whose small fruits could be used for bruises. He also found the dark, purple berries of belladonna, whose poison would cleanse his system if mixed well with bits of tallowleaf and honeysuckle. Next he dug for herbs and tubers, small shoots and plant bulbs for curing. When he had sufficient for his needs, he turned back to where his horse had resumed munching grass.

The deer sat it the grass a short distance away, her large intelligent eyes following his every movement. Minesh placed his precious ingredients in a tidy pile on the ground and then went about collecting wood and dry tinder for a fire. He refilled his water skin. When he returned, the doe had not moved.

He rested several minutes before arranging the tinder and striking flint to steel. The swift movements sent flashes of pain ripping through his chest. Minesh ignored it, and on the fourth attempt, a spark caught. After building up the fire, he lay down beside it and waited for the ache from his exertions to subside. When he sat up to prepare his medicines, the deer was still there.

It occurred to him to reach out to her through True-Speech, to find answers to his questions. For that matter, he could call Galin, whom he felt certain was in some way responsible for the deer. He did neither. He had taken the drug; how could he use his faculty now? A faculty he had been so proud to gain without the drug. True, he had already summoned his horse. But that was before he'd had time to think; the guilt had not yet encompassed him. How could he face Galin? Or the deer who even now observed with utter calm his awkward attempts at healing?

When the fire burned low, he retrieved the tin cup from his saddlebag, set it among the coals, and poured a splash of water from the refilled water skin. He then crushed the herbs and leaves he had collected on a flat rock, working them into a powder. When the water began to steam, he added the powder to the cup, stirring the mixture into a paste with a twig. Then he pulled the cup from the fire and gritted his teeth.

His fingers burned when he stuck them into the boiling concoction and a low groan escaped his lips. Urgently, he daubed the bubbling paste onto the wound in his chest. New pain set Minesh's head to spinning, but he had to apply the poultice hot in order to activate the herbs and to seal the wound. He forced air into his lungs in short gasps and when he was done, collapsed onto the grass. Then he closed his eyes, his last sight that of the deer watching him.

The manea dreamed.

It is night. No stars hallow the sky. The three larger moons – Rhea, Hergo, and Lalantha – are full and tinged with red, haunting. Beneath the moons Skin-Runners and Demons dance, performing their rites. Wolf skins flutter in the frosty night air. Animal cries echo among the shadows.

Tall wooden posts rise up from the ground, their dark surfaces slick and greasy. Good, honest people are lashed between the posts. Blood, laced with the drug, is poured down their throats. There are knives, and violations, and butchery.

Then Corin is there, wielding the Hest. The Mastren. But the Skin-Runners do not flee. Instead they howl with rapture, dancing round and round. Corin turns. His eyes burn red, the eyes of the Beast.

Minesh woke to the shrieking of his own lungs. Sunlight burned his eyes. Sweat beaded across his face. Dreams. Only dreams. Truth, let it be so.

The manea forced his body upright and looked around. He had slept two, perhaps three, hours. The deer was still there, watching. He checked his wound; it seemed improved beneath the poultice. Hunger rumbled in his stomach and he ate some dried rabbit meat from his saddlebag, after which thirst forced him to the stream for more water. When he returned, the deer was still there.

Guilt continued to gnaw at him, although now it was a new guilt. He suspected the deer would not leave until he spoke to her. Hesitantly, Minesh opened his mind. "Thank you." He still felt unworthy to use True-Speech.

"It was a small thing," the deer answered, using words that only an adept of True-Speech could comprehend. "You are welcome." With that the animal climbed to its feet as though to leave.

"Wait! Who sent you?"

"One who awaits your touch. Your guilt is your own to banish or embrace as you will." She turned and bounded into the trees.

It was when she turned that Minesh saw the seared wound upon her flank, the mark of the Hest. Only then did he recognize the deer for what it was.

"Galin?" He reached without thinking.

The voice that answered was rife with sarcasm. "I am hurt that you would sooner speak with a horse and a deer than with me."

Anger hardened Minesh's thoughts. "This is no time for joking." Then the guilt returned. "I've used sagcryl, the drug."

Galin's tone shifted from humor to compassion. "No. The drug used you. You were the victim, not the perpetrator."

Minesh wrung his hands. Tears burned his eyes as self-loathing threatened to overwhelm him. "But it took me, Galin! It ran through my veins. My blood! My voice!"

His True-Friend grew clinical. "The physical damage is secondary. It is the mind that counts. Do you crave to use the drug again?"

The breath caught in Minesh's throat. "No! Of course not."

"Do you desire to subjugate the will of others? To use them to fulfill your own lusts?"

"No, never! Galin, you have never spoken to me this way!"

"If you do not feel these things, then your mind has not been damaged. Be at peace."

Minesh breathed again. "The deer, Galin. Corin's deer. The one I shot for Corin's test and would have died if not for Corin. You sent her. All the way across the Serpent's Tail. Truth knows how long ago you must have called her. She licked away some of the drug, prevented it from killing me."

"Perhaps."

"Why? You could have let me die." A pause. "I might have preferred it."

"We cannot always have that which we desire. Such is the hunger of the Beast. You are needed, Minesh. Remember? At Stonepast."

Minesh sighed. "Stonepast."

$$\Omega$$

Herlen hardly knew his own city when he rode in through Haven Gate at midday. But for a few anxious guards at the wall, the streets were deserted. Not a barker hawked his wares. Not a child played with his dog. There was not even a dog.

Pale faces peered out through shuttered windows as Herlen and his escort rode down Freedom Avenue toward the Sanctuary. Ominous stains marked the street. Herlen saw one man hurrying to his house with an armload of wooden planks. When he saw the King, the man dropped his load and fled.

"By the Demon, what has happened here?" Herlen said, not realizing at first that he had spoken aloud. No one answered.

Outside the Sanctuary he was met by men of the Tower Guard; they looked embarrassed and were quick to lead the horses away.

"Send Minesh to my quarters," Herlen barked.

"The manea is not here," said a soldier. "Left day before yesterday, just after you did."

"Demons! I don't suppose Corin is back?"

"H—He was. Arrived after you left."

Herlen stared at him. "Was?"

The soldier looked down at his feet. "He left again, yesterday morning."

"Double Demons! Send Ceric to my dayroom."

As he climbed the Tower staircase to his rooms, Herlen knew that he should be pondering the state of the city. What could have happened during his two-day absence to cause such fear and disorder? But his thoughts kept returning to Corin. His son had returned. And now he was off again. Herlen paused and gripped the staircase railing. No one was ever *off again* after finding their True-Friend. Something must have happened. To Corin. To Toroth. Sweat trickled down his forehead and into his eyes. He released the railing and continued climbing. Even Minesh was gone. Something terrible must have happened.

He entered his dayroom and went immediately to the wine cupboard. The rich vapors helped to calm him. Herlen drank his cup empty and refilled it, then went to the window. The streets outside were empty in all directions. And then suddenly he knew.

A barely audible knock came at the door. Herlen grunted and the door opened, then closed. He did not need to look at his visitor. He allowed a word to escape his lips; it came out as little more than a whisper. "Skin-Runners."

Ceric sucked in his breath. "You were told? Somebody had to. I was afraid it would be me."

Herlen sighed and turned to face the Peace-Ruler. "No one has said anything, Ceric. Not even *Welcome Home*. How bad was it?"

Ceric moved to the divan and sat down. Herlen had never seen the Peace-Ruler's shoulders so stooped. He studied Ceric's face; the Circle Elder had aged years in the past two days.

"The word bad does not begin to describe it," Ceric said.

The man looked a stranger without his smile. Herlen had never seen him not smile.

Ceric wrung his hands. "It was a nightmare! They were Demons, Herlen. Demons! The Skin-Runners were possessed. All of them. Our people were butchered from midnight to daybreak."

Herlen's hand trembled as he lifted his cup to his lips. He thought he had prepared himself for the answer. It still came as a shock. "How many?" he asked.

Ceric hesitated and his hallmark quiet voice became stony. "Do you want it in identifiable corpses or in cart-loads?"

Herlen started, spilling his wine. "That was in incredibly bad taste. And coming from you..."

The Peace-Ruler's face paled. "I'm not joking, Herlen! We don't know how many they killed. Many... many were hacked to pieces! And... and eaten." Ceric's shoulders drooped even further. Tears trickled from his eyes. "Elder Dumas spent the morning collecting pieces of his two grandchildren from outside the courtyard."

Herlen poured a second cup of wine and thrust it into Ceric's hands. "Of course. I'm sorry. Where is Dumas now?"

The Peace-Ruler stared into the cup. "Dead. When he was done, he hanged himself."

"Gibbering Demons!" Herlen tried to imagine Dumas's despair, and failed.

"Oh, Herlen, If only you had seen—"

"I've seen enough." Herlen straightened and shook the image of Dumas and his grandchildren from his mind. "Are the Guard preparing?"

Ceric blinked. "Preparing? For what?"

"For tonight." Herlen raised his cup to his lips and then lowered it again without drinking. "You can't believe we've seen the end of it."

Ceric's eyes went wild and his hands shook, spilling wine onto his white robes. "Gracious Spirits! That's what Dumas feared. It can't be true. Not again! Not again!"

Herlen leaned over and yelled into the Peace-Ruler's face. "Snap out of it, man! Get control of yourself. I need you. Have we heard from the towns?"

Ceric raised his cup to his lips, slowly, his hands still trembling, and took a small sip. "No," he said. "From no one."

"Maybe they haven't attacked anywhere else." Herlen slammed his cup down and began pacing the floor. "I can't afford to send riders. We need every man we've got right here. They wouldn't be safe, either, alone on the road." He stopped. "Corin's out there."

Ceric resumed sobbing. "It doesn't matter. Nowhere is safe. No one!"

Herlen yanked the Peace-Ruler's cup from his hand and threw its contents into the old man's face. Ceric sputtered and pushed away.

"Blast you, Ceric! I need you now. Last night Toroth was surprised. Tonight we'll be ready. I want all the guardsmen assembled in the courtyard. Their first duty is to round up every able-bodied man they can find. We'll arm everyone and post them on every street corner in Toroth. Tonight," Herlen returned to the window and stared out into the deserted streets. "Tonight when the Skin-Runners come, we'll have a surprise waiting for them."

The Hunt of Orion

Seven men sat together in Bruenor's warehouse crowding a scarred wooden table that creaked and wobbled with the shifting weight. Each remained silent and stared at the stone walls. An eighth man entered from the dockside door. He wore a heavy cloak tied at the neck. It gave him the appearance of a much larger man. He took an empty chair at the table and sat down.

Bruenor kept all emotion from his face as he appraised the new arrival. "Have all the priests reported, Arnor?"

"Yes, Bruenor. All who can will be in place in the neighboring towns and villages before nightfall."

"How many did we lose?"

"Two. I was surprised when last night's skins didn't win them over."

Bruenor grunted. "Those were the weak ones. Did they give your people any trouble?"

Arnor grinned. "No, the knife found them easily. Their replacements were much more cooperative."

"How many will we have in Toroth tonight?"

"A hundred. Perhaps more."

Bruenor scowled. "That will have to be enough."

"They'll be waiting for us, Bruenor," said a third man. "We won't have surprise on our side this time."

"Are you weak too, Roman? Was last night's run not evidence enough for you?" Bruenor stood and hammered the table with his fist. "Our time has come! The Day of the Demon! Tonight will make last night's run seem like a children's game. Tonight we shall drink Toroth's blood until the cup is empty!"

"The Hest," asserted Roman. "After last night the Mastren is sure to come."

"I hope so," Bruenor growled. "I truly hope so."

Arnor's hands gripped the table. "What about the Hest, Bruenor? Doesn't the Circle have a legend about the Hest being used against us, wiping us out before the Hunters arrive?"

Bruenor rose from his seat and paced around the table until he stood behind his man. "Are you afraid, Arnor? Do the fanatical ramblings of senile old men frighten you? Are you one of their flock to be intimidated into obedience by empty fables? All the Circle knows is that the Mastren is the Herald of the Hunters. They have forgotten the Day of the Demon, that the Hunters will come because their Mastren is defeated by the Beast. They lose their last weapon against us and have no choice but to come themselves. The Hest wiping us out? Who's been feeding you this rubbish? Roman?"

Arnor slowly nodded.

"I should have known." He cast Roman a cold stare. "That one is a coward. I should have stretched him out long ago."

Roman shrank into his chair, saying nothing.

"Even so," Arnor continued. "Regardless of who or what the Mastren does, the Hunters will come. No one denies that. Our histories tell how thousands of years ago the League of Orion all but exterminated Mankind, and how they continue to search out those who fled the known worlds. When they do arrive, you, I, and everyone else on Sindarin will die."

Bruenor returned to his chair and ran a finger along a groove in the tabletop. *This is why I am priest and not these fools. They forget. They are told, and told again, and still they forget.* "These so-called True-Friends of the Circle are in league with the Hunters. It is they who lead them here."

The Skin-Runners all gawked at him, as though hearing this for the first time.

"The Demon is Mankind's only friend. And we," he pointed a finger at Arnor, "you and I, and all who keep the oath, are friends of the Demon. Remember our oath."

Bruenor cast his gaze around the table. "When death takes us and we cross the Shroud, we will become Demons ourselves. We will continue to hunt through Gorgings on other worlds, worlds the Hunters have not yet found!"

Arnor stared back at him, as did the rest of the men in the room, their heads nodding.

"The oath," Keliel whispered.

Bruenor clenched his one hand, watching his knuckles turn white. "Forever, Arnor. You and I will run with the wolf forever!"

$$\Omega$$

Corin held Serl's reins loose, giving the horse its head. Alethea sat behind him, her long, lean arms locked about his waist. Together they cast a shadow that at times formed familiar shapes: the Sanctuary tower, a city guard in full regalia standing at inspection, his father ambling down a hallway, vegetables in a bowl, and once he swore he imagined a turkey fully dressed and steaming on a silver platter, though that could be his hunger speaking to him. Most times, however, the shadow was as indecipherable to Corin as the girl breathing into his back.

"Where are we going?" Alethea asked.

They had been riding since yesterday morning with hardly two words between them. It amazed Corin how long it had taken for Alethea's anger to cool over his words in the courtyard. For his part, he didn't know what to say to her. The Peace-Ruler had pushed them together and he didn't know why. To answer Alethea's question, he shrugged. "Does it matter where we go?"

Serl walked at an easy pace through humming fields of tallow-grass and oxalis. Small insects and flitting birds flew past, hardly seeming to notice Man's intrusion into the wilderness.

Abruptly, Alethea's arms about his waist tightened their grip. "Listen! Do you hear it?"

Corin pulled in Serl's reins and cocked his head. But the sound came from within, not without, a seraph hymn.

"Angel-fly," Alethea murmured.

Her arm came up and Corin's gaze followed its sweep. A lone flutter of golden wings stained with red and blue tumbled toward them, spinning drunkenly.

"When we were children," Alethea said, "my sister and I watched them for hours. See how it moves? Dancing through the fields, searching for lost loves."

Corin watched the moth-like insect spin several uneven loops, the steady cadence of its song belying its awkward movements. "You hardly ever see them this far north," he said, but Alethea did not seem to hear. She was still listening to the angel-fly's song. He flicked the reins and Serl moved forward.

The sun rose to its zenith and started downward before either of them spoke again, when hunger forced them to stop and take a meal by a large, clear pond.

"You do realize that we're cheating," Corin told her. He leaned back in the tall grass, a thin strip of rock-hard bear meat between his teeth.

Long strands of rich, auburn hair seemed to almost glow in the sunlight as Alethea swung her head to face him. "Cheating? How?"

"We're supposed to be alone. And we weren't supposed to bring food."

Alethea picked at a dry piece of week-old bear meat. "You call this food? Besides, you said you killed the sten-bear yourself. I don't call that bringing food."

Distracted by the way sunlight coaxed fire from her otherwise dark brown hair, Corin ignored the jibe. "In order to find our True-Friends, we're supposed to suffer in the wilderness."

Alethea did not look particularly concerned. "Who told you that?"

"Minesh. It's how he sent me out the first time, with nothing but a knife."

"How would starving help you find your True-Friend?"

"I don't know," Corin admitted. He shrugged his shoulders. "It didn't help before."

Alethea glanced away, and then rose to her feet.

Corin sighed and sat in dejected silence, reminded once again of his failure to find his True-Friend. Idly, he watched Alethea walk to the edge of the grassy slope, kneel down, and drink several swallows of water with her cupped hand. Then she sat and began unlacing her boots.

The air in the glade was hushed, the pond still and serene. Alethea pulled off first one boot, then the other, and set them in the grass. Corin felt his foul mood evaporate as he watched her graceful movements. He even smiled when she touched the cotton of her breeches and gently rolled them up past her knees. Her feet and legs were tan and smooth; soft skin gleamed in the brilliant sunlight. Corin sat still as he watched, his heart pounding in his ears.

An image of Alethea's white bosom heaving beneath her old tunic, the one with the missing buttons, flashed through Corin's memory. He silently cursed Ceric for Alethea's new clothes, and then poked a finger at the shabby sten-bear coat that lay rumpled in the grass. The Circle's Man of Peace had not extended the favor to him.

Alethea squealed as her toes dipped into the icy water, and her whole body shivered. The pond's rippling surface glistened in the sunlight, reflecting the young woman's laughing image, water shimmering like a poorly crafted mirror when she wiggled her toes. She squealed again, clenching her teeth as she immersed both feet up to the ankles.

When she turned her head to glance back at him, Corin flushed. He didn't know why he felt uncomfortable. Perhaps it was shame for the way he had been looking at her. Or thinking about her.

"Your feet must be as sore as mine, prince. The water isn't that cold." Alethea laughed and turned away, her long hair swinging free with the motion.

Corin stared. *Why have I never noticed her hair before today?*

Climbing to his feet, he lumbered toward her and then stood at the pond's edge gazing down into the water. His reflection gazed back at him, rippling with the gentle movements of her legs, the water darkened by swirling mud where she disturbed the floor of the pond. It was hypnotic, like peering into another world. It was himself he saw in the reflection, and Alethea standing near him. Yet they were different people entirely. Happy people.

Alethea laughed. "Are you going to stand there all day?"

Embarrassed, Corin plopped down on the grass and pulled at a boot. He grew even more embarrassed when it wouldn't come off. "These always were too tight," he admitted.

"Here, let me help." Alethea moved toward him, stepping carefully through water that rose past her ankles, halfway up her calves; she gave no sign that it was cold.

Corin should have known what would happen next. So should Alethea. She put one hand on the boot's heel, the other grasping the toe, and yanked. Both boot and girl went flying backward into the pond. The icy splash hit Corin full in the face.

Alethea came up sputtering, hair plastered to her head, her cotton tunic clinging to her body in a way that Corin appreciated. "You did that on purpose!" she screamed.

"I didn't!" Corin widened his eyes with innocence. While it was exactly the kind of thing he might do on purpose, this time he hadn't.

Alethea cast about herself, appearing lost, squeezing water out of her hair. She turned on Corin, her look imploring. "I'm soaked! What am I supposed to do now?"

"Well," Corin suggested. "I do have another boot." He held up his booted foot and waggled it.

Uttering a snarl, Alethea grabbed and yanked. Not pulling the boot off, but pulling Corin off the bank.

"Demons!" Corin yelled as he slipped off the grass and into the pond, freezing water biting into him. Quick as an eel, he leapt to his feet, slipped in the mud, and fell back into the water.

Alethea stood laughing, shivering with the cold.

Climbing more warily from the water, Corin tried to appear mad, but almost laughed with her. "What did you do that for?"

"Well, you did say you wanted to suffer in the wilderness."

This time he did laugh.

It took Corin longer than he would have wished to find his missing boot. Longer still to wash the mud out of it. Building the fire seemed to take forever, even with the flint he had taken from the Skin-Runners' camp. The touch of a rising breeze against his wet clothes didn't help.

He had to admire Alethea, though. Not once did she complain, though she was certainly just as cold. Without his asking, she had followed him into the trees to collect small twigs and branches.

Together they sat by the fire, Alethea wearing the blanket Ceric had given her before leaving Toroth, and Corin wrapped in his sten-bear coat. Their clothes lay draped over nearby bushes, drying in the breeze.

Corin toyed with the fire, poking it with a stick and tossing in bits of twig and dry grass. His eyes strayed to Alethea's face, however, taking in the tangles of wet hair, then drifted lower, glimpsing white skin behind the blanket.

Alethea stared into the flames, humming to herself.

"Ceric shouldn't have given you that blanket, you know," Corin said. "Minesh wouldn't have allowed it."

Alethea pulled the blanket tighter. "Well, I'm glad I have it now. If you want to suffer you can go stand in the pond again."

Corin blushed. "I'm talking like an idiot, aren't I? You must think me a lunatic."

Alethea pursed her lips and gave him a long, appraising look. "Actually," she said, letting the word roll off her tongue. "I think you are the finest man I've ever met. Except for Ceric."

Corin blushed deeper. He opened his mouth but nothing came out.

"I'm not used to men being nice," Alethea explained. "For the longest time I didn't think it was possible. Thank you for proving me wrong."

Corin blinked, not knowing how to respond. Being nice was a poor quality in a prince. Since childhood he had expended considerable effort in being cold and blustery, something the

Sanctuary Guard could respect. They would not respect nice. When was I nice? He pondered this question for a long time while Alethea went back to her humming.

Ω

Alethea finished tightening her belt and straightened her shoulders. Though no longer wet, neither were her clothes exactly dry; it would have to do. While dressing, she had recalled where the sturdy pants, shirt, coat, and boots had come from, and remembered also some of what Ceric had told her. "Who are the Hunters?" she asked.

Corin poked his head up over the bushes, and then moved to join her. He looked ridiculous, lumbering through the brush covered in sten-bear furs.

Alethea giggled.

"What?" Corin asked.

"I can just picture the expression on some poor hunter's face after shooting his Prince in the behind with an arrow."

Corin winced. "What about the Prince's poor behind? Do you think I enjoy walking around like some archer's target? What's all this about hunters?"

Alethea considered Corin for a moment. Even with the pathetic bear furs, he did look rather handsome now that he had washed his face. His nose was sharp, but not too sharp, set nicely above slightly parted lips that seemed to beg to be kissed.

Kissed? Where did that come from? Alethea moved her attention to his gray-blue eyes and prayed that she wasn't blushing. She couldn't recall ever seeing such clear and intelligent eyes; they seemed to penetrate into her soul.

Demons! What's wrong me? I must be red as a rooster. His hair. I'll focus on his hair. Black. That's safe. How could hair get me into trouble? Short, but not too short, for a man. And thick. Clumped in tight locks that on anyone else would be unruly, but on Corin looked... Bloody demons!

Alethea turned away. He must think me some fool child. Staring and blushing and ducking my head. She coughed to cover her actions. Perhaps he'll think I had something caught in my throat. Yes, that will do.

"It—" Alethea coughed and then cleared her throat. "It was something Ceric said. About Hunters. Orion's Hunt." She looked up, peering at him from beneath her bangs.

Corin peered back as though puzzling something out, and then shook his head. His expression turned grim. "You're better off not knowing."

Alethea blinked. What was he questioning? My cough? My blushing? Or what I said? But his response surprised her. "I remember something from my childhood about Orion and his Hunters coming for us if we were bad. We called him Mr. Onion. Ilsa would do something she oughtn't and I'd say, *Mr. Onion will come for you*, and we'd both laugh."

Corin continued to frown. "Onion's... Orion's Hunt is no laughing matter. It's why we came to Sindarin in the first place. To hide from the Hunters. It's why we live the way we do, without technology, in order to stay hidden."

Alethea was uncertain what technology was – the word was unfamiliar – but it sounded unpleasant; she was glad to live without it. But she didn't like the worried tone in Corin's voice. "Ceric said that the Hunters would find us."

Corin nodded. "They will. Someday."

"What happens then?"

The Prince's reply surprised her a second time. "Then we die. Come on, we had better get going." He pointed at purple clouds gathering over the Serpent's Tail. "I don't like the look of that sky."

Ω

Herlen stood at one of the windows of his private study, staring out across the city and beyond its gray walls to thick purple clouds that hung like a blanket above the Aenlaen Mountains far to the north. Sheets of rain streaked down against the horizon, watering the vast grasslands of Nume and the foothills beyond. It would not be long before the storm broke over the city.

Is Corin out there now? Traipsing through the rain in search of his True-Friend while all Sindarin awaits its death? Is my son the Mastren?

The King stepped away from the window to his wine

cupboard. He could look as long as he wished, but the sky would tell him nothing.

A knock at the door interrupted his pouring of the wine. A guard's voice announced that the Peace-Ruler of the Circle sought an audience. Herlen supposed he responded. The door opened and Ceric drifted in like a ghost and sagged into a chair.

"Well?" Herlen asked. "Are the people ready? Is the Guard in place?"

He didn't know why he asked the question. The Circle Elder had done what he could during the Skin-Runner attack. Herlen had been as impressed with Ceric's actions as he had been disappointed with himself for not being there. *But now I am here. If an attack came tonight, it is my responsibility to see to the city's defense.*

The Peace-Ruler took the question for what it was, however. "Ready? They are resolved to dying, if that's what you mean."

Herlen cast the Elder a sour look. Now was not the time for defeatism.

"I have been wrong," Ceric added. "All my life I have proclaimed the coming of the Mastren as the Herald of a new era of Mankind, a time when we would rise up from barbarity into a Golden Age of Peace. But that was only half the Legend. The Skin-Runners have their own version— the Day of the Demon, the Great Feeding."

Herlen snorted. "Where did you hear this nonsense?"

"The archives. I spent the past few hours going over the Legends. The notes. The commentaries. It's all there. In Arwyth's own words. She knew. The Mastren is a two-edged sword, Herlen, heralding either the ascension of Man or our extermination. It is the crux; the one Legend the Elsan gave us with no sure outcome. The most important Legend of all."

Herlen did not reply. He had spent time in the archives as well. Ever since Minesh had suggested that Corin might be the Mastren.

But Ceric wasn't finished. "I have been wrong, Herlen. The entire Circle has been wrong. All these centuries we have contented ourselves with guiding a few questing souls to the Path while the majority of Sindarin wallows in its own excrement. We needed to teach everyone, not just a few. And now it is too late." The old man looked up. "Judgment has come, Herlen! The Mastren has arrived. The Hunters follow after. But Sindarin will be judged as a whole, not individually. And as a whole, well, the Hunters are right— Mankind is better off dead."

Herlen grunted and turned back to the window. "That's your fear talking."

The storm was closer now, sweeping toward Toroth like a straw broom, ready to whisk away the dirt and the filth. Herlen knew what Ceric was saying. He had pondered the same words himself after his visit to the archives. But he was not ready to give into them. Not yet, anyway.

"The Judgment isn't here yet," Herlen said. "And we don't know for certain that Corin is the Mastren."

Ceric's answer was a whisper. "Don't we?"

"No," Herlen said. "Until the Hunters arrive and tell me to my face that Corin is indeed the Mastren, I will have room for doubt."

The chair squeaked and Herlen turned to see the Peace-Ruler rise from where he sat and place a trembling hand upon the doorknob. Ceric cast him a grave look. "May your doubt save us all." Then the old man stepped out into the hallway and closed the door behind him.

$$\Omega$$

Corin sat in darkness, listening to distant thunder while, overhead, stars twinkled like friendly fireflies. Hergo, Sindarin's second moon, peaked out from among a stand of trees as though reluctant to join its cousins. Storm clouds concealed the heavens further north and to the west. A chill, rain-damp wind had begun blowing up from Toroth-way. Corin drew his sten-bear skin coat closer about his shoulders.

Alethea must have been awake and heard his movements. "I'm cold," she said.

Corin grunted. "You're the one with the blanket. But if you come a little closer, perhaps I'll share my poor animal hide with you."

Dark on dark shadows blotted out the stars, accompanied by soft rustling noises. Then Alethea was beside him. Despite her claim of being cold, her body felt warm beneath her clothes. She said nothing as he lifted the edge of the fur to cover her.

"Rain must be flooding the streets of Toroth," he said, hoping to break the awkward silence.

But Alethea had something weightier than small talk on her mind. "Tell me about the Mastren."

Corin hesitated as an odd melding of fear and anger flooded through him. He clenched his teeth and felt his muscles harden. As a prince raised in the Sanctuary, Corin had rarely known fear. Since leaving Toroth with Minesh three short weeks ago, he had known little else. It was an emotion Corin was not comfortable with. Anger, on the other hand, was Corin's closest friend.

When he was eight years old, Corin's mother had died giving birth to his second sister. Short hours later, the newborn also died. Corin had loved his mother. He remembered her as a sweet woman, beautiful and always cheerful. She had given Corin and his younger brothers and sister all the love that their father seemed incapable of giving.

Not that Herlen did not love them. Corin was certain that he did. But his father was King. Showing affection was a sign of weakness and Herlen was not a weak king. He was cold and ruthless and quick to make difficult decisions. He was much respected by his people. And by those who understood him and the sacrifices he made, Herlen was loved.

Corin hoped to one day earn as much love and respect.

However, after the death of his mother, his father had grown colder and even more ruthless, withholding even the small affection that had sometimes slipped out when they were together as a family. Corin's brothers and sister had been sent to Phenos, far to the south, to be raised by their mother's sister. Corin, the eldest and heir to the Square, had grown to adulthood in the Sanctuary, training with the Toroth Guard and tutored by the First Circle.

Corin's chest tightened. It was not fair that his mother had been taken. That his second sister had been taken. That his brothers and sister had gone to live in a distant keep. That his father treated him like a soldier rather than a son. It was not fair that he had been forced to grow up alone and seemingly unloved, feared by the guardsmen he trained with and despised by the Circle Elders who held no love for the Square.

Corin had had but a single companion growing up— anger. And nowhere more pronounced than with the Circle. He strained to suppress that anger now.

"The Mastren is a fiction," he said, answering Alethea's question. "A fable created by the Circle to give hope to a hopeless people."

"You can't believe that!" Alethea said.

Corin grudgingly tried to recall the words that had been beaten into him by the Circle. "I have to believe it. Listen. According to the Circle, the Mastren is supposed to lift Mankind out of barbarity. You've seen the Skin-Runners. You've seen men like Lathan. No one man can do anything about people like that. And believe me, there are a lot of them. My father has spent a lifetime fighting them, and his father before him, and his father before that, all the way back to the days when our ancestors first came to Sindarin. The Legend of the Mastren is impossible."

"Then what about the Hunters?" Alethea asked. "Are they fiction too?"

Corin sighed and felt his muscles relax. Alethea spoke to him like no other had, honestly and easily. Weighing what he said before deciding how to respond. Not a yes-man, like the Toroth Guard, eager to please and fearful of giving offence. And not a no-man like the Circle Elders, self-righteous and disdainful of Corin's opinions. Corin could not recall a time since the passing of his mother when anyone had simply talked with him, as Alethea seemed happy to do. It was refreshing.

"The Hunters are real enough," he said. It's the Square's duty to watch for them. The coming of the Mastren is said to herald the Hunters' arrival."

He felt a small fist punch him in the ribs. "You can't believe half of a legend and not the other."

Corin smiled. No one but Alethea would dare punch him in the ribs. It was a welcome discomfort.

"Who are these Hunters?" Alethea asked. "And why would they come?"

"Minesh would know better," Corin said. "Or Ceric. But I'll tell you what I can. What I remember. It all started long ago, in a time before Man came to Sindarin. In a time when Man roamed freely in the heavens, like birds winging from tree to tree."

"What? We moved among the stars?" Alethea sounded impressed.

"Yes. It was a time when Man used technology, artifacts like those kept locked away in the Dome of the Ancients in Sanctuary Park. Many things were commonplace then that are unthinkable now. That's how the trouble started."

"Trouble?"

"There are other peoples among the stars, Alethea. Some, very much like us. Others inconceivably different. Our ancestors responded to them first with fear, then with awe, and finally with brutality. There were Lathans back then, and worse. They killed. They ravaged. They stole. They thought very highly of themselves. That all changed when they found peoples who would not be bullied— the League of Orion."

"The Hunters!"

Corin let out a deep breath. "Orion is more than that. They protect civilized peoples by hunting barbarous ones. It's like how the Square hunts Skin-Runners to protect the common folk. Minesh says that Demons used to roam the stars as well, but that the Hunters killed them all a long time ago."

"But we're not Skin-Runners or Demons. Why would Orion hunt us?"

"We are Skin-Runners, Alethea. If Sindarin were dead, there would be no more Skin-Runners. Demon spirits would no longer reach through the Shroud to possess men in frenzy from sagcryl."

"But that's killing the hens to get at the fox!"

Corin shrugged beneath the bearskin. "In many ways the League of Orion is like the First Circle. Their society follows Arwyth's Path. Unlike the Circle, they are willing to enforce their beliefs. In that they are more like the Square. They will not permit Sindarin and other peoples like us to disrupt their peace, and have no qualms whatsoever about hunting us down or slaughtering the hens with the fox."

He paused, struggling to fit the pieces together. "The Elsian world is involved somehow. The League is very powerful there. True-Speech and sageroot have something to do with it as well. I don't understand it all."

Alethea's voice fell to a whisper. "Then there really is nothing we can do?"

"We hide. And we wait. When the Hunters do come, I doubt they will find anything to change their opinion of us."

Beside him, Alethea withdrew into thoughtful silence. Corin looked up at the twinkling lights. Somewhere out there, the Hunters searched for signs of Man's technology and waited to strike. No longer did the stars seem so friendly.

A Worst Nightmare

Midnight came to Toroth amid a torrent of icy rain. Water mixed with hail pummeled against boarded doors and windows, the pounding of a thousand relentless hammers. Thunder boomed against a black, Stygian sky, pierced by baleful lightning blasts. The City Guard along with four hundred conscripts stood their posts uneasily, their oiled vestments poor protection against the downpour. Near the docks, Bruenor's warehouse lay cloaked in sodden darkness.

Bruenor himself sat at the table, biding his time, waiting for the proper moment.

"Rain." Roman ground his teeth as he paced the warehouse floor. "It's wet out there. Cold. Slippery." He stopped his pacing and turned to Bruenor. "We should stay inside tonight. Tomorrow will be better."

"The wolf has no fear of rain, Roman." Bruenor stood and

waved his arm. "We are no longer the dog nipping at the heel but the wolf tearing at the throat. We won't even notice the rain."

Roman shook his head. "You know what I mean. The meat is easier to cut when it's dry."

Bruenor stared at Roman. "What do you know of cutting meat? You have been a phyte-runner for a single night. There is so much more for you to learn. Anyway, the cutting is just a means to an end. It is the terror that counts. The storm will add to the terror. Keliel! Is the elixir ready yet?"

The sober faced niac came and stood by Bruenor. His hands held a tall, silver flask. "I've mixed sagcryl into the wine. I've yet to add the blood."

Bruenor peered into the flask, his eyes wistful. "Blood isn't really necessary. A matter of protocol is all. Still, I'm rather fond of protocol." Abruptly, his arm came up. Something small and shiny left his hand and sailed across the room.

Roman's eyes went wide, and he clutched at his throat with both hands. Red liquid sprayed between his fingers. Harsh gurgling noises escaped his lips. Arnor rushed to grab him and dragged him before Bruenor.

The priest took the flask from Keliel and held it below Roman's severed jugular. Bright blood steamed as it gushed into the flask. Bruenor murmured into Roman's ear. "Are you learning from this?"

The phyte-runner gurgled an unintelligible response.

"Was that necessary?" Arnor asked, his voice low.

Bruenor's eyes blazed. "Do you challenge me as well, Arnor? Do you wish to mix your blood with that of this coward?"

Roman's dying body slumped to the floor from Arnor's hands. "I'm just thinking of you, Rule-Master. You'll need every man to support you at the Pae-thn."

Bruenor twisted his lips into a scowl. "Roman was a liability. In addition to being a coward, he questioned my judgment. He can best support me by being an example to the others." Bruenor paused and then decided that he would confide in Arnor after all. He needed a strong second. One who understood his motives. Bruenor dropped his voice to a whisper. "Last night I failed to summon the Demon. I need to rebuild the trust of the pack."

Arnor's gaze strayed to Bruenor's shoulder. "What of tonight? How will you join us?"

"I'm already taking the drug," Bruenor told him. "Slowly, in small doses. I'll reach frenzy with the others without the sudden onrush of a large dose. Summoning the Demon will be child's play."

Arnor nodded and backed away.

Moving to the center of the room, Bruenor raised the elixir-filled flask with his one hand. His gaze took in his men, reading the lust that burned in their eyes.

"My brothers, the Day of the Demon has come! Tonight's storm is an omen, a sign of the rain of death that the Demon shall bring upon Sindarin!"

Touching the flask to his lips, he took a small swallow and then lowered it again after a much longer than necessary pause.

"Drink deep, for tonight we shall feast on Toroth's flesh! As will our brothers in towns and villages all along the coast. Tonight even the Demon shall be sated!"

Grunts of approval echoed among the men as they moved forward to drink from the cup.

Bruenor watched and nodded. *Tonight the Mastren will come and I will be ready to serve him up to the Demon as a sacrifice. Then none will question my leadership. Not phyte. Not niac. Not Demon. The Great Day of the Demon will be mine!*

$$\Omega$$

For a second straight night, Death visited Toroth. Howls of fear and ecstasy rose above the wailing of the wind and the rush of rain. Doors were broken. Windows smashed. People taken. Corpses littered the streets. Blood ran through the gutters, mixing with rainwater.

Through it all Herlen stood at his window high in the Tower of Toroth, his cup abandoned on the table. No wine touched his lips. He simply stood, knuckles white where his hands gripped the grating, listening at the open window as the hours crept by and screams filled his ears.

It is not enough. Even with the Guard forewarned and four hundred conscripts, it is not enough. Even with the citizenry hiding in their deepest cellars and boards nailed across the doorways, it is not enough.

My fault. My own, Demon be damned, fault. I should have worked harder. Hunted them all down. Slaughtered every last one of them.

New screams erupted just streets away. A dozen rain-shrouded figures raced into view and were gone in an instant. The screaming never ceased.

How can there be so many? That's what offended Herlen most. Skin-Runner sightings had been rare. Unexplained disappearances were few. And now this. How did I not see it? They were there all along. Experts at hiding. Taking only those no one would miss. Vultures. In front of my nose the entire time. Now they are vultures no more. Hawks. Wolves. Rampant in the streets. The Square's worst nightmare come to life, my own worst nightmare. Demons loose in the city. Monsters who feed on the fear and suffering of good people too frightened to protect themselves.

The rain hid most of the devastation, though occasionally Herlen glimpsed a guard running through the street below, as often as not away rather than toward some new burst of wailing. He could not bring himself to rebuke them. The Demons were a fate no man should have to face.

Once he even imagined a three-legged wolf loping after one of the fleeing guards. Herlen stared as the animal stopped, rose up on its hind legs, and waved its single foreleg up at his window. Its eyes glowed with an unholy, crimson light, its body draped in what could only be human skin. Herlen blinked and it was gone.

It was enough to make him consider going for his cup, but he denied himself. No, I must face this with my people. I must not abandon them.

$$\Omega$$

In the vaulted Tower of Toroth, Herlen sat at the head of the great table in the Breakfast Hall. Breakfast had been dispensed with hours earlier. In its place, a labyrinth of unrolled scrolls littered the tabletop and the scent of recent rain lingered in the air. Around the table sat eighteen commanders of the Square gathered from Toroth and the surrounding area, those who still lived and could join him. After a second straight night of Skin-Runners raids, many familiar faces were missing.

Behind him and to his right, as though eschewing the Council, sat Ceric, robed in the king's formal crimson instead of his usual white. Present at Herlen's insistence, the Peace-Ruler's face expressed discomfort at both his being there and the proceedings.

The discussion thus far had consisted of little more than grievous descriptions of Skin-Runner atrocities, the like of which had never before been witnessed in living memory. The reports had finally waned and a troubled silence had descended over the room. It was the calm before the storm. Everyone now waited for the true discussion to begin.

Knowing that delay would avail nothing, Herlen set down the scroll he had been reading and looked up to meet the solemn gaze of those around the table.

"That decides it, then. From this we can assume that the rest of Sindarin is no better off than we are. Skin-Runners have enacted their vile evil in every community. We cannot expect to receive aid, neither can we send any."

"But we die each night!" cried a voice from far down the table.

Across from Herlen, Sarimon of Aarinlea rose from his seat. "Terthal is right. The Skin-Runners eat — the commander's face darkened at his poor choice of words — eat away at our people. Sixty of us made it here from Aarinlea. Sixty of a town of two hundred! Aarinlea is no more. What was a garden a few short days ago is a ghost town now, a city of open graves."

Herlen gazed wearily at the white-haired commander. "We all feel for your people, Sarimon. For all the people of Sindarin. There is not one among us who hasn't felt the cold touch of this great evil."

Sarimon remained standing. Clearly, he had more to say and, just as clearly, he was having difficulty saying it. "I have the highest regard for the sentiments of the First Circle," he said at last, not meeting Ceric's gaze. "But it is them or us. Either we become as savage as animals and destroy the Skin-Runners utterly, or they will destroy us. And it will not take them many more nights." He sat down quickly.

Herlen grimaced and prepared to defend the Circle; not that he disagreed with his commander, but it fell to the King to keep the peace. Ceric beat him to it.

"I know your heart, Sarimon," said the Peace-Ruler. "And I will not condemn your words. There have been times, it saddens me to say, in the past two days that I myself have felt exactly like you." Ceric rose from his seat and stepped over to a window. Sunlight gleamed from the king's crimson of his robes endowing the old man with an aura of majesty. He bowed his head and spoke to the floor. "I am much ashamed of those thoughts."

Whispered grumbling echoed around the room, joined by the nervous rattling of parchment. Several cups lifted from the table. Herlen waited; he was certain Ceric was not finished.

As expected, the Peace-Ruler of the First Circle raised his head. The Elder's eyes were watery with tears. "It is exactly such thoughts that brought our ancestors to Sindarin in the first place, where we must crawl beneath the rocks and hide from the Hunters. It is exactly such thoughts that make the Skin-Runners what they are." Ceric's gaze searched around the table. "I am a weak, old man. Frail. Awkward. Undeserving, perhaps, to be at this council. But I am not so weak that I will give myself over to such wickedness."

Sarimon jumped to his feet and curled his hands into fists. "You would have us welcome slaughter? Like you, I have followed the Path all my life. I, too, am a Man of Peace. Countless are the times I have turned the other cheek. Day by day, I have treated my neighbor as my brother. But this? This is madness!"

Ceric said nothing. He turned. Returned to his seat. Sat

down.

Sarimon clenched his teeth. "The Skin-Runners are not people. They are animals. When the tree-lynx threatens my goats, I cast stones. When the mountain fox calls for my chickens, I snare him. What makes the Skin-Runners any different?"

Ceric spoke in a whisper. Herlen strained to hear him. "When you cast the stone at the tree-lynx, you do not become the tree-lynx. When you snare the fox, you do not become the fox. But when you turn your thoughts to slaughtering people, as deserving of slaughter as the Skin-Runners may be, you become no better than a Skin-Runner."

Sarimon opened his mouth, closed it again. Then he frowned and also sat down.

"But..." came a guarded voice from further down the table. "Then... then we shall all die."

Herlen answered. "Perhaps we shall. If not beneath the knives of the Skin-Runners, then by the mercies of the Hunters."

Silence filled the room. Silence and cold fear.

A voice whispered, "You—You've seen them?"

Herlen shook his head. "No. But most of you have heard about the Skin-Runners found killed at Karlac. And about the priest they had at Kelmar."

Whispers echoed around the table. Herlen heard the words *arm* and *Hest* mentioned several times.

He took in a deep breath. "All of you know the Legend. The Mastren will fight the Skin-Runners. Then the Hunters will come."

Sarimon spoke. "The Mastren is a two-edged sword, Sire. The Legend says that he will fight the Skin-Runners. It does not grant that he will win."

"That is true," said another. "The Mastren merely portends the time of the end, the Advent of the Hunters."

"Many of us know Minesh," said Sarimon, "and honor the manea. I, for one, am pleased that he has taken up the Hest against the Skin-Runners. But does that mean he is truly the Mastren?"

"It is not Minesh," Herlen said.

Several around the table gasped at this admission and murmured voices swelled with questions and conjecture.

Sarimon's brow wrinkled in confusion. "Not Minesh? Then... who?"

Herlen shook his head, surprising even himself that the words were able to leave his lips. "My son has taken up the Hest."

The room fell suddenly quiet and all eyes turned to the King.

"Is he...," Sarimon began, and then faltered. "Is Corin the Mastren?"

"I don't know," Herlen said. "I hope..." To himself he said, *not*.

Sarimon took in a deep breath and then spoke in a loud voice. "Corin is a brave young man. A leader of our people. You do well to be proud of him, Herlen. But he is one man alone. The Skin-Runners will take him, if they haven't already. He needs our help."

Herlen raised one eyebrow. Strong praise, but followed by doubt. The commander saw Corin as nothing more than an untried boy. He studied Sarimon's face carefully. "Our help? We do our best to fight the Skin-Runners now. What are you suggesting?"

Sarimon's response was a low, harsh whisper, as though his words were not fit for public speaking. "The vaults."

"Never!" Herlen slammed his fist on the table. "You know the consequences. Use of the proscribed technology will reveal us to the Hunters."

The commander to Sarimon's left waved his hand in dismissal. "The consequences are as old as legend. None of us has ever seen a Hunter. The Skin-Runners, however; they kill us now."

Herlen ground his teeth. "If you are foolish enough to dismiss the Adjudication of Orion, you have no place at this council. Do you not speak to your True-Friend? Does he not confirm that Orion's Hunt continues? That the Hunt grows to include still other races that benefit the cause of the Demons?

That Mankind is just one among a growing slate of vermin to be hunted down and burned?"

The commander cowered in his seat, his mouth a tight, uncomfortable line.

"None of us denies any of that," suggested Sarimon. "It's just that... what certainty do we have that the Hunters will find us if we do open the vaults? For just a little while. Long enough to put down the Skin-Runners."

Herlen clutched his cup in his hand. "I don't need certainty. The threat is certain enough."

"But what purpose serves the vaults? If our First-Landers had not intended us to use them, they would never have wasted precious resources building the Dome in the first place."

Herlen stood and passed his gaze around the room, gauging, measuring. "The vaults are a last resort against desperate times, in the event that we face extinction."

Sarimon also stood, slowly, his stance one of pleading rather than conflict. "And what are we facing now, Sire, if not extinction?"

Herlen shook his head and remained silent for a long moment. He had known it would come down to this. Last night, as he stood watching the slaughter in the streets, he had known.

The Dome of the Ancients was the guardianship of the Square. No king had ever ruled without the constant fear that he would be the one called upon to open the Dome. Herlen was no exception. Still, now that the unthinkable moment had arrived, he felt somehow calm. It was as if opening the vaults was inevitable. The fact that he was king when it happened was of no consequence.

His True-Friend knew this. In last night's darkest hour, when the screams had become too much to bear, the Elsian world had remained silent. It was then that Herlen knew as well. The final act of the Legend of Four was in progress. The Hunters were coming. The Skin-Runners were making one final rampage. The Mastren... There was no doubt in Herlen's mind. The time for the Dome had come.

Herlen peered from face to face around the room. What he saw were good men. Sarimon, Terthal, the others. Afraid, perhaps, but not fearful. They knew what they asked. And were no more happy about it than he. But they, too, understood that the time had come.

"Yes," Herlen nodded, gravely. "You are right. We shall open the vaults. We have no choice. If we are to have any hope at all of survival, we must take the risk."

From the corner of his eye, Herlen saw Ceric shake his head, but the Peace-Ruler spoke no words.

We must do this to save our people, Herlen told himself. We must do this to save my son.

Shelter

By mid-morning, the rain that had assailed Toroth through the night had moved east into Rhedan and south through the Tildis Dells. For Alethea, it began as a drizzle that steadily grew worse. By late afternoon a full-fledged storm soaked her clothes with icy rain. Beneath her, Serl flinched with each lightning strike. The storm was too close, too frightening. Alethea could taste the black stallion's fear. Returned it. She buried her face into the back of Corin's bearskin coat, but it, too, was slick with water. Her arms, wrapped tightly around his waist, shook from the cold.

Lightning crackled the air, so close this time that Alethea couldn't help but scream. Electric heat pricked her skin. Serl reared back on his hind legs and Alethea had visions of dashing her brains out on the sharp mountain rocks. She clung to Corin even more fiercely.

They were in a narrow mountain pass of the lower Aenlaen, the Serpent's Tail, sharp with salis stone and thinning trees of fir and aspen. Karlac's Bane towered off to their right, a dark, menacing shadow. The sky loomed as thick and gray as the rocks around them. Even the trees appeared dull, as pounding rain battered needles and leaves from lonely branches and dashed them against the ground. Thunder roared with satisfaction, the air growing colder, the sun long since blotted out, its yellow warmth dead and gone. Mist lifted from the mountain rock, weaving in and around trees and shrubs like twilight ghosts. Alethea shivered, her teeth chattering together like stones in a jar.

Three days they had searched since leaving Toroth. Three days without a glimpse of the Elsan. Three days of doubt, wondering why they were here, wandering in the wilderness. What were they doing wrong? Why was the Elsian world silent? Alethea was no longer certain there was an Elsian world.

She tried more often than Corin. Wanted it more. Needed it more. Desperately, she needed someone to take Ilsa's place. To justify their separation. Between attempts, she encouraged Corin, remembering Ceric's words. "He is for you, Alethea. And you for him." She clung to those words throughout the storm.

It wasn't until Karlac's Bane rose up ahead of them that they realized they how far south they had travelled.

"We can't go back there," Alethea had said, images of the Skin-Runner grotto flashing through her mind.

"No, of course not," Corin agreed. "There should be a pass through the Serpent's Tail just ahead that will take us to the Ilden Plain. It's further south than the one Minesh and I took several weeks ago, but it is marked on my father's maps."

The sinister mountain grew much taller before they found the pass and was much too close for Alethea's comfort. But the rising storm quickly overshadowed those fears.

Beneath the pressure of her chest and arms, she felt Corin shiver. His body seemed hard and cold, like stone. "Are you suffering enough now?" she asked through chattering teeth. Corin didn't answer. She doubted he had heard.

They had used up all of their provisions from Toroth. Even the sten-bear meat. As Corin had begun his quest, so now they were living off the land: breadroot, wild mushrooms, spring yams. Alethea blended them skillfully with shoots and tubers, as she had in Lathan's camp. Everywhere they found sageroot. It seemed to grow out of bare rock. Though edible, they left it alone, knowing there was already too much sage spore in the food they did eat and in the water they drank.

The mountain trail grew especially narrow as it wormed left around a collection of tall shattered boulders partially hidden by trees, bushes, and moss. A blinding flash of light exploded among the trees. Lightning strike. Fragments of gnarled wood flew in all directions. Despite the rain, small patches of fire burned like startled fireflies. Serl reared again, this time spilling Alethea into the mud.

The ground was hard, though not as hard as Serl's saddle. Alethea landed on her back, looking up as Corin peered down at her. Above the noise of the storm, she doubted he had heard her scream as she fell, but knew he would have felt her missing from behind him. Through the curtain of rain, she saw him jump down from the saddle, holding tight to Serl's reins. The great black fought him, trying to bolt, but Corin prevailed in calming the beast.

"Are you all right?" he yelled. A flash of brilliance rocked the mountain pass as Corin's free hand reached toward her.

"We have to find shelter!" she shouted, grasping his hand. Serl gave a tug on the reins, yanking Corin with him and pulling Alethea to her feet.

Ahead of them, the lightning-blasted trees burned madly, despite the rain. Serl twisted from side to side, eyes white with fright. Alethea saw Corin's face stiffen as he opened his mind, felt emissions of calm and resolve directed at the horse. She opened her mind as well and felt the fear and desperation in the stallion subside. Eventually, Serl calmed enough for Corin to again control the reins.

Alethea felt him pull her in close. She moved to embrace him, not knowing why. He stopped her, brought her around, and pushed her toward Serl. Her disappointment tasted like bile. She yelled above the noise. "What are we going to do?"

"You ride. I'll lead Serl."

"Where? We can't take much more of this!"

Corin's voice was nearly lost in the wind and rain. "I don't know. Shelter. Somewhere."

Alethea could see that he was shaking badly. His exposed

skin was blanched, drained of blood. She knew that she fared no better. She had heard of people dying in storms, had always wondered how; it was only rain. Now she knew. "Somewhere" would not be good enough.

Lightning flashed, illuminating the mountainside. The trees no longer burned, the flames extinguished by the downpour. "Look!" she cried, pointing to the ruined trees among the boulders.

Corin turned and squinted into rain. "What?"

Alethea pulled her hand free of his and ran toward the trees, then on into darkness. Turning, she imagined the bewildered expression on Corin's face; the rain prevented her from actually seeing it. "A cave!" she shouted.

Corin, leading Serl, came closer.

Darkness engulfed Alethea as Corin urged Serl into the tall, narrow opening, blocking the entrance. Alethea didn't mind the dark; at least it was dry. She crept further into the cave until she came to a wall. Outside, the storm raged on, the rush of rain echoing like a river canyon. As Corin and Serl moved past her, she could just make out a narrow column of dull indigo marking the entrance.

"Some luck to have those trees burn away just in time to reveal this cave," she said through chattering teeth.

Corin, a mere shadow in the darkness, answered. "Was it luck?"

"The luck of the Elsan, then," said Alethea, a phrase used when someone ascribed his or her good fortune to the intervention of a True-Friend. Could that be it? Was the cave a sign that they would soon find their True-Friends?

She helped Corin unsaddle Serl, her fingers numb as she fumbled with the straps. When they finished, she stood there, shivering. All of their meager possessions were as soaked as she was.

She felt Corin take her frozen hands in his and rub them. The cold was bone deep and reluctant to depart. "You'll have to wear the bearskin," he said from beside her. "It's the only thing we have that's even partly dry."

"What about you?" she asked, knowing he was just as cold.

"Can we make a fire?"

Corin's voice echoed in the darkness. "I doubt there's enough wood. And even if there is, the flint is wet."

"We can share the bearskin."

"There's not enough. And I don't think cutting the coat in two would leave enough to do either of us any good."

Alethea held his hands tight, prevented his warming motions. "We will share the bearskin."

Corin said nothing. His hands left hers and Alethea heard his fingers moving against the wet of the fur. The sound seemed unnaturally loud in the cave, even against the heavy fall of rain outside.

She drew her own fingers to the buttons of her coat, found the wet fastenings difficult to undo, her fingers clumsy. She worked them through and slid the coat to the floor of the cave. Her shirt beneath was just as wet and clung to her skin. Corin's hands found hers, helping to peel off the slick cloth.

Corin's touch was warm, grew warmer as he pressed closer, tentative at first, then more boldly. Alethea found herself welcoming his touch, pulling him against her as she shed the last shreds of wet clothing. Together they sank to the cold earth of the cave floor, drawing the damp bearskin about them like a blanket, embracing each other for warmth.

Soon, the hardness of the floor and the chill air were all but forgotten. Outside the cave, the storm continued. Rain, sudden light, and heavy thunder.

$$\Omega$$

Minesh peered from his makeshift shelter out into the storm, his face set in a crimped frown.

Rain, thunder, lightning, ice. You'd think our ancestors could have found a more hospitable place to hide. Ah well, the worst of it seems to be over.

He threw another stick onto the fire and rubbed his hands over the flames.

"You realize I shall have to walk tomorrow," he said to Galin. "First I am attacked by drug merchants. Then this storm. And now my horse has thrown a shoe. It's a conspiracy!"

"There are many conspiracies," Galin replied. "Some good. Some bad. None of them control the weather or cause horses to throw shoes."

"You say that now," Minesh told him. "But I wouldn't put it past you." He touched his hand to the partly healed wound on his chest.

"Walking is no harder on your injury than being jostled on a horse," Galin suggested.

"It will take me longer to get to Stonepast."

"We can afford the delay."

Minesh threw another stick onto the fire. "How is Corin doing?"

Galin's response was slow, the words carefully selected. "He fares well. Better than you might expect."

Minesh grunted. "Well, at least something is going right."

Ω

Lathan stood with his men before Haven Gate, waiting to be questioned by the Toroth Guard. Night was almost upon them and the gate was a flurry of last minute activity.

When a guard at last he turned his attention to Lathan's band, he glared at them with impatience. "State your business, man! It's almost curfew."

"Curfew? Since when did Toroth post a curfew?"

"I'll ask the questions here. I didn't catch your name." The remark was not a question.

"Lathan. But, what—?"

"Lathan? That's all? Where are you from?"

"I'm a wandering trader. My home is nowhere. I am best known at Thadan's Market as a dealer in fine merchandise."

"Spare me the barker's call. What do you want in Toroth?"

"For one, a place to sleep. We've come a long way through wet weather."

"You have business here?"

"Of course! I—"

"Drop your barriers."

"What? This is outrageous. By whose order..."

Lathan's voice trailed off as armed men turned toward him. He raised his arms, placating. "Please, please, I mean no offense. I've done nothing wrong. We have been traveling."

"Your skin is stained, trader. Your neck and arms. All drug traders are to be executed before nightfall."

Lathan widened his eyes. "Drug traders! No, no, we are all of us clean, honest people." He waved his hands. "We travel a lot. Not every place is as pure as Toroth. It is well known that Barshan is high in sage. We've just come from there."

The guard eyed him warily.

"Please," Lathan said loudly, to alert his men. "We'll all drop our barriers. You can see for yourself that we are but simple traders."

One by one, they were tested. Lathan suppressed a smile as the guards exerted their pitiful wills in an effort to unmask them. All of his men knew enough to get through the gate, leaving nothing for the guards to wonder at. Years of drug use had left them more adept than Herlen's gatekeepers. It was a simple matter to lower their barriers, yet still disguise their innermost thoughts.

"Choose quickly where you will stay," the guard told him. "No one is allowed in the street after sundown."

"We have our own means of shelter."

The guard eyed the trader's luggage. "Your tent dwellings will not benefit you tonight. You must secure yourselves within walls of stone."

Lathan frowned. "We hadn't counted on the expense."

"Even in Toroth the Skin-Runners roam the streets at night. If you value your lives you'll want good stone and strong doors around you."

"Skin-Runners in the streets?" Lathan shot the man a perplexed stare. "In Herlen's city? Is there no place safe?"

The guard sighed. "None. If you have any sense at all you will buy secure lodgings."

"Of course. Of course." Lathan led his people into the city at a sober gait.

He chose the Hall of Deltis, an inn on Freedom Avenue where he'd had dealings in the past. It stood near Herlen's Sanctuary, but not too close. The building was almost a palace in its own right, with thick walls and strong oak gates. The

Keeper there, Abo, a round-bodied man who smiled too much, owed him some favors. Though not enough, apparently. People from surrounding towns had flocked to the city, and now Deltis and similar inns overflowed with affluent landowners seeking refuge. Lodgings were at a premium. Lathan grudgingly handed over a full purse for a single large room for his entire band.

"What now?" Nagram asked, after Abo had left them.

Lathan cast a dispassionate gaze at the room's rich furnishings. At least a dozen soft chairs sat around the largest fog table he had ever seen, but none of that was important. He folded his massive arms across his chest, saying nothing.

"You saw?" asked Hyrmus, an older trader with thinning gray hair and chin whiskers who had joined them on the journey north from the Sethnin Plains. "The Dome of the Ancients as we passed near Sanctuary Park? Herlen's opened the vaults!"

"So it would seem," Lathan said. "All that activity."

"Those lights weren't torches," Hyrmus suggested. "Glare-beams. The legends mention them."

Lathan gazed at his men with cold, measuring eyes. "Herlen's bringing out the banned technology. No doubt to fight the Skin-Runners the gate guard mentioned. I thought Abo's claims of nightly murders was a ruse to raise his prices, but—"

"Good." Nagram interrupted, then spat on the polished floor. "Those Demon bastards deserve a good shaking down. Getting too powerful for my taste."

"Don't be an idiot," Lathan said. "With those weapons, Herlen could wipe them out. Then where would we be? No drugs; no business. I've got to think."

"I thought we came here for the girl," Nagram said.

Lathan stared at his nephew. "Demon take the girl! Don't you see what's going on here? Those weapons are worth more to the Skin-Runners than any girl. Than any hundred girls!"

"What about the Legends?" asked Hyrmus. "The vaults were locked to keep the Hunters from finding us. Now they are open."

"Bah! Superstitious drivel. Fictions made to keep a weak Circle in power."

Nagram raised his voice. "What about the Skin-Runners, Lathan? What has brought them out into the open? Running the streets of Toroth?"

Lathan whirled. "How the Demon should I know? They've got their own power structure to maintain. Their own superstitions to follow. Any man knows that a Skin-Runner is as crazy as a starving sten-bear."

As he spoke, a sound like a thousand fletched arrows whizzed past the window. Lathan rushed to the edge of the room and pushed open the shutters. Something large and metallic flashed in the failing light as it sped out of sight.

"Grav-sleds!" exclaimed Hyrmus. "Flying machines! Herlen's using everything."

Lathan closed the shutters and walked back to the fog table. His hands shook. If he had known the vaults would open in his lifetime, he would have taken time to study them in the Legends. Instead, he glared at Hyrmus. "You're sure? You saw it?"

Hyrmus shrugged. "There were stories when I was a lad growing up in the Circle. I never really believed them. But this is what they described. There's nothing else it could be."

Lathan nodded. "If the Skin-Runners come out tonight, then they and we will all know exactly what those machines are worth."

"What are we going to do?" demanded Nagram.

Lathan paced the floor, rubbing his chin with his hand. "We wait and we think."

Forbidden Technology

Bruenor kept a wary eye as almost a hundred Skin-Runners prowled about the dockside warehouse, swaying, scratching and growling in their throats as frenzy threatened to take them. Three score niacs had abandoned rival priests in order to run at his side, a sure sign of his upcoming victory. His pack had never been so strong.

He breathed deep as his own frenzy pressed against his mind, threatening to crush his control. It was more difficult since the loss of his arm, but got easier each night. He couldn't afford another episode like two nights earlier, when the drug had left him a useless carcass, unable to run.

As he had last night, he'd ingested sagcryl slowly, a little at a time, taking strength from the drug without being overcome by it. He would need strength. Already a few of the newer niacs had thought to test him, pressing him with their drug-induced will. Bruenor had resisted, pressing back roughly. Others had supported him, not that he needed it. No one dared take it past a tentative prodding. Tonight was his. It would not be so easy at Stonepast.

The side door opened and Arnor and two other niacs slipped inside holding between them a thin, timid-looking man. His throat moved rapidly as he talked, pleading for mercy. The door closed and Arnor led the man to the center of the room. His eyes boggled as Runners in wolf-skins circled him on all fours, snarling and licking their lips.

Bruenor retrieved an iron cup from the table and raised it to the man's lips. Behind him, his pack took up a low chant.

"Please," the thin man said, even as he swallowed the sagcryl-laced blood. "Please."

"You're welcome," said Bruenor. He passed the empty cup to Keliel and took the knife from his belt.

"Please," said the man again. Bruenor caressed the mottling skin on the man's cheek and then began cutting his shirt with the knife.

The chanting grew louder as the priest peeled back skin from the man's drug-mottled jugular. The drug had taken hold; no blood flowed from where the skin tore free. Even so, it was difficult work with one arm. But Bruenor cared less and less; the Demon was coming.

The thin man, still horrified by what was happening to him, suddenly stopped saying, "Please."

Bruenor stared at him, his mouth splitting into a grin, his eyes burning red. In a low, low voice, Bruenor croaked, "I am the Demon!"

The man gurgled something incoherent in his throat. Then Bruenor, who was Bruenor no longer, fed.

$$\Omega$$

While his men slept, drunk on sage wine, Lathan sat alone in darkness at a window, listening. Screams filled the night. The wailing of damned souls entwined with animal howls wafted up like music in the dark. It surprised Lathan to learn that he enjoyed the sound, that he took reassurance from the savage emotions that poisoned the night.

As he listened, he took sagcryl. Not enough to send him into frenzy, though he was tempted. The drug brought him closer to the slaughter, in tune with the ravaging of the Skin-Runners. He knew it was not a good thing, but it felt good, his heartbeat throbbing in time to some primal rhythm deep in his soul. Almost unconsciously, he bit the inside of his cheek and tasted blood, sucked it from the veins as the drug would not allow it to flow freely. The bitter, metallic taste complemented the night's sounds.

Lathan had always despised the Skin-Runners' blind zealousness. Their theological mysticism. Their religious rituals. Their eager willingness to become possessed by beings from beyond the Shroud. He considered himself a practical man. Intelligently hedonistic. And it was for that same reason that he could not deny the rapture he was feeling. *They know something, these lovers of Demons. Something that makes all the ugliness worthwhile.* The realization that there was something more, something he had not yet attained, grated at him.

A grav-sled whizzed past the inn, its unnatural whine oddly offensive. In its wake, the light of a glare-beam flashed like lightning onto the street below. The pale, even light was obviously not lightning, but something foreign, alien, unwanted. Only the dark, and the screams, and the dying felt natural.

Lathan shook himself and concentrated on the technology. Grav-sleds. Glare-beams. And who knew what else from a buried past. A more powerful past. There was opportunity here.

Business, he told himself. Practical. Profitable. He smiled and tried to shut out the baleful enticements of the Skin-Runners.

Outside the window, the howling continued all through the night.

$$\Omega$$

Morning came and with it the raising of the curfew. Bruenor paced the warehouse floor like a caged animal, his face a heavy scowl while he stroked his stumped shoulder with his fingers, searching for satisfaction and finding none. His thoughts reeled with images of the previous night.

The door opened and Arnor slipped inside, his face a mask of non-emotion.

"Well?" demanded Bruenor.

"It's inconceivable," Arnor said.

"It is many things," said Bruenor. "What I want to know is why no one learned of the vaults being opened before glare-beams were used against us."

Arnor strode over to the table and sank into a chair. "I loitered near Sanctuary Park and overheard some of the guards outside the Dome of the Ancients. Herlen opened the vaults just after curfew. He wanted to take us by surprise."

Bruenor took a chair across from Arnor and poured himself some wine. Suddenly he laughed. "Well, he did that well enough. Who would have thought a coward like Herlen would open the vaults? Even in the days of the Sagan Priests, the vaults remained locked. Kings were stronger back then." He faced Arnor. "It is through desperation that they turn to the forbidden technology. Another sign that the Day of the Demon is upon us." He took a swallow of wine. "What are they doing now?"

"There is much activity around the Dome," Arnor said. "I'm not sure what's happening, but the vaults are still open."

Bruenor stood and resumed pacing. He couldn't sit still. Too much was at stake. Too many important decisions needed to be made.

"We'll have to do something about those weapons," Arnor

said.

Bruenor shook his head. "Later. We must leave today for the Pae-thn." Then he stopped and snorted. "This may work in our favor."

"Oh?" Arnor arched his brow. "How?"

Bruenor stroked his chin with his hand. "Herlen will think he's scared us off. He'll relax. Then, after the Pae-thn, we'll bring hundreds of niacs to Toroth and take Herlen's toys away from him."

Arnor snorted. "How? Glare-beams can kill at a hundred paces. More."

"Idiot! A weapon is nothing without a mind to control it. When we return from Stonepast, the Demon will be with us. We will strike such fear into the King's pitiful Guard that they'll drop their weapons and flee before us."

Bruenor's thoughts fell inward, his lips twitching with pleasure. When he looked up again, he saw discomfort on Arnor's face. *He is still weak. The Pae-thn will change that.* "Is all in readiness?"

Arnor nodded. "Yes. Everyone has been told."

"We'll should collect more sageroot on the way. We'll want plenty for the Cavern." He paused. "I want no mistakes at Stonepast. Clear?"

Arnor's jaw was tight. "There will be no mistakes."

A Oneness of Being

Alethea awakened to the smell of sage. Opening her eyes, she saw sunlight at the cave opening, a narrow doorway of whiteness leading to a world vastly different from last night's storm. She took in a deep breath of morning, freshly washed, and peered about at the emptiness of their refuge. It was a cave like any other, running deep into the mountain, its end lost in shadow.

Something moved near her breast. Corin, asleep beneath the bearskin. Memories of the previous night flooded into remembrance. Darkness and wet clothing. Huddling together for warmth. Tender caresses. Lips, soft and gentle. Joy and ecstasy. Then sweet surrender into sleep. A happy smile crept across her lips.

More movement. Corin's face emerged from beneath the thick fur. His noble lips and chin held a soft, fuzzy expression that turned into a wide, gaping yawn. Corin opened his eyes and stopped cold.

Alethea grinned at him, and then kissed him on the nose. "Time to get up. Serl is already outside having breakfast."

Corin's ears flamed red and his eyes blinked. He worked his jaw, but no words came.

Alethea laughed and pushed him away, gathering the entire bearskin around herself.

Corin sprawled naked on the earthen floor, peering about the cave as though in a daze. His eyes focused on Alethea. "I—I'd better get a fire going. So we can dry out our clothes."

Alethea choose not to answer. Instead, she nestled herself within the bearskin, luxuriating in its warmth. It was only later when Corin, looking oddly vulnerable in his nakedness, reentered the cave with an armload of sticks and moss for a fire that she felt a twinge of guilt. *Well, he's the one who wanted to suffer in the wilderness.*

The naked prince arranged the wood and struck flint against his knife. Sparks scattered into the kindling, seeding the dry moss with flame that quickly spread to twigs and small branches. He built the fire in a recess in the wall that concentrated its heat and directed smoke up a natural chimney. Spindly stalagmites rose above the flames, providing ready perches for damp clothing.

When he finished arranging their things about the fire, he turned to Alethea. "The smell of sage is strong here." Was he too embarrassed to speak of last night? "Odd for an empty cave."

"I noticed that myself," Alethea said, willing to play his game. "Do you think someone has been storing sageroot in here?"

Corin wandered deeper into the cave to where the shadows were darkest. "It goes on for a distance then turns. I should go have a look."

Alethea grinned at him. "Do you make a habit of exploring caves naked?"

Corin grinned back. "It's better than wandering around outside, naked."

Alethea climbed to her feet, still clutching the bearskin around her. "I'll watch that our clothes don't burn. Otherwise, we'll both be wandering around naked. Don't go far."

"I won't," Corin said. "I'm not that brave."

Left alone, Alethea ran her fingers through her hair, working out the knots. Then she poked her head outside to check on Serl. By the time the clothes were dry, Corin had not returned.

"Men!" Alethea whistled between clenched teeth as she dressed herself. She considered shouting for him, but was concerned about the stone ceiling. Yelling at the top of your lungs inside a cave was not the most intelligent thing to do. She realized then, that except for that one time in Ceric's Council Chamber, she had never used True-Speech with Corin. Not even during last night's intimacy. Ilsa was the only one with whom she had ever Spoken True. It had always been something special between them. Well, maybe now it could be something special between her and Corin. At least, she hoped it could.

"Corin?"

In the confines of the cavern, it was like trying to speak to rock. She had no idea how far away he might be. Perhaps he couldn't hear.

"Corin?"

"Alethea. Is that you?"

"No, it's your True-Friend." She laughed aloud, knowing that he was too far away to hear.

"Very funny. It would be pretty humiliating to find my True-Friend while wandering naked through a cave."

"I thought you enjoyed suffering."

"I—I think I enjoyed last night better."

Now he speaks, when they can't see each other's faces. Even so, Alethea found herself smiling. "I thought you weren't going to go far? Your clothes are dry."

"Good. You'd better bring them."

"What? In there?"

"I think you'll want to see this. Trust me."

Reluctantly, Alethea gathered up Corin's tattered clothing and the bulkier bearskin. She tied the bundle together and swung it over her shoulder. The prospect of moving deeper into the cave did not appeal to her.

She cast one last glance at the cave entrance, knowing that Serl would not wander far. Knowing also that she and Corin should be out foraging for food instead of poking around old caves. Gritting her teeth, she shuffled further into the darkness, following the turn that led deeper into the mountain. Light crept in behind her from the entrance, but faded quickly, along with her courage. After about twenty steps, the passage turned again and the light from the opening was gone.

"It's dark in here."

"Just feel your way along the right wall. It twists a few times, but it's fairly smooth."

"How am I going to see anything when I get there?"

"Oh, you'll see something. But you won't believe it!"

Alethea placed one foot in front of the other and kept moving. The rock wall was hard and cool to the touch, its rough edges blunted and smoothed by time. The floor was level and clear of debris. Man's hand was evident. But whose? And why hadn't they arranged for some light?

The darkness of the passage seemed to stretch time and Alethea lost all sense of direction. Did the tunnel turn just now? She couldn't be sure. The weight of the mountain grew above her, pressing down. Alethea's breath stuck in her throat. Corin was a help. She spoke to him ceaselessly through True-Speech. How long, she had no idea. Corin mostly just listened, offering occasional words of encouragement.

After a time, Alethea thought her eyes were playing tricks on her. Vague outlines of wall and floor seemed to match her steps, ghost-like, elusive in the darkness. If she focused on them, they disappeared. If she ignored them, they fit right in where the wall and floor belonged. Another ten paces and the ceiling and opposite wall appeared. She could see the passage, and was surprised at how narrow and well-formed it was.

She walked faster now. Fifteen paces. The passage turned and Alethea saw light, pale and red and full of shadows, like scarlet blood. It glowed with an opalescent fire. The light repelled Alethea with its deathly hue, yet drew her by the warmth it emanated, real or imagined. A few more steps and the passage turned again, ending in a large cavern.

Alethea stepped into scarlet light that seemed to breathe a life all its own. Her eyes took in Corin, naked, and beyond him the source of the lustrous glow. Both hands flew to her face as she screamed.

In the center of the chamber, a pair of stone posts the color of blood rose up like monstrous fangs. Deep gouges marked the stone where unwilling participants in the Gorgings had pulled and strained against their bonds.

Corin jumped as her cry split the stillness, her scream reverberating again and again off the walls. He ran to her, pulled her into his arms, and clutched her to his chest. "I'm sorry. I wasn't thinking. I should have warned you."

Alethea pushed him away, more scared than angry. "How could you! They nearly killed me! Skin-Runners! What kind of place is this?"

Corin took her hands into his and squeezed. "I truly am sorry. I forgot about what happened before. Please, don't be angry with me."

"How could you forget that? How could you!" But she didn't pull away.

The chamber was large. Against one wall stood a row of drums. Shadows revealed small alcoves on the left. The place stank of sage. Further back, beyond the posts, towering above the twin points of bloody stone, was the source of the scarlet light. Corin led her toward it.

It was a wolf's head. Thirty feet tall and carved into the wall. The eyes, large as loaves, gleamed with fire, like pools of liquid blood. They seemed to follow Alethea as she moved, menacing. Additional light issued from deep in the wolf's throat. The jaws were open, snarling, the tongue, red stone, protruding. Corin brought Alethea to a stop facing twin rows of white, quartz-like teeth, sharp as knives and as wide as laundry stones.

Everything had been reproduced with graphic clarity. The sides of the mouth and jaws, the roof of the mouth, even the tongue that lolled before them.

"A giant effigy of a wolf's head," Corin said, stating the obvious. He reached toward a lower incisor, stopped, and pulled back his hand. "It's so life-like."

"No!" Alethea shook her head. "Not life. Death. Life is never like this." She stifled a gasp as she peered closer. The dark red light and the steamy warmth made it seem as though the stone were alive, breathing. The tongue seemed poised to roll up and swallow her whole. How she wished that Corin would hold her again.

Corin studied the wolf with intent eyes, his mouth a tight, narrow line. "We have to go in," he said.

Alethea shook her head, unable to speak. She turned to stare at him.

Corin took his bundled clothes from her and began dressing. His movements were slow, calculated, like a man going to his death.

"Can't," she said. The word stuck in her throat.

Corin pulled the bearskin over his head and tugged it into a comfortable position. He looked again at the wolf's gaping throat and white teeth. "Close your eyes," he said. "I'll carry you."

Alethea clenched her teeth and closed her eyes, then felt Corin lift her. His arms were strong. A whimper escaped her lips.

"Don't struggle." Corin's voice was soft, soothing. "The teeth are sharp. You may cut yourself. It'll take but a moment. There. We're through."

Alethea felt Corin swing her legs toward the floor. Her boots clipped and scraped against stone and she opened her eyes to find Corin's face bathed in deep red light, his gray eyes glinting like flaming stones. An image of Lathan's high forehead and square jaw replaced Corin's and she tensed, remembering when Lathan had tried to take her, the red glow of sagcryl in his eyes, the bleeding of the skin, the rasping, deep-pressured voice.

Corin read her expression. "It's just the light, Alethea. Don't be afraid."

"It's just so awful. This place. This blood-red light. I'm sorry for being so frightened."

Corin pulled her close, cloaked her in his arms. "I'm afraid too. I'm just doing a better job of hiding it."

Alethea reached up, ran her palm across her face. Her skin was damp. "I feel hot."

"It's this place," Corin said. "It's warm, and warmer further in." He removed his arms and took her hand. Together they crept forward, deeper into the wolf's throat. "Careful," Corin said, when Alethea almost stumbled. "The floor dips here."

The slope continued for about thirty paces, then ended. A crystal barrier blocked their path, its surface an enormous jewel, each facet no larger than the palm of Alethea's hand. Light glittered within, pulsing and throbbing, like gemstones set by a fire.

"At least now we know where the light comes from," Corin said.

Alethea nodded. "And the warmth." She watched Corin reach out to touch the barrier, tentatively at first, then with both hands. He pushed along its face and near the edges. After a moment, he stood back.

Alethea couldn't help herself. Afraid as she was, the crystal was beautiful. She put out her hands. The stone, if that's what it was, radiated subtle heat and felt very smooth. The edges were precise, but not sharp. She ran her fingers along its surface, all the way to the natural rock of the tunnel, which appeared to have been cut to make place for the jewel. Then she, too, stood back. "What is it?"

Corin shook his head. "Some kind of door, I think. From the time of the Settling, perhaps. It's important though. I was suspicious before, but now I'm certain. Finding this cave was no accident."

Alethea looked at him. His face was serious, concerned, wise. "You're changing, Corin. I used to see only anger in you. Now it's gone."

"Changed?" he said. "I don't feel any different. Except for wandering in the wilderness these past days. And being with you." He smiled, and a white light seemed to burn in his eyes, stronger than the red pulsing from the crystal barrier.

Alethea pressed against him and ran her fingers over the scar above his right wrist. She could tell the wound went deep, deep in more than just the physical. A shudder passed through her body as she sensed the power she was touching. "Does it hurt?"

Corin sighed. "I remember asking Minesh that question. It seems a long time ago. No, it doesn't hurt. At least, not just now."

She peered up at him, into his eyes. "What are you going to do?"

He avoided her gaze and instead studied the scar on his arm and flexed his hand. "I think you know."

Alethea let out a slow breath. "There must be a way to make it open. If it is a door. Doors open."

"We've both tried. And you know as well as I that we have to go forward. We didn't come this far only to turn back."

She cast a quick glance at the crystal barrier. "Do you think we'll find our True-Friends in there?"

Corin shrugged. "I don't know. Something brought us here for a reason. I'm not turning back."

Confidence shone from Corin's eyes, a vast change from the anger and doubt that had seemed a part of him since they'd met. Alethea liked that change and wondered if she could ever feel so self-assured. "Do you really believe something brought us here?"

"I do," he said. "Something brought us together and then brought us here. I don't know why. I accept that there must be a reason. I'm glad for it."

Alethea leaned forward and hugged him, then kissed his cheek and stepped back.

$$\Omega$$

An uncomfortable weight settled in Corin's stomach as Alethea back away. The warmth of her touch faded leaving a chill emptiness, as though he had lost a part of himself. It struck him that over the past few days he had grown to enjoy her presence, her laugh, her smile, her arms wrapped around his waist as Serl carried them through the wilderness. But it was more than that. He also valued her direct questions that made him examine difficult matters he had always avoided. Then there was her boundless faith and persistence. He had never met anyone like her, and couldn't imagine having come this far, here, deep in the bowels of Karlac's Bane, on his own.

He forced himself to look away and focused his attention on the crystal barrier. What a tale this chamber would make over his father's wine, though the thought of its telling brought him no satisfaction. As little as a week ago, the telling of such an adventure would have pleased him. Now he wished only to be left alone, with Alethea beside him. What did that mean?

The question brought discomfort, so he narrowed his thoughts to the task at hand. There was work to do. A barrier to cross. True-Friends to discover. The tale to complete, whether it be recounted over anyone's wine or no.

His eyes shifted and he found himself gazing once again at Alethea, thankful for her understanding, her companionship. For the small kiss just now that lent him strength. He wanted to say something, but what? His own feelings were so new, so unexplored.

Focus. He turned away and stepped toward the jeweled wall. Taking a deep breath, he held out his right arm and formed his hand into a fist. With his left hand, he gripped his right wrist. He had summoned the Hest three times before. First to save the deer. Then to fight the sten-bear. And finally to rescue Alethea from the Skin-Runners. It had not been easy and he was still unsure exactly how he had done it. All three times he had been under tremendous stress. The word *desperation* came to mind. Would he be able to summon the Hest now? On command?

He formed no words in his mind — unsure of what words

he would use as well as who or what might receive them — but merely expressed an emotion of need. He needed the Hest to come to him. He needed—

Light and pain washed over Corin. He gasped and staggered sideways. A soft cry reached his ears and he realized it was Alethea. He turned his head and saw her slipping further back into the tunnel that had brought them here, her eyes wide, but her expression one of awe rather than fear. The brightness of the Hest illuminated the small space, surpassing the paler glow from the jeweled barrier, which now reflected the blue-white light of the Hest in a thousand different directions.

The agony was more than Corin remembered; every nerve in his body seemed on fire. Eager to end it, he turned back to the barrier and brought the blade down against the crystal surface.

The Hest entered the barrier slowly, like a hot knife piercing ice. It seemed to him that the myriad lights behind the barrier retreated and that the stone had grown less warm. Corin pressed down with all his weight. Slow. So slow. The Hest seemed to move hardly at all, like cutting wood with a toothless saw. Breath rasped through his lungs, and sweat poured from his body. He could hear himself groan from the effort, a pain almost as severe as the agony of the Hest itself.

Behind him, Alethea wept. She had lowered her barriers and her thoughts boiled like a storm. He could sense her distress, could touch her compassion. Her tears joined his in a unity of anguish.

Little by little, Corin lost awareness of his thoughts and then his body. Legs, arms, back, neck. All ceased to exist. There was only the jewel and the pain. The Hest burned like the sun, obliterating everything in its sphere.

$$\Omega$$

Alethea gasped as Corin collapsed to the floor. He had been grappling with the crystal door for what seemed hours, but had yet to make any kind of opening. The Hest still burned from his wrist, its once-bright light dimmed to dull yellow. She ignored the likely danger and rushed to his side.

Corin's chest heaved in spasms, his breath coming in short gasps. Perspiration washed across his face like an ocean wave.

"Let it go!" she shrieked. "It's killing you! Please! You have to let it go!"

Muscles twitched along Corin's jaw, His eyes were clamped shut against the agony. Alethea knew he could not hear him. She tried again, Speaking True. "Corin, Please! Let go of the Hest!"

Nothing. Alethea waved her trembling hands in the air, unsure of what to do. In desperation, she called out to the Elsian world. "Please, where are you? By all that is good, help him! Please, don't let him die!"

No answer came.

Having to do something, she reached down and touched his chest with her hand, searching for his heart. A faint pulse touched her palm. She frowned and slapped his face, hard. Then again, and again. Corin's head rolled from side to side like a useless sack.

I can't let him die! I won't! She looked at his arm and saw that the Hest had grown nearly as dull as the cavern wall. It was dying and seemed to be taking Corin with it. Dropping once more into True-Speech, Alethea thrust her mind at Corin, more urgently than she had done anything in her life. "Corin, hear me!"

His barriers were there, weakening, even as his life weakened. Alethea pushed against them, seeking passage, worming her way inside. There! A gap! Mustering her strength, she thrust her mind past his barriers, and met... pain. It was as though she'd stepped into a furnace. Agony. More than Lathan had tried to thrust upon her. More than Bruenor, even when the demon had taken him. Alethea felt waves of fire flow back along their link and instinctively moved to stop it, to break the connection, to intensify her barriers. Somehow, she held on, letting the pain flood back inside her, accepting it as her own. Her entire body shook as she closed her eyes, allowing the blaze to build, drawing it away from Corin.

"What? What are you doing?"

Alethea forced open her eyes and saw that Corin's were now also open. He blinked several times. The passageway brightened as the Hest flared to life. Even so, the pain felt somehow less intense rather than more. "Corin, I thought you were dying."

"I—I was. I have to finish. The Hest won't go until it's done. Help me."

"Of course I'll help."

Alethea felt strength flood into her as Corin stirred. He still seemed weak and she helped him to sit. Kneeling beside him, she draped his left arm over her shoulder for support and wrapped her fingers around his right wrist. The Hest glowed fiercely again, but she no longer feared it. Strength filled her, seemingly coming from the Hest. She poured that strength into Corin, even as a portion of his agony rushed back into her. The light of the blade flowed through her as she knew it flowed through him and there was a oneness between them, deeper and more sure than what they had shared the night before.

Together in motion, their movements like lovers, they cut through the remainder of the jeweled barrier. Time stood still. No sound. No smell. No sight. Just Alethea and Corin, the jewel and the Hest.

A grating sound filled the air as a segment of the barrier, large enough to admit Serl, shifted and slid inwards for perhaps an inch before stopping. Then the Hest winked out, leaving the cavern in utter darkness.

The Dome of the Ancients

With the approach of evening, Lathan's men returned to their room at the Hall of Deltis. In short order a tall flagon of sage wine and a scattering of cups littered the fog-table.

"I trust you were all successful," Lathan said, taking in their tired faces.

Hyrmus took a long pull from a wide, black goblet. A trickle of wine dribbled down his chin. He wiped at it with the sleeve of his tunic. "This might be easier than we thought," he said. "I saw only two guards at the vault. I don't think they've seriously considered that anyone might try to steal the technology."

"How many glare-beams did you see? How many grav-sleds?"

"Few that worked," Hyrmus admitted, running an age-spotted hand through his thin hair. "Most everything is still deep inside the vault where I couldn't see, but they were working on equipment in the sunlight near the opening. Herlen was there, and a few others. They stood around staring at the technology, scratching their heads. I guess it never occurred to anyone what they might find, opening the Dome after all these centuries."

"Right, right," said Lathan, losing patience. Hyrmus thought himself a wit, and always spoke ten words when one would do. "How many are working?"

Hyrmus shrugged. "No more than a dozen grav-sleds appeared usable. Perhaps twice that many glare-beams."

Lathan checked a laugh. "They call that an arsenal? I bet Herlen was mighty disappointed when he opened his precious Dome. Well, we'll take what they have. If we can supply Bruenor with the lion's share of Herlen's toys, he'll be that much more generous."

Hyrmus paused from raising his goblet to his lips. "Herlen's son, the Prince, wasn't at the Dome, Lathan. Were you able to learn anything?"

The master trader shook his head. "Gone. He and the girl have vanished into the countryside. To find the Prince's True-Friend, if you believe the gossip around town."

"True-Friend?" said Hyrmus. "But I thought—"

"Yeah, yeah. He would have gone alone. But I wouldn't have believed that cock-and-bull excuse had the Prince left the city knifeless and naked. More like Herlen's sent his brat into hiding. The pampered Prince must have taken the girl to warm his bed. Well, she's not important now."

Hyrmus licked his lips. "With raiding the city, Bruenor's probably had his fill of Gorgings anyway. He'll be much more interested in the arsenal."

Lathan turned to his nephew. "Speaking of Bruenor; Nagram, how did you fare? What is the word on our friends the Skin-Runners?"

"Not good, I'm afraid. They're gone."

"What!" Lathan hammered the table with his fist.

Nagram put down his cup. "That list of names you gave me. Everyone on it has disappeared."

The master trader glared at his nephew. If he shirked his duty... "They can't all be dead. Or captured. Herlen had no more than four grav-sleds in the air last night."

Lathan smiled inwardly as the idiot youth lost his arrogance and cringed. His lips moved quickly as he spoke. "They've left town, Lathan. Witnesses saw them leave, in threes and fours."

Lathan straightened and pressed both hands down on the table. "You're telling me that one night of resistance has sent the Skin-Runners slinking away like beaten curs?"

Nagram shook his head in quick, short movements. "Not slinking. From what I could tell, they've all headed east toward the Aenlaen Mountains, the Serpent's Tail. More like they're going *to* something, than away. Some of them were provisioned yesterday, before Herlen opened the Dome."

Lathan snorted and began pacing the floor, considering. "Well then, we'll follow them. With grav-sleds we can find them on the road before they get to where they're going."

"Uh, Aenlaen is wild country," Nagram said. "No one goes there. Especially the southern Tail. The only thing out there is the old Sagan ritual grounds."

Lathan halted and peered at his nephew. "You're not afraid are you, Nagram? I'd hate to think that one of my own men is afraid of our business partners."

Nagram's mouth narrowed and an arrogant coldness returned to his eyes. "I just want you to consider the risks."

"There is always risk!" Lathan pounded his fist into his palm. "The greater the risk, the greater the reward. In just a few short days, we shall all be wealthy men."

"Or dead," Nagram suggested.

Lathan pulled his knife from its sheath. Cold metal glinted in the light of the fog table. "Better a dead gambler than a live coward. Which would you be, Nagram?"

The youth remained perfectly still, but his eyes retained their coldness. "As you say, Lathan."

I'll have to do something about that boy. But now is not the time. Lathan sheathed his knife and cast a cool gaze around the table. "Tonight then, as darkness falls. We will hit the vaults before the King's Guard arrives to collect our weapons."

Hyrmus rubbed his chin. "Tonight! What about curfew?"

Lathan laughed. "By curfew we will have flown over the wall."

The old trader nodded. "What do we do in the meantime?"

Lathan tapped a finger against his lower lip. "We need more information. And I think I know how to get it."

Ω

Lathan observed Elder Layou with caution as the white-robed Circle-man narrowed his eyes and gazed about the room of the Deltis Inn. He peered at Lathan, white brows arching against a high forehead. "You said there was a son of the Path here, dying and in need of solace."

Lathan grinned and cocked his shaved head.

Many hands grabbed the Elder from behind, forcing him facedown onto a lavish bed. The door swung shut and was bolted with a loud thud. "What?" the Elder gasped, flailing with his arms. Then he arched his body and screamed as Nagram's blade found his back and buttocks. Red blood washed across his hips, down his legs, soaking into his robes. Layou screamed into the bedding. "Skin-Runners!"

Lathan turned him roughly and spit in his face. "Hardly. We may just let you live. That's more than the Skin-Runners would give you."

"Who are you?" Layou demanded, straining against the pain that racked his body.

Lathan glared at him. "Why would the Skin-Runners go to Aenlaen?"

"What? What are you asking?"

"The Serpent's Tail? What's there?"

Layou shook his head, wincing from the pain of his wounds. "Mountains," he said. "That is all. Mountains."

Lathan sighed. "You Circle clowns and your secrets. Get the drug, Eraed. This one's going to entertain us for a while."

"No, no!" Layou cried. Tears that had not come with the knife now burned in his eyes.

Eraed passed around white tablets of Sagcryl and the men took them. Lathan had already taken a small dose, a precautionary reinforcement to his barriers before calling on the Circle. Soon his men would be ready for a controlled search. Not like with the girl, Ilsa. He read the fear in the Elder's eyes; this one was too frightened to run.

Twenty minutes later a corpse lay on the bed, the sheets and blankets drenched with blood. The Elder's mind had died shortly before the body.

Lathan drifted over to the window and stared out into the street. "Stonepast? What the Bloody Demon is a Stonepast?"

"I guess we'll find out when we get there," Eraed said. He nodded at the corpse. "What should we do with that?"

"Leave it," Lathan said. "A lesson to Abo for overcharging a friend."

$$\Omega$$

Twilight came to Toroth with the locking of doors and the shuttering of windows. Before retreating inside their houses, sorrowful faces lined with fear and hopelessness cast lingering looks at the guards and conscripts who stood an uneasy watch at street corners and along boulevards. Tardy citizens, racing through the streets to the dubious safety of a roof and four walls, met challenges from the guards, who questioned their destinations and urged them to greater speed. "Curfew," they called. "Curfew. Night is falling!"

Some of those challenged on Freedom Avenue did not reach their declared destinations, but slipped instead into the thick, spring foliage of Sanctuary Park and assembled atop a small, tree-cloaked hill on the west side that overlooked the Dome of the Ancients. It was a good place of concealment and Lathan took advantage.

"Only two guards," said Eraed. The small man gazed down

at the nearer vault's open entrance with beady eyes. "I've seen brighter minds weaving rope for door coverings."

Lathan poked him in the chest with a thick finger. "There are others, off to the left and right, and doubtless more on the far side. See! There! Look at those two by that other vault. Hyrmus, you didn't tell me they were opening the entire Dome!"

"They weren't," the older trader said. "A single vault stood open this morning. I swear."

"Well, never mind. We need a diversion. Eraed, you and Hyrmus go down there by the nearer vault. Fake an injury. If Hyrmus isn't convincing, give him a real one. Take the two guards. The rest of us will come around behind them."

Hyrmus swallowed. "What if something goes wrong?"

"Make certain nothing does," Lathan said. "Now get on with it. The sun's going down. Patrols will be arriving soon to collect our weapons."

Eraed and Hyrmus stumbled off to the left while Lathan led the others to the right, following the concealment of shrubs and small trees. The setting sun worked to help conceal their movements. When everyone was in position, Hyrmus groaned and the two men approached the open vault.

Herlen's guards raised their pikes, squinting into the sunset. "Halt! Drop your barriers!"

Hyrmus groaned louder and leaned into Eraed. Both men stumbled. The guards lowered their pikes as Hyrmus fell crashing to the grass.

"What's wrong with him?" snapped one of the guards, a stocky man with a thick, black beard.

"It's almost curfew," said the other, taller and clean-faced.

Eraed was down on one knee pretending to care for Hyrmus, who groaned again while clutching his side.

"I said, what's the matter with him?"

Eraed glanced up, his eyes wild, a quiver in his voice that mirrored the worry lines on his forehead. "We were attacked. Something... an animal... broke through the door. We got away. Others weren't so lucky. Help me lift him."

The bearded guard put down his pike and crouched to

help.

"It's too early," said the other, scratching his chin. "Sun's not even down."

Hyrmus opened his eyes and whispered to the helpful guard, who leaned closer to hear. He died instantly as Hyrmus' knife slid just beneath his sternum and into his heart.

"It's never too early to die," said Hyrmus.

"What?" asked the remaining guard.

With lightning speed, Eraed straightened and had his knife to the man's throat.

"Uh," grunted the guard.

"Inside!" whispered Eraed, his voice no longer quivering. "Quickly. At the first sign of resistance, you'll be breathing out your windpipe. Understood?"

The two of them sidled toward the vault as quickly as two men could with one pressing a knife against the other's throat. Hyrmus followed, dragging the dead guard after him.

Lathan met them inside the vault where he had arrived with the others.

"Why is that one still alive?" Lathan demanded.

Eraed jerked his wrist and let the dying guard fall to the floor. "Why drag the man here when he can walk?"

"Never mind. Let's get busy."

The vault reeked of age and dust. Equipment lay everywhere. Stacked along the walls. Spread across the floor. Sitting on tables that looked to have been brought in by Herlen's men. Most of it appeared to have been piled up and locked inside, which probably it had. Any order had likely been imposed by Herlen's men sorting through it. Near the door stood two rows of grav-sleds. A row of glare-beams lined a wooden table. There were other things, too, nameless even in legend.

Nagram picked up a round metallic object with three knobby protrusions. He turned it in his hands.

"Put that down!" Lathan snapped.

"But it might be useful," Nagram said.

"We don't know what it is and we haven't got room for it.

Let it blow up in Herlen's face instead of ours. We've got work to do. Put as many glare-beams into the sleds as you can. Then let's get out of here. We've only minutes before someone comes to investigate."

Each sled was little more than a padded bench with a carry box fitted behind it. The metal frame held the same hue as plasteel, with smooth edges impossible to fashion on anything metallic made on Sindarin. Lathan frowned, reminded of the plasteel knife Alethea had stolen. He tossed several glare-beams into the box on one of the sleds, sat on its bench, and frowned. This was going to be more difficult to use than a knife.

A stick rising up from the front of the bench seemed shaped to be grasped by a hand. Lathan did. Nothing happened. Experimenting, he found that the stick moved—forward, back, left, right. He pulled it around in a circle. Still nothing. In anger, he pressed his thumb on the stick's top. The sled shot up in the air about ten feet, then stopped. Another two feet and Lathan would have smashed into the ceiling.

In the dim light, he could see his men grinning at him. "What are you all gawking at? Take a sled and let's go." Out of spite, he didn't tell them what he had learned.

With obvious awkwardness, the others tossed glare-beams into the boxes of the remaining fourteen sleds and crawled onto the benches. The five extra men doubled up on five sleds, the bench apparently designed to accommodate two.

"What's going on here?" came a shout from the doorway. Unnatural light washed through the room. Muffled shouts came from further outside.

"I'll show you," Lathan yelled, grabbing a glare-beam with his free hand and pointing it at the source of illumination. A high-pitched whine culminated in a small explosion. Shattered pieces of glass flew everywhere and someone screamed. More high-pitched sounds echoed inside the vault as Lathan's men cleared the doorway. The glare-beams with their handle and trigger were much simpler to learn than the sleds.

Lathan eased the steering stick forward and the sled

banked left, avoiding an immobile sled. Lifting his thumb slightly, he lowered the craft and then pushed the stick again. The sled shot forward, striking two guards in the head, probably killing them. With his glare-beam, he shot a wide arc, clearing a path for his men. The entrance whizzed past and he was free of the vault. Banking eastward, he pushed the stick all the way forward for speed and pressed his thumb down hard to gain more height.

The city passed beneath him at a blinding speed. In the space of heartbeats, he was over the city wall. Laughing, he sped on to the rendezvous east of the Garden Bridge where his people would meet up with him. Lathan had never felt more alive.

$$\Omega$$

"Attacked? Stolen?" Herlen paced his dayroom, waving his hands. He felt an urgent need to strangle somebody. "Who could have done such a thing? Why? What happened to the guards?"

"It was between shifts," Captain Rejin explained, his eyes shifting with discomfort. "The guard was light."

"And the thief who was killed? Was it a Skin-Runner? If Skin-Runners have the weapons, then all is lost."

"Not a Runner, no," Rejin said, his lean face brightening at having a piece of good news among all the bad. "The gate guards identified him as a trader who arrived yesterday with a group of others. They all submitted to a mind-search and were allowed in."

Herlen waved Rejin away, not wanting to hear any more. He turned to the Ceric. "Well, we all know where the weapons are now, don't we? In the hands of thieves and murderers. Blathering Demons! They'll terrorize the populace with our own sleds and beams!"

"I was afraid this might happen," Ceric said, rising from his seat. The Peace-Ruler had recovered somewhat from the melancholy that had plagued him since the raids started. He spoke and moved now with a cool detachment. Herlen didn't know which was worse. Ceric continued. "The drug-users are more proficient at True-Speech than our guards. They can get past a mind-search."

"Why didn't you mention this earlier?" Herlen demanded.

Ceric shrugged. "You could guess as well as I. Besides, what could we have done differently?"

"Increased the guard!" Herlen said. He reached for his wine.

Ceric sighed. "How? We have already conscripted every capable citizen, some of whom are likely thieves themselves. As it is, the men watch the streets at night and clean up the dead in the day. They have no chance to sleep."

Herlen stared at the Peace-Ruler. He had known Ceric all his life, knew him as the kindest, most compassionate soul one could hope to meet. How all this must be wearing on Sindarin's foremost man of peace.

He shook his head and turned back to Captain Rejin. "And tonight? It's already well past dark. How many weapons do we have for tonight's watch?"

"Sufficient," Rejin said. "They only raided the first vault. Some of the arsenal in the other three chambers is already in working order."

"Good." Herlen closed his eyes and pressed his palm to his forehead. "Tonight... tomorrow, have the guard sleep in the vaults. The real guard, not the conscripts. We can't afford any more such incidences." He opened his eyes and reached for his cup. "Now, on top of everything else, I have to figure out how to reclaim what was stolen."

Stonepast

The sky was bright, with no cloud and little wind. Birds twittered in the trees. Breakfast smells wafted through the air. It was a perfect spring day.

Herlen, King of Sindarin, stood in Sanctuary Park before the Dome of the Ancients, his hands on his hips and a scowl on his face. The Dome itself was a hive of activity. Shouted orders echoed within the vaults. Men ran from place to place, arms filled with technical arcana. Equipment clanked and squealed and bobbled. The soft hum of battery motors charged the air. The end result was a growing line of grav-sleds on the south grounds.

Herlen cocked one eye skyward and measured the sun. "Almost mid-morning. We should have been halfway to Kelmar by now."

"Are you certain that is where you want to go?" Ceric asked.

Herlen turned his gaze on the Peace-Ruler. The eldest of the Elders had never seemed older. His pale and wrinkled skin appeared paler and more wrinkled. Thin, white hair fluttered in the breeze. His face was gaunt, ancient jowls sagging with hopelessness. His smile, Ceric's eternal smile, was missing.

The Peace-Ruler had remained withdrawn since Herlen's decision to open the vaults. Ceric's condition, surprisingly, had worsened when the Skin-Runners failed to put in an appearance the previous night.

The people of Toroth, on the other hand, had greeted the rising sun with cheers and dancing in the streets. For the first time in four days, laughter rang through the city as wine, not blood, flowed through the gutters.

Little wine had been poured in the Sanctuary or the Tower, however. The Circle and Square knew better. Ceric, with drawn face and trembling hands, knew better. It was not over yet.

"Kelmar is just a detour," Herlen said. "I'll take no conscripts on this trip. I need experienced men, and Peradean has the largest garrison within reach. Olwen will be a boon as well. That healer thinks faster on her feet than anyone I know."

"And then?" asked Ceric. The words implied doom.

Herlen narrowed his eyes. "I think you know where I'm going, where the Skin-Runners most certainly have gone. And where our stolen equipment has likely gone."

The Peace-Ruler's face sagged even further, if that was possible. He gazed at the surrounding activity. "All these machines. Working at once. In one place." A lone spark flared in the old man's eyes. "It may not be too late. We could put the sleds back in the Dome. Reseal the vaults. The Hunters may not have noticed us yet."

Herlen shook his head. "What's done is done, Ceric. For good or ill, we have chosen our path. I gave this a lot of thought last night while I stood at my window, waiting for Skin-Runners that never came. If... if Corin is the Mastren, I don't think we could have done differently."

Ceric grudgingly nodded his head. "If Corin is the Mastren, then the Hunters will come. Opening the vaults was perhaps inevitable. But if Corin is not the Mastren, then by opening the vaults you have doomed us all."

Herlen took a deep breath and straightened his shoulders. He couldn't count the number of times that same thought had haunted him since he had opened the vaults. "It's too late for second-guessing. We have chosen our path. Now we must follow it to its conclusion."

"Even if that path ends at—"

"Yes, Ceric. I know the Legends too. Even if that path ends at Stonepast."

$$\Omega$$

Alethea stood alone before the breached crystal barrier, warming her face and hands by the blood-red glow that pulsed from within. A full day had passed since she had helped Corin cut through the jewel. The memory of that encounter with Corin, with the Hest, still filled her with wonder. Except for the uneven line that cut a rough oval through the barrier, and the huge block of crystal that had shifted within that cut, she could have thought the entire experience a dream.

From behind came a staccato echo of hooves clicking on stone. Alethea turned to find Corin leading Serl toward her through the wolf's throat. Bundles tied to the saddle contained the roots and berries they had collected the previous afternoon.

"I still think you're crazy bringing a horse inside a cavern," she said.

Corin grinned. "A horse is a man's best friend. Besides,

who else is going to keep us out of trouble?" He patted Serl on the nose. "He did put up less of a struggle entering the wolf's throat than you."

Alethea ignored that and turned back to the jeweled opening. Red light flickered through the facets like slow-moving flames. "You're intent on going in there?"

Corin came up beside her and took Alethea's hand in his. "I must. It's no accident that we found this place."

"Then you do believe that you're the Mastren?" Her question hung in the air, an arrow shot skyward at the peak of its arc.

For long moments, Corin gazed into her eyes, saying nothing. Then he turned away. "Help me push the jewel." He set his hands against the shifted segment. "I don't know how heavy it will be."

Alethea joined him and together they put their weight against the large block of crystal cut by the Hest. A grating noise filled the tunnel as the cut segment protested. It slid several inches and then stopped. The illumination behind the jewel had receded.

"Again," grunted Corin.

More noise. The crystal block sank another inch. It was like moving a mountain.

"Again."

Alethea threw her weight against the jewel. The grating picked up again, then stopped as the segment fell inward, almost taking the two of them with it. Acrid air rushed out into her face, followed by a resounding thud as the cut jewel hit the cavern floor on the other side of the opening.

Silence reached out from the dull, blood-red emptiness beyond, and with it the most pungent odor of sagcryl Alethea had ever encountered. She forced her lungs to work, to breathe despite the stench. Even with her mouth closed, she could taste the drug on her tongue, gritty, caustic. She almost turned and ran.

"Wait here." Corin's voice was hushed. The smell had so overwhelmed Alethea that she had forgotten he was even there.

"You can't go alone," she said, forcing her tongue to work.

"I won't go far. Just a few steps."

"No, don't—"

"Alethea."

Something in his voice made her stop. Corin turned and put his hands on her shoulders, his face washed red in the bloody glow that was slowly returning within the cave. "Serl will be with you. And I'll only go a few steps."

"I'll come with you."

Corin's face was blank for a moment. Then he smiled. "Of course you will. You're braver than I am."

Before she could respond, he seized Serl's reins and coaxed the animal through the tall opening. Taking her hand, he led Alethea through as well.

The world beyond the jeweled door was a pool of blood. Where they stood, all was dark, blackness. Alethea could just make out the edges of the opening they had made, and was aware of stone beneath her boots because it prevented her from falling. But beyond the immediate darkness lay a sea of red. Dull, featureless, and growing brighter.

"See the stars," Corin said. He raised his arm.

Alethea looked up to find a blood-red sky, the same as the emptiness before them. Then she saw.

Pinpricks of white twinkled amid the red. First here, then there. "Pulsating," she said, "like the lights beyond the jewel before we disturbed it."

There was orange now. It seemed a cycle— tiny points of light, first white, then orange, then red, then white again. And everywhere the smell of the drug. Clinging. Lingering.

Serl seemed oblivious to his surroundings, following without complaint as Corin led Alethea forward, out of their small pocket of blackness and into the light.

$$\Omega$$

Minesh slumped against a wide, smooth rock and gazed up at the mountain rising before him. He was at the edge of Ethan's Green, bordering the Karlac tombs. The jagged peak of Karlac's Bane towered above him, the southern tip of the Serpent's Tail.

This was an unlucky place. More men had died below this mountain than anywhere else on Sindarin. First at the time of the Settling, when the colony ship had made planet-fall with rather more force than the pilots had intended. Then again when the Sagan Priests had risen, followed by years of ritual violence. Travelers these days went north through the Rhedan Pass or south through Kemplar Steeple. Only outlaws ventured near the mountain. Outlaws and Skin-Runners.

Karlac's Bane had another name, unknown except to a select few. A name given by the Elsan shortly after Man's arrival on Sindarin, a time when many men had died by fateful accident and by murder not far from where Minesh sat.

Stonepast.

Minesh turned his head and spat.

The sun angled up toward noon and had all but dried out his clothes, soaked for a second time in as many days by a pre-dawn shower. He suspected that the cold Aenlaen winds had done more drying than the sun.

"I'm too old for this," he complained in True-Speech. "Traipsing around through storms, on foot, catching my death."

"Must I hear this again?" Galin answered from the Elsian world. "You have become poor company in your dotage, old man."

Minesh waved a hand in the air. "All right, all right, you've made your point. I just wish we could get this over with." He rubbed his fingers against the arrow wound in his chest. "Things seem to be going from bad to worse, that's all."

Galin made no comment. This, more than anything else, told Minesh that things must be worse than he knew. It would be the Skin-Runners, of course. The severed arm and the wolf ring were just the beginning. It was possible that the Skin-Runners had known, even before he did, that the Mastren had come.

What, he wondered, would that knowledge do to them? Since leaving Toroth, he had asked Galin many times what the Skin-Runners were up to. Galin's response was always the same: "More active than usual." What was that supposed to mean?

He shook his head and returned his thoughts to the matter at hand. Between him and the mountain stood a grove of alders. Jonquil and sageroot grew profusely among the trees. He could smell their freshness after the recent rain. According to Galin, an entrance into Stonepast lay hidden behind those trees.

"Are you sure this is the place?" he asked, pushing himself back to his feet.

"If my information is correct," replied Galin.

"And if it's not?"

"We shall know soon enough."

Minesh worked his way through the trees, the ragged remnants of his vestments catching on sharp branches and thorn bushes, until at last he discovered a rugged stone wall—the foot of the mountain. Working his way to the right he found a collection of large boulders. Old scrapings indicated that the stones had been moved. Cobwebs filling deep crevices suggested they had not been moved in some time.

"Just how current is this information of yours?"

"Time is meaningless," suggested Galin. "Accuracy is everything."

Minesh rolled his eyes and pressed his shoulder against one of the boulders. Pain from his wound shot through his chest. He took several slow breaths until it dissipated. The boulder had not moved. He might as well have pushed against the mountain. "Any idea how to get in?"

"Have you lost faith in me now, as well?" Galin asked, sounding insulted. "There should be a smaller stone near the bottom that supports the rest. Use a stick for leverage. A child could roll the larger boulder above once the smaller is removed."

Minesh found a sturdy branch and then searched for the smaller stone. Grunting, more to show Galin his discomfort than out of any physical need, he worked the smaller stone free. His chest tore with the strain, throbbing like hot knives piercing his flesh. Abandoning the branch, he pressed his back against the larger stone above and pushed backward with his legs. The boulder grudgingly rolled to a new position, revealing a narrow opening.

Minesh sagged against the rock and wrestled for breath. "A large child, perhaps," he murmured.

Galin made no comment.

Taking one last look at the green of the grove and the blue of the sky, colors he feared never to see again, Minesh squeezed through the opening into darkness.

The tunnel inside was tall and wide enough to walk upright, but disappeared into blackness after a short distance.

"My torches are soaked from the rain," he grumbled irritably.

"There is light where you are going. You will find your way."

"How?" demanded Minesh. "The tunnels of Stonepast are said to be a thousand miles long. The meeting place could be anywhere."

"Legend tends to exaggerate," Galin replied. "Your destination is the Singing Cave. It is aptly named. Let your ears be your guide."

Minesh listened, but could hear nothing beyond the wind whistling through the alders outside. He shook his head and began working his way along the tunnel wall letting his hands find his path.

$$\Omega$$

Corin inched forward with a hesitation born of cautious curiosity. Alethea came up beside him, close enough to be his shadow. Serl followed easily, calm to his surroundings. All about them surged a sea of pulsating stars — white, orange, red — pulsing, quivering, dancing. The tiny lights were everywhere, even beneath their feet. Corin felt a softness with each step, like walking on moss.

Reaching down with nervous fingers, he touched the glittering floor. His hand came back glistening with color. There was little weight there. And tingling. He stared intently at his hand — white, orange, red — and brought his fingers ever closer to his eyes, straining to see.

Alethea hovered nervously at his side.

He shifted his fingers, turning the bits of color. He could see now, almost make out shapes.

"Insects," Alethea whispered, speaking the word even as it suggested itself to Corin. How she had guessed, he didn't know.

"Small," he said, "like whiskers. Black bodies with the changing colors at one end. Miniature caterpillars?"

"Do you think they're dangerous?" Alethea asked. "Maybe that crystal door was meant to keep them in."

"More likely to keep them hidden," Corin said. "I'm sure the Skin-Runners are very protective of their tiny friends."

"Insects? Why would the Skin-Runners hide insects?"

"You already know. Smell the air. The drug is in here. These insects are involved somehow." With rapid motions he brushed the bits of color from his fingers, and then wiped his hands on his sten-bear coat. "Come on," he said. "There has to be more to it than just insects."

They continued forward, stepping blindly through the dull light. The path curved down and to the left following a smooth floor. Ahead of them, a large pocket of insects blinked hypnotically, like crystal sand on a moonlit shore. The ceiling dipped toward them and the passage narrowed.

Above and in front of them was what seemed the brightest colony of insects in the cavern. Hundreds of thousands of them formed a wide orange band, wriggling and twisting, a teeming mass of lights clinging to the ceiling and the upper reaches of the walls, moving and throbbing, in and out of tiny pores in the rock.

They passed beneath the colony through the neck of the passage into a wider tunnel that curved to the right, and then opened into a large chamber. Walls, ceiling, floor. All pulsed. White — orange — red. Corin paused, unsure of which direction to take.

"What do they eat?" whispered Alethea.

"What?"

"There are millions of them. Millions and millions. What do they eat?"

Corin saw what appeared to be a large shadow off to the

left and turned toward it. "Insects eat leaves, don't they? Or... or other insects?"

"There are no leaves down here. And some insects bite people."

"They haven't bitten us. Yet." As they approached the shadow, Corin stretched out his hand to touch it and then moved his fingers along its surface. It was a large boulder, oddly shaped and sitting out in the open. He traced a larger part of it with his hand. There were no insects on it. "Why not this rock?" he said. "They're over everything else."

"Not us," said Alethea, with thankfulness in her voice.

"They must digest rock," Corin suggested, realization falling into place. "And they don't like this kind, so they leave it alone."

Larger shadows loomed ahead. Corin led Alethea toward them. Serl followed.

"Do you hear that?" asked Alethea.

Corin stopped and listened. "What? I don't hear anything."

"It's faint," Alethea said. "But... I swear... it sounds like singing."

$$\Omega$$

Minesh observed the Gorging posts with disgust. A body hung between them. Man or woman he couldn't tell. Not from what remained. It looked to have been there a long time. Months. Perhaps years. Dried blood covered the posts and the surrounding cavern floor. Wide strips of human skin dangled from tall stone poles along one wall like futile flags, banners of obscenity.

He paced around the cavern, peering at unreadable wall markings, very old and painted, seemingly, with blood. He poked his head into alcoves. A stone obelisk, taller and as thin as the offering posts used in the Gorgings, stood in the center of each. Minesh couldn't fathom their purpose until he reached the final recess. Inside stood one of the obelisks, with bones, human bones, stacked around it to shoulder height in some obscure arrangement. The bones, like the wall markings, were very old.

"Sagan Priests built this place," Galin said, "and others like it." Minesh listened carefully; it was one of those rare occasions when his True-Friend offered information without being strong-armed first. "Skin-Runners use it now on special occasions, thinking themselves as grand as the Sagans."

"And are they?" Minesh asked. "As grand as the Sagans?"

Galin's voice took on a strange blend of sorrow and distaste. "The Sagan Priests were masterful in their way, carving stone as skillfully as they carved human flesh. It was their design to bring about a culture of purely Demonic origin. They built homes of stone, herded people like cattle, and used the skins from their Gorgings as currency. Kelmar was a Sagan fortress, built on the backs of slave labor, slaves who afterward were taken in the Gorgings. If not for the Hest, the Sagan Priests would have held irrevocable control of Sindarin."

Minesh was both amazed and appalled. Never before had Galin been so forthright in his revelations. "I never knew it was so bad. No wonder history from before and during the Sagan wars is clouded."

Galin went on. "After the collapse of the Sagans, the Demons knew they were beaten. Knew we would not allow them to reestablish their vile culture, not vicariously, not even on so small a rock as Sindarin. And so they push as far as they dare with the Skin-Runners, taking the little bit they can without incurring the full and final wrath of the Elsan."

"Why are you telling me this?" Minesh asked. "Before, you always said it was not allowed. That you could guide in small ways, but were limited in the information you could reveal. That the Elsan had to allow Mankind to find its own path from barbarity into the light. I've asked you about the Sagan Priests before."

"I could not tell you," Galin said. "If I had, you would have told others. Eventually the Square, in a fit of supposed revenge, would have doubled its efforts against the Skin-Runners and wiped them out. The Sagcryl traders would have been next. After that, the penalty for suspected drug use or Demon possession would be death. There would be no need for the Mastren. And when the Hunters finally found

Sindarin, they would find not the Sagan Priests herding and executing Mankind, but the Square. And that, my friend, would be as good a cause for extermination as the Demons ever were."

Minesh nodded, seeing how all these things could be true. "But why are you are telling me now?"

"At this juncture," Galin said, "your knowing makes no difference."

There was a sadness in Galin's voice that shook Minesh to the core. His True-Friend could as easily have said, "Your death is at hand." His meaning was that clear.

Leaving the bone alcove, Minesh approached the cavern's last feature, a giant wolf-head with large, red eyes that glistened with something akin to life. "How many murders have you witnessed over the centuries?" he asked the wolf. "And do you care?"

The wolf gave no answer, and Galin, too, remained silent.

Minesh breathed deeply, and then peered past the stone teeth down into the wolf's cavernous throat. He was not surprised to find a tunnel. An entrance? Into what? What besides my own death? Stepping carefully over the sharp, stone teeth, Minesh entered the jaws of the wolf.

$$\Omega$$

Lathan the Klep peered out from between twin, jutting rocks that blocked one end of the clearing. Stands of tall alders rose up on all sides, hiding his people from unfriendly eyes, as few eyes as there were in the Aenlaen wilderness.

Behind him, the grav-sleds formed a disorganized circle around which loitered twenty men. Nagram swaggered over to join his surveillance.

"Those aren't Bruenor's men," Nagram said, squinting. "And look, Skin-Runners walk straight into the mountain without walking out again. There must be a cave, or a tunnel."

"Stonepast," Lathan asserted, confident that he had discovered the Circle Elder's secret. "We'll wait until the last of them go in and then follow at a distance."

"Why?" Nagram squinted at him and sneered. "Why not approach them out here where we have room to maneuver?

We don't have to sell the weapons to Bruenor. Any Skin-Runner will pay."

"You are a child, Nagram. Skin-Runner packs from all over Sindarin flock to this... this Stonepast, and you are not the least bit curious? There is opportunity here. I can smell it."

Nagram said nothing, but his eyes went cold.

"We may just have an auction here," Lathan explained. "Grav-sleds to the highest bidder. Glare-beams for the man with the heaviest purse. They'll be fighting each other just to throw coin and sagcryl at us!"

Nagram shook his head and slipped away to rejoin the others.

Lathan stared after him. *My nephew thinks I'm mad. Walking into a den of Skin-Runners and setting them to argue. Perhaps I am mad. But he will follow me. They all will. They always do. They are sheep and I the shepherd. That is the natural order of the universe.*

Without provocation, his thoughts went back to two nights earlier in the Hall of Deltis and the sound of wailing rising through the city outside the window. Lathan felt his heart quicken and hastily swept the memory from his mind. *Not sheep then*, he decided. *A wolf pack. With myself as pack leader. Others are the sheep and we the predator.*

The thought boosted Lathan's confidence as he resumed watching the Skin-Runners enter the mountain. *The most dangerous sheep of all.*

$$\Omega$$

Bruenor was having a difficult time with the door. The unlocking mechanism, with its many crystal faces, was designed to require two hands. Several niacs in his pack knew the secret, but to ask for help would be to debase himself. He could not afford that. Especially not now. Not here.

On the fifth try he succeeded and the oval jewel swung inward, revealing a wall of blood-red light. He entered without hesitation, thrilling in the pungent smell of sagcryl. Once inside the cavern, the one-armed priest stood and drew breath, filling his lungs. He groaned with ecstasy as the drug-imbued air lent him new strength. The sensation almost made up for not performing the Gorging before entering. Almost.

Arnor had complained bitterly about omitting the rite, forcing Bruenor to draw his knife to convince the fool that speed was more important than protocol. "We must be first to arrive at the Paē-thn," Bruenor had told him. "It is paramount that we entrench ourselves firmly. There will be challenges to my supremacy. And if I die, Arnor, you die also."

Or you will die here, Bruenor implied with the knife. Arnor had been dissuaded.

Over a hundred Skin-Runners followed Bruenor through the crystal door, many of them leading animals. He had thought to order the horses left outside the mountain, but there were too many of them. If Herlen did find the courage to send out patrols, the animals would surely be spotted. He reached to scratch his phantom arm, cursed, and then massaged his shoulder stump instead. Doubtless the horses' hooves would trample many of the drug-makers, but there was no shortage of those. A smaller supply of the drug might just suit his purposes. People were always a little more respectful, more subservient, when what he offered was harder to find.

"Let's move," he called to his men. "We shall be first to arrive or all of you will be tied to the poles. Clear?"

Grumbles echoed within the cavern, but the men quickened their movements. Bruenor grunted and marched forward.

The Legends of Arwyth

Minesh pressed his palms against the final two stress points. A grating sound followed by a sigh of air met his ears as the crystal door shifted and swung open. Beyond the doorway stood a cavern of inestimable size bathed in blood-red light. A pungent stench of sagcryl assaulted his senses, reminding Minesh of his encounter with the traders in Rhedan. He pushed the unpleasant thought aside and studied the door.

The lock had been complicated, certainly more sophisticated than the lock on his hutch and much better concealed. A design from before the Settling? Without Galin's guidance, it could have taken days to figure out. But what truly astounded Minesh was the crystal door itself.

"Child's play," suggested Galin. "Created by mixing certain chemicals and crystalline compounds, like the fog tables that your craftsmen still make today. Much knowledge was lost at the time of the Settling. More lost through the Sagan years. Little has been rediscovered."

"Would such knowledge have benefited us?" Minesh asked, curious and a little uneasy. He was still not used to Galin's candidness.

"No," Galin said. "Knowledge is a dangerous tool in unskilled hands. Better to learn first the skills of fellowship and social enlightenment as laid out in the Path of Arwyth. Once civilized, Man may then wield knowledge without becoming a threat to Himself and to others."

"And the Hunters would accept us," Minesh concluded. "All of this was told to Arwyth, wasn't it? The Elsan were as candid with her then as you are with me now. Your rules were broken then, too, weren't they?"

"Arwyth was told," admitted Galin. "She was a civilized woman at the time of the Settling when there were few civilized men." The otherworldly voice grew somber. "Few of those who survived the landing had achieved any semblance of enlightenment, and most who did were killed in the name of peace by their fellow settlers who fought to conquer the land as well as establish their own selfish hegemonies. Although settlers is too kind a word; refugees is more accurate. Arwyth, seeing that peace had no place among them, fled alone into the mountains searching, for what, she did not know. What she found was the Elsan.

"For twelve years she lived alone, her only fellowship coming from beyond the Shroud. At times she thought herself insane, and at other times the sanest person alive. In the end she decided to return to her people and attempt to share what she had learned.

"The Elsan helped her, framing her knowledge into a Path that could help those who were ready to receive it. They also gave to her the Legends, called legends and not prophecies because that is what they are. The Elsan cannot see the future, but have all of history behind us and can well fathom how events will unfold given certain catalysts."

"And the Hest?" asked Minesh.

"Arwyth made it herself. Crystals and chemicals. And, of course, the will of the Elsan when the Hest is used. If Arwyth would attempt to bring civilization to her people, the Elsan could not refuse to help."

"And all this?" Minesh waved his arms at the crystal door and the cavern. "You knew that the Sagan Priests would rise up?"

"It was inevitable," Galin said. "Sindarin has the crysalis mineral. And with the arrival of Man, came the sage plant. The same way that Arwyth found the Elsan, others were certain to find the Demons. And the Demons are very predictable. They are the chief catalyst of the Legends."

Minesh shook his head. It was all too much. If Galin had told him these things years ago, his life could have been so much different. But, no. Nothing would have changed. Yes, he would have had the answers to questions that had eluded him. But he would have been like Arwyth, alone in his sanity. His knowing would have accomplished nothing; Arwyth had already done what was required. His, he realized, was a different role. And the Legend of the Mastren remained before him.

Taking a deep breath, Minesh straightened his shoulders and stepped through the crystal door into blood.

Ω

Corin and Alethea gazed with apprehension about the wide chamber before them. There was additional light here, its source hidden behind a multitude of grotesque rock carvings that reached toward the high ceiling, shadowed silhouettes in the blood-red light. The scenes they portrayed echoed the worst of Skin-Runner legend. Corin felt Alethea stiffen at his side.

The singing they had followed to this place could be heard clearly now, like the rush of a river or the hum of a strong wind. That, and the statues... There was no doubt in Corin's mind that they had reached their destination.

"I'm not going in there," Alethea said. She crossed her arms and turned her back.

Corin nodded. When they had first met, Alethea had been an unwilling participant in many of the scenes the carved stones depicted.

After brief discussion, he led Alethea back through a winding, smooth-floored corridor to an empty chamber they had passed earlier. The cavern was huge and very dark. Near its center stood one of the black stone formations, the kind the insects ignored. It was smooth and featureless, except for a deep recess on one side.

"A cave within a cave," Corin joked, trying to set Alethea at ease. "You and Serl will be safe here." He hoped that was true. It had to be. "I won't stay away long."

"No," Alethea said. Her voice shook as it had when she was freezing from the rain and Corin knew how scared she was. The wolf-head cavern and the rock carvings had awakened memories of her time among the Skin-Runners in the Karlac grotto.

His own first sight of her, tied between the Gorging poles and surrounded by frenzied men in wolf-skins, passed before Corin's eyes with astonishing clarity. Alethea's face had been white with horror and fear. And a presence had filled the grotto, infinite evil beyond the malice of Men. The Skin-Runners, those he had killed and the others who got away, had been less than men in that place. And what they had intended for Alethea was too hideous to contemplate.

"I-I should go with you," Alethea said, drawing Corin back to the present.

The image in his mind faded as he pulled Alethea inside his arms and held her tight. Alethea returned the embrace and it seemed as though their bodies had become one. After a long moment, he released her and wiped the tears from her cheeks with his fingers.

"You are the most fearless person I know," he told her. "The most fearless person who ever lived. But I should go on alone. Whatever is going to happen in there…" and here he faltered, "I would rather that you hid yourself here. Safe."

Alethea said nothing, but took the one remaining sack of roots and berries from Serl's saddle and opened it. They sat against the dark stone and shared the modest meal between them, then drank the last of the water. When they finished, Alethea nestled her head into the nook of Corin's shoulder, and he held her. How long they sat like that, he didn't know.

At last Corin stood. "If I don't return before you get hungry again, take Serl and go back the way we came. There is food in the forest. You're as good at finding it as I am. Better."

"You will come back to me." Alethea said it as a command, though her voice still shook.

"Of course I will." Corin tried to smile. "But if you get hungry first…" He patted Serl's nose and Spoke True. "Protect her."

The horse nickered and nodded its long face.

Abruptly, Alethea rose and flew into his arms. Her lips brushed his ear. "Be careful," she whispered.

"I will. I have you to come back to."

And then he left her.

$$\Omega$$

Lathan was the first through the mountain opening, a narrow crevice obscured by rocks and brush. He took his grav-sled in slow and low to the ground. Feeling along the front of the bench, he found the pad he had discovered earlier that lit a torch positioned just below it.

"Two of you get down and walk ahead," he called over his shoulder. "Make sure the tunnel doesn't get too narrow for the sleds. Also, if we catch up with the Skin-Runners, I want to see them before they see us. Stay as far ahead of our lights as you can. One of you run back when you find anything. On your lives, I want no mistakes."

"I still think this is a bad idea," Nagram growled from the grav-sled behind him. "It was dangerous enough meeting Bruenor and a few of his animals in daylight. Confronting the entire Skin-Runner population on their own ground is madness!"

Lathan turned in his seat and pointed his glare-beam at his nephew. "I should have done this a long time ago," he said, and pulled the trigger. In a fury of flames that lit up the crevice, Nagram's head exploded on his shoulders. The grav-sled he had been piloting halted and hung in the air, as lifeless as its driver.

"No mistakes," Lathan repeated. "That includes dissension in the ranks."

His men said nothing; the only sound was the wind and the low hum made by the hovering grav-sleds. Then Eraed climbed up onto Nagram's sled and pushed the corpse of Lathan's nephew out onto the rocky crevice floor.

Lathan waited until two men had run far enough ahead, then he moved his sled forward, the others following. He had never killed one of his own before. It surprised him how good it felt.

The crevice narrowed into a tunnel that led deep into the mountain. Lathan lost track of the passing minutes as he contemplated what he might find. Why would the Skin-Runners gather here? Inside a mountain. What is Stonepast?

He almost didn't see the returning man and halted the grav-sled only inches before slamming into him. Lathan smiled as the man thrust out his hand toward the flying machine, as though he could somehow fend it off like it was a small bird.

"T—They've st—stopped just ahead," the man sputtered. "I—In a c—cave."

Lathan climbed down off the grav-sled and slapped the man on the shoulder. "Wait here with the others." He then walked alone along the tunnel running his hand along one wall as the light from his grav-sled faded behind him. In his other hand he carried a glare-beam.

He found the second man standing in a section of tunnel softly lit by a red glow from somewhere up ahead. The man shifted from foot to foot and wrung his hands. When he saw Lathan, he opened his mouth to speak, but Lathan motioned him to silence and then indicated he should go back with the others.

He continued along the tunnel at a much slower pace, listening for any sound as the dim red light grew stronger. He soon reached a small cave littered with broken wooden boxes and decaying cloth sacks. He examined a few and determined they were empty, though a few of the sacks looked less decrepit than the others. A break in the wall at the far side of the cave opened into a larger corridor. The source of the red light emanated from the far end.

Lathan paused as he discerned the slow tom-tom-tom of drumbeats echoing somewhere ahead. Skin-Runners. Something deep in the trader's gut told him to turn around and go back. Nagram had been right; meeting the Skin-Runners in this secret place of theirs was a bad idea. Would they even let him live long enough to tell them what he had to trade? His grinned at the realization that the glare-beam would buy him time, one way or another.

The drumbeat beckoned; he had to go see what they were doing.

He slunk along the stone corridor keeping close to one wall. The drumbeats grew louder and faster as he approached, arriving at last at a much larger cavern filled with activity. A large rock carving jutted out from the wall near the entrance and Lathan slipped silently behind it. He swallowed hard as his eyes took in what was happening.

At the center of the cave a score of Skin-Runners circled two tall posts, prowling on all fours and howling like the wolves whose skins they wore. Between the posts they had tied a terrified young woman. Lathan snickered when they tore the clothes from her lithe body. She was a pretty little thing, and he burned with envy as the Priest began violating her, taking her mind as well as her body.

He was so absorbed in watching the woman that several minutes passed before he noticed the rasping sounds that emanated from the priest were only vaguely human and that his eyes glowed red. By then the woman was beyond shrieking and Lathan no longer snickered. He had heard that Skin-

Runner priests allowed themselves to become possessed by Demons during their rites. He had never truly believed it. Now he was not so sure.

The priest held a knife. Lathan had watched him play it across the curves of the woman's body. Then the knife did more. Sheets of something fell to the floor. Wolves, or men dressed as wolves, scurried in to scoop them up and stretch them across their faces with their hands.

Bile rose in Lathan's throat. Skin! Of course, there would be little blood; the drug would see to that. Lathan swallowed hard as the woman moaned. Faster now, the priest's knife worked, across her back, her arms, her breasts. Then he finished and put the knife away.

Lathan realized that he had stopped breathing. His head spun as he drew oxygen back into his lungs. Would they kill her now?

The woman made no sound as the priest bit into her flayed breast.

Lathan stared at the woman's lidless eyes. The irises moved, following the Demon-priest's actions. She was aware of what was happening! He continued to stare as the other Skin-Runners sank teeth into the woman's arms, legs, and back.

This went on for some time. Then, without warning, the priest roared and dove for her throat. The woman's eyes, unable to close, went vacant.

A short while later the drums stopped and the Skin-Runners shed their wolf skins. Lathan licked his lips and tried to breath. His throat felt drier than he could remember and his heart beat faster than the drums at the peak of the Gorging rites. He knew he should race back to his men and tell them to turn around, that the Skin-Runners would be coming back out. Outside. Outside would be a better place to trade them Herlen's technology.

But he found he couldn't move. They might see him as he slipped from behind the stone carving and back into the corridor. They might do to him what they had done to that woman. And so he hid himself as the Skin-Runners laughed and collected up their gear.

After a few minutes it dawned on Lathan that the Skin-Runners were not going back into the corridor. He could hear them still at the other end of the cavern, their laughing, talking, and movements becoming less and less. Taking a deep breath, he poked his head out from behind the carving and immediately pulled it back. But he had seen enough. The Skin-Runners were leaving the cavern through the gaping mouth of the giant wolf head that had overseen the proceedings. The wolf head that was the source of the blood-red light.

Yes. He nodded to himself. Where were the others? This is but one band of Skin-Runners. Bruenor and other bands were also coming to this place. The auction. It could still happen. There must be another cavern, a larger cavern, deeper inside the mountain. Stonepast.

After ensuring the Skin-Runners had gone, Lathan slunk back into the corridor, through the smaller cave, and along the tunnel to where his men waited. He tried to think of what he would tell them. That he had witnessed a Gorging? Certainly. That the Skin-Runners had violated and killed a woman? That too. How they had done it? No. How he felt about what he had witnessed? Of that, he was not even sure himself.

$$\Omega$$

Bruenor brought his people to a halt and flashed his eyes about the cavern. Stone platforms stood everywhere, carved daises of varying heights. A series of stone steps had been carved into the side of each platform, allowing ease of access from the cavern floor. At the center of each dais, like upright fangs, stood a pair of tall, stone posts. Though they had seen little use in centuries, not since the days of the Sagan priests when the Pae-thn had been a regular occurrence, they glittered deep red in the bloody light.

Below the platforms, scattered throughout the cavern, stood sculpted works of ordinary stone: granite, feldspar, basalt— minerals the drug-makers ignored. Massive wolves sprang up from the floor, frozen in mid-leap, curled lips stretched over pointed fangs. Offerings shrieked and cowered in frozen silence. Vivisected near-corpses wailed at the loss of limbs and organs, waiting for death. On frameworks of long stone poles hung row after row of thin, translucent veils, decaying human skin that muted the bloody light.

From the ceiling loomed gargoyle shapes, lupine Demon faces leering over a scene of frozen suffering. Song murmured from their hideous lips, a resonant hymn to those with even the smallest ability of True-Speech. Behind the faces, unseen, lay the larval nests— gaping cavities where Skin-Runner priests set heaping piles of sageroot. The place where drugmakers came to nest. The place where the drug was harvested.

Bruenor grunted and waved to the left and right. Several of his pack ran ahead, peering behind stone statues of screaming women and cowering men. They returned after several minutes.

"We are first," Arnor confirmed. His tone implied that there had been time for the Gorging after all.

Bruenor ignored him. "The highest dais is at the center. Settle yourselves. I want us to appear as though we own the place when the others arrive. Clear?"

His pack, Arnor included, moved quickly to obey.

$$\Omega$$

Minesh rummaged among the glowing insects with the nail of his forefinger, turning them over, looking for clues. The tiny bodies were soft and fleshy. Their squirming tickled his skin. He watched intently as they changed color. Red — white — orange — red. The air was full of the drug; it was difficult to breath.

How? he asked himself. Then it hit him. The nature of the stone over which the insects swarmed. "Crysalis!"

"Ironic, is it not," said Galin. "Hundreds of refugee ships flee a doomed Earth carrying precious cargo that includes sageroot, a medicinal herb. And the ship that crashes on Sindarin hits a mountain of crysalis, the one mineral in the universe local insects can consume along with sageroot to produce sagcryl. There have been many tears and laughter shed over that twist of fate, I assure you."

"The drug," Minesh asked, casting his gaze about the seemingly endless cavern. "Can there be so much?"

"More than you could know," answered Galin. "But you must hurry. The crux approaches."

$$\Omega$$

Two grav-sleds separated from the rest and edged toward the foot of the mountain.

"Are you sure the trail leads here?" Herlen called to the other sled.

Olwen, Peradean's healer, sat in the second sled's carry-box cradling a golden sphere in her hands. The flat top held several small gauges and dials. Olwen screwed up her face as she peered at it. "If I read this thing right. I'm a healer, not a soldier."

"That's precisely why I gave you the job," Herlen said. "Let's go see."

It took several men scouring the mountainside to find the hidden entrance, a wall of shadowed rock that concealed a deep crevice.

One of the scouts shouted from inside the mountain. "There's a body in here."

"Do you recognize him?" Herlen demanded.

The scout poked an ashen face out from the shadows and Herlen feared the worst. Corin. Spirits, don't let it be my son!

"His head's gone," the scout said. "Looks like a glare-beam did it."

Herlen leapt off this sled and raced past the scout into the crevice. The corpse was of a size with Corin, though skinnier, and wore rustic garb. A trader, then. Or a highwayman. It wasn't Corin.

"It must be one of the thieves who stole the technology," Olwen suggested, joining him.

Herlen nodded. "At least we know we're on the right trail."

"And what a trail," Olwen said.

Herlen looked up and followed the healers gaze down the dark tunnel into the mountain. "Karlac's Bane," he agreed. "Stonepast. We should have known."

"We probably did," Olwen said. "We just didn't want to

admit it."

"Let's get the sleds." Herlen swallowed a deep mouthful of air. "There's nowhere to go now but forward.

$$\Omega$$

Corin reached up as far as he dared without risking his balance. Raw fingers scrambled for purchase. Pale light, blood-red and full of shadow, made his destination uncertain, while choral singing filled the ears of his mind. Below him, the animal noises of a growing assembly of Skin-Runners competed with the song of angel-flies. How the delicate, winged insects came to be singing deep under a mountain, Corin had no idea. He did know, however, that their presence must be significant.

The Skin-Runners had begun arriving shortly after Corin returned to the carving-filled cavern. Skin-Runners! He'd briefly considered going back to Alethea and leaving Stonepast. But as he'd told her earlier, the Legends had pushed him here for a reason; he had to discover what that reason was.

Within minutes, hundreds of Skin-Runners lined the cavern floor and many had climbed narrow steps up onto the several platforms. Most of the demon worshipers came from other directions. Other caverns? Or other entrances into the mountain? But he soon heard footsteps approaching from the way he had come and quickly hid himself within the shadowed base of the nearest gargoyle.

After this new band had passed – herding several frightened people none of whom were Alethea, thankfully – Corin had begun climbing the outcropping carved from the cavern wall. Though difficult, it seemed the best hiding place.

Grunting, he kicked off with one foot, found a new base of support, and then hoisted himself up over the gargoyle's lip and into its monstrous maw. He landed on something soft and fleshy. For one breath-stifling instant, visions of an enormous, Demon tongue flashed through his mind. Corin wanted to retch. Then he looked. What he saw filled him with wonder.

There were insects. Thousands of them. But they didn't pulse orange and white like the others. These glowed a steady red. There was more. Bent, stumpy sticks wound with coiled vegetation protruded up through the layer of insect bodies. Despite the tiny, glowing insects that covered the vegetation, Corin recognized it. Sageroot. The insects eat sageroot?

Corin lifted his hand and discovered silver beneath where he lay. He leaned closer and smelled sagcryl, its scent so powerful that his nose began to bleed. He made an effort to breathe through his mouth, choking on the acrid taste on his tongue and in his throat. Why would the drug be here?

The block of sagcryl beneath the insects seemed thick as well as wide, its surface coarse and flat, patterned. Corin had seen that pattern before— the facet faces on the crystal door. In places he could see insects at work, building, making the sagcryl block larger. A hive?

He stared again at the sageroot, then at the sagcryl block. Sage and crysalis, combined into the drug. He allowed his jaw to fall open. *They're not eating the sageroot. They're making a nest out of it!*

Something brushed Corin's ear. He ducked and turned, only to spot something small with wings fluttered near the ceiling. Bats? The wings dropped closer. Smaller wings than a bat's, and not leathery, more like a moth. An angel-fly. Corin concentrated through True-Speech and found its lone voice, hidden among a multitude of others. Many angel-flies. They seemed to congregate near the ceiling. Seeking a way out? To the surface? That had to be it. But why?

Again, Corin watched the insects building the nest. *Like bees. Or ants. Their color is different. They're building a nest. A nest! They're laying eggs.* Of course they had to lay eggs. The insects had to come from somewhere. But why the angel-flies?

To make new nests. To migrate. To find other sources of the crysalis mineral they need as food. To find sageroot. Angel-flies are the insects!

Corin didn't understand the mechanism, but he knew he had to be right. It was like how some ants have wings, while most do not. *Angel-flies are the queens. I must tell Minesh.*

Casting his gaze further, Corin saw a tunnel leading down

from the far wall. The gargoyle's throat. He knew it would be there. Just like in the wolf head. It was why he had climbed into the gargoyle mouth in the first place. The tunnel should take him to the cavern floor behind the platforms. He would have to go that way. That, or fight his way through the ranks of Skin-Runners that had filled the cavern floor.

But he didn't move toward the tunnel. *I should observe from here. I'll never get a better vantage point.* He nodded to himself. *I'll wait until the time is right.* For what, he didn't know. He had no idea what he was supposed to do here. What the Mastren was supposed to do. *If I am the Mastren.*

Setting aside thoughts of what he had learned in the nest, and what he hadn't learned about the Mastren, Corin twisted himself around the way he had come, and from his perch in the Demon's leering mouth, he peered down into the cavern of carvings.

Ω

Alethea wakened to the sound of Serl nickering in the shadows. She knew horses well enough to know he was agitated. Her barriers were up in an instant. At the same time, she searched for other minds... and found them.

Serl's snorts become threats. His body blocked the entrance to the hollow where she had fallen asleep, but Alethea could see that he was kicking forward with his hooves. Suddenly there came a burst of light, brighter than lightning, and an animal scream. Serl went down, thrashing his hooves once, twice, and then lay still.

A shaved-headed man stepped over Corin's horse. He held a plasteel device in his hand and wore a cruel grin on his face. Even in the darkened chamber, Alethea could see the mottled skin, sense the creviced eyes, and smell the sick stench of drug-soured sweat. "Lathan!"

Alethea redoubled her barriers and sent out a cry through True-Speech. "Corin!"

Lathan laughed. "He can't hear you; my men have you blocked. Hmmm? Well missy, you've grown stronger since last we met. Good. You'll be that much tastier. Get up, slut!"

When she didn't move, the trader shoved the weapon

under his belt and reached for her. Lathan's hand slapped her face, hard, before clutching her arm. "I said, get up!" He yanked Alethea to her knees.

Others moved in to join them. Alethea knew she would have just one chance. Setting on her left leg for support, Alethea lunged forward, her right knee slamming hard into Lathan's groin. The trader howled with pain and relaxed his grip on her. She was on both feet in an instant, leaping past startled men who sported amused grins for their fallen leader.

"Arghh! Get that bitch!" Lathan shouted. "I want her alive!"

The trader's voice echoed as Alethea ran. She felt her barriers pummeled as her pursuers' feet pounded against stone. Risking a backward glance, she saw Lathan stagger out from the hollow, his hands grasping the stone surface for support. "Use the sleds, you idiots. The sleds!"

Alethea had no idea what the trader meant, but ran all the harder, quickly becoming lost in the darkness, the distant pulsing red lights offering no landmarks. The sounds of pursuit faded quickly, cloaking Althea in a silence broken only by the low humming of the cavern Corin had entered. Despite the horrible images of that place, she turned toward the sound, hoping to find the chamber entrance before Lathan's men captured her. With luck, she could lose them among the stone carvings and perhaps even find Corin.

In front of her, a patch of darkness like a large bird swooping through a field rose up to obscure the pulsing lights. Then a blinding light replaced the darkness and Alethea squeezed her eyes shut as something sped past, buffeting her in its wake. It had to be a horseman with a lantern, but the light was too bright for any lantern she was familiar with and there was no pounding of hooves. She opened her eyes, but could see nothing. Something fast and silent swept past her head, a rush of air with a hum unlike that of the carving chamber. Then the sounds of men were everywhere. Alethea wheeled about, but there was nowhere to run. She remembered the plasteel knife hidden beneath her clothes. It would take time to dig it out.

Before she could move her hands, Lathan loomed before

her, his fist a blur in the near darkness. Alethea's jaw throbbed with pain and her legs collapsed beneath her. Lathan raised his hand again. Hesitated. "No," he said. "It is too soon to join your sister."

"Ilsa!" Alethea choked.

Pae-thn

Bruenor stood atop the center-most platform, slowly taking in the sea of glaring eyes, anxious grins, and flashes of wolf-skin that filled the cavern. He and his pack had shed their clothes. He now wore a fire-red wolf pelt about his loins and the skull of a wolf like a cap. Or a crown. Torches wedged among the stone carvings flickered and flared, adding to the lurid glow of the drug-makers upon the walls. A low rumbling of voices echoed throughout the cavern, almost as loud as the singing gargoyles overhead.

They were all here now. Every pack of Skin-Runners on Sindarin. He watched impassively as other pack leaders contested each other for the remaining platforms. Some blood was spilled; it worked to excite the pack members more. This was the Pae-thn, the Grand Summoning of the Beast. And he, Bruenor, would be the summoner.

Near the center of each platform, priests in wolf skins oversaw an offering being tied between the Gorging posts. Where a compromise had been reached and two packs shared a platform, two offerings were bound back-to-back, a priest on either side.

On his own platform, Arnor and Keliel had tied a young man whose rabbit eyes darted back and forth, seeking escape. They had discovered him on the road just outside Toroth, where he had begged to join their company for protection.

"There are Skin-Runners, good sirs," he had whined, "within the city and without. No place is safe!"

Bruenor had smiled in agreement, then clubbed and bound the man. Bruenor leered at him now. It was obvious he had no idea what was going to happen. Bruenor would enjoy enlightening him.

He returned his gaze to the cavern and signaled to Arnor for the drummers to begin. The murmur of voices faded as the drums found their rhythm. He signaled again and the drumming softened. When he spoke, his voice filled the large cavern.

"Priests! Niacs! Phyte-runners! Hear me! The time spoken of in Legend has come. Legend passed down from priest to priest, renewed in the rites and promised anew. Now is our Day of Glory. The Day of the Demon. The Great Feeding! When we shall run openly in the streets, taking what is ours and answering to no man—"

"What of the glare-beams?" shouted a voice.

Bruenor looked down. It was Kyrin, a scar-faced priest from the Sethnin Plains and one of the few female Skin-Runners to secure position as pack leader. Bruenor had few uses for women, but admitted that the right woman could be as cruel and bloodthirsty as any man. Kyrin had proven herself among the southern packs and a large body of supporters surrounded her.

Bruenor had known this would happen. When Kyrin failed to lay claim to one of the lower platforms, it could only be because she wanted the chief place. Kyrin was a snake, and she was dangerous.

"What of the Mastren?" Kyrin shouted. "Where is your arm, Bruenor? I hear that Herlen keeps it in his trophy case."

Laughter echoed throughout the cavern.

Kyrin continued. "You've been a poor leader, Bruenor. Your arm on display in Toroth. Your pack lying dead in Toroth's streets, slain by Herlen's glare-beams. I think it is time you stepped down."

Bruenor raised his hand to signal his men. Several dozen had remained below the platform. He had observed them move into position during Kyrin's insults. Not that he minded the belittling words. He wanted Kyrin to appear strong before cutting him down. Eliminating a weak claimant would do nothing to dissuade others. One good fight was all he needed. He just hoped that his men were competent enough to handle

Kyrin's pack.

He spread his fingers, giving the signal, but before his men could attack, a bright flash of light erupted across the cavern. Bruenor blinked. When he opened his eyes, he saw Kyrin crumple to the cavern floor, her face a charred ruin. Kyrin's supporters vanished into the crowd like so many ghosts.

"Does anyone else dispute the leadership of Bruenor?"

Bruenor sought the voice and finally found it, up near the gargoyles. A grav-sled hung there, a shaven-headed man's face peering over the side.

"And as for Herlen's glare-beams," announced Lathan the Klep. "Bruenor has them now."

$$\Omega$$

Corin crouched low behind the Demon's lip in case additional grav-sleds hid among the gargoyles. He had already felt his heart stop once when a one-armed Skin-Runner priest had strode out on the center dais and begun his speech. Even from this distance he could see it was the same man who had held Alethea in the Karlac Tombs. Corin knew only too well how the man had lost his arm.

His heart had stopped again when the sudden flash of light blinded him. And then a third time when his sight cleared and he spotted the floating bench only a few feet away from his perch. It wasn't until after the shaven man had completed his exchange with Bruenor that the full meaning of the words hit him. Glare-beams? Was it a glare-beam that had burned the Skin-Runner woman's face, brighter and more fearsome than any of the stories? And that floating bench must be a grav-sled.

The vaults, Corin realized, hoping somehow that it wasn't true. His father had opened the vaults.

The very thought of the Dome of the Ancients standing open under the sky sent chills inching along his spine. Of all the responsibilities of the Square — his father and soon himself — keeping the proscribed technology locked in the vaults was paramount. Since the time of the Settling, when parts scavenged from the colony ship had been hauled to the fledgling city of Toroth and built into the domed vaults, there to lock away all technology that might attract the Hunters, the vaults had never been opened. Not even during the Sagan uprising. And now, here, before his very eyes, was that technology. In the hands of Skin-Runners!

Peering out again from the gargoyle's mouth, Corin watched a dozen grav-sleds land in a protective ring before the central platform. Their riders dismounted and stood by them, their movements nervous and their hands clutching glare-beam weapons. The Skin-Runners kept their distance, circling, but making no sudden moves. The drumming had stopped.

The shaven-headed man who had fired the glare-beam eased his sled down to join the others and Corin watched as the Skin-Runner leader, Bruenor, descended from the platform. Together the two men examined the contents of several of the sleds' carry boxes. Bruenor waved his single arm while the two men spoke fervently, but Corin couldn't hear them. The singing of the gargoyles was too loud in his mind. He watched as Bruenor and one of his men bent down to remove something from a grav-sled carry box while the shaven-headed man stood by. It was a person. A girl. Alethea!

$$\Omega$$

Bruenor stared at the girl Lathan had brought him, eyeing her up and down, reading the terror in her eyes. There was no doubt. It was the same one. The one who had brought the Mastren to the grotto. That she was here? Now? It could not be coincidence. A portent, then. But of what? The elbow of his arm that no longer was began to ache. Bruenor kept his face hard, while inside his anger roiled. I owe you, girl. I owe you good!

"I offer weapons," Lathan said, interrupting his thoughts. "Glare-beams and grav-sleds." He nodded toward the girl. "And an offering. As clean as a newborn, this one."

Bruenor weighed the options in his mind, suppressing a smile. Of course, there was only one option. "Coin," he said. "Sagcryl. Either or both. All you can carry."

He did smile then, as Lathan's jaw dropped at the offer. Doubt and distrust washed across the trader's face. His eyes grew wide and nervous. He licked his lips and glanced around. Now, thought Bruenor, comes the deal closer. Greed. He could always count on greed.

His smile faded as Lathan turned an ashen face back to his own and leaned in close so that his men might not hear. There was no hint of greed in the trader's eyes. Only hunger.

"I don't want your money," Lathan hissed.

Bruenor narrowed his eyes. "Then take the drug."

Lathan leaned closer, his breath puffing in quick bursts. "I don't want the drug either."

"What then? You want something. Otherwise you wouldn't have come."

"I want...," Lathan dropped his eyes and swallowed noisily. "I want to be a priest."

Bruenor laughed. A full belly laugh. Heads turned. Lathan's face darkened. The girl stared at the trader, sickened. She had overhead.

Bruenor rubbed at his chin with his fingers. "Of course you shall be a priest, my friend. Second only to me. I would be only too happy to oblige."

$$\Omega$$

Lathan let his face relax and tried to steady the shaking of his hands. He concentrated on appearing calm while Bruenor passed orders to his followers.

What if my men suspect? No. By the time they learn, Bruenor will have the weapons.

He wiped his hand across his face. His fingers came back damp.

Until a moment ago he had fully intended to take the drug, and had marveled at the size of Bruenor's offer. And in that moment, when visions of endless coin and sagcryl danced before him, he remembered what he had seen in the outer chamber, and realized that he no longer cared. It wasn't wealth he craved. It had never been wealth. It was power. The ability to hold a life in his hands and do with it as he pleased. And what he had seen the Skin-Runners do — what the Skin-Runners had done! — pleased him greatly.

Lathan swallowed and his whole body trembled. He still

could not believe the bargain he had struck. Lathan the Klep, a Skin-Runner! The realization scared even himself.

$$\Omega$$

"Corin!"

Alethea closed her eyes and sought to wipe from her mind what she had just witnessed, tried to forget what Lathan had told her in the outer cavern, that Ilsa was dead. That the trader spoke the truth she had no doubt; for a man like Lathan, killing was easy. She concentrated instead on reaching Corin through True-Speech. He was here. Somewhere. He had to be.

"Corin!"

No answer. Either he could not answer, or Lathan's men still blocked her. Alethea gritted her teeth to hold back the tears. Please, Spirits, let him be alive.

Someone grabbed her roughly by the arm and Alethea opened her eyes. It was Bruenor, his angular face an evil leer. One of his henchmen took her other arm and together they dragged her up narrow steps to the top of the platform. When they were apart from the others, the priest hissed at his man. "When we have the weapons, Arnor, I want all of the traders tied to posts. None of them must be allowed to leave. Clear?"

"And Lathan?"

"Save that one. He wants to meet a Demon. I think we'll introduce him to the Beast."

Arnor laughed.

"And you, my pet," the priest whispered into Alethea's ear. "You and I have unfinished business."

Alethea struggled but knew it was futile. These monsters had developed the taking of captives into an art. They could grip her arms and not let go no matter how she squirmed.

At the center of the platform a young man was already a tied between the posts. Alethea watched the fear on his face turn to wretched hope when he saw them bringing her.

"I guess we'll have to let this one go," Bruenor said. He nodded at Arnor.

Arnor put his knife to the ropes, and at the last moment pulled back to carve a large, ragged "U" into the man's abdomen.

The man screamed as his intestines spilled out onto the platform, his eyes bulging as organs pulsed and liquids spilled across the stone. Arnor flicked his blade within the man's abdominal cavity; additional organs joined those on the stone: stomach, kidneys, pancreas. Blood steamed as it poured out of him. The man no longer screamed. His jaw hung open. His eyes dimmed. He fainted or died; Alethea could not tell which.

"What a shame," Bruenor said, shaking his head as Arnor cut the man loose. "His dying could have been magnificent. Viands for the Demon." The priest kicked the disemboweled corpse with his boot, pushing it away from the posts, and then laughed as the bloody flesh tumbled off the edge of the platform to land messily near some of Lathan's men, who yelped and danced away in startled abhorrence.

Alethea turned away, her stomach roiling. Again she struggled, unsuccessfully, as Arnor and another Skin-Runner tied her to the posts in the dead man's place.

Corin! Where are you?

$$\Omega$$

Lathan the Klep, master trader for almost twenty years, watched in silence as his men grudgingly handed the grav-sleds and glare-beams over to several of Bruenor's followers who had descended from their platform. His men shot him questioning glances, mouths tight, eyes sharp with accusation, almost as though they knew what he had done, knew that they were giving up more than just the weapons.

They are giving up their lives and still they obeyed me. Out of blind habit? Or do they wish to lay the weight of their deaths on my conscience? What does it matter? What is conscience to a man like me? To a man like I'll become!

Visions of the woman in the outer chamber, bound and helpless, wilting beneath the carving knives, flooded before Lathan's eyes. He scarcely saw as the Skin-Runners seized and bound his people. His men's pleas for mercy and cries for help failed to evoke a response in him. Hyrmus gibbered like a lunatic as Skin-Runners tied him to a makeshift post below the platform. Eraed merely stared, his beady eyes now dead as stone. Some of the others struggled and received near-fatal blows for their efforts.

When it was done, Lathan turned and climbed the narrow stairs to the top of the platform.

Bruenor was waiting for him. "You are one of us now," the priest said. With his one arm, he tossed the trader a long strip of wolf-skin.

Lathan clutched the fur and lumbered over to the posts where Alethea stood bound. He stared at her. Read the fear in her eyes. Her incomprehension at what he was doing. Tongue wagging and parched lips curling, he spoke his first words since fixing his deal with Bruenor. "Your sister was good. You'll be oh so much better."

Alethea screamed.

$$\Omega$$

Bruenor turned his back on Lathan and stepped to the edge of the platform. He didn't trust the trader, but doubted he would try anything foolish. Even so, Arnor, who stood vigil near the top of the stairs, would keep an eye on him. Arnor could be trusted, as much as Bruenor could trust anyone.

But now, Bruenor had work to do. The Pae-thn had already been delayed too long. And yet, the expected challenge had turned out better than he could have dreamed. Who would have thought he'd so easily gain control of Herlen's weapons?

He filled his lungs with sagcryl-sweet breath. *I'm unstoppable now. From this day forward, I rule Sindarin! Not even the Sagan Priests had risen so far.*

Curling his fingers in a tight fist, Bruenor raised his arm, feeling stronger and more powerful than ever in his life. Throughout the vast chamber the drums resumed beating and a low chant joined itself to the song of the gargoyles. Bruenor gazed out upon his people, eager, respectful, ready to follow him. *I am a god. A god among men who would be gods!*

"Phytes!" he cried. "Niacs! Priests! Possessors of the ancient secrets of murder! Guardians of the minions of Hell! Takers of the essence of dreams! Crushers of minds! Ravagers of bodies! Hear me now. Hear the words spoken in secret. Feel the power that is ours!"

Bruenor paused, casting his eyes across the cavern. "From the ancient ways of those who went before, those who have followed the Beast, who have lived and died in Arazmud's name, we begin the ritual that opens the gate to the nether world. We bring forth the power of the Beast. We bring forth Arazmud's awful presence. To run with us. To kill with us. To dwell within us!"

The drums beat slowly, in time it seemed, with the singing of the insects. The many packs had begun to leap and jump, circling, some upright, others on all fours. Deep moans rumbled in their throats, a counterpoint to the drumbeat.

Bruenor turned to Alethea, ignoring Lathan who hovered too close, whose tongue lolled from a gaping mouth, saliva dripping to the platform floor. He approached and stood before her, rising above her. "He's here, isn't he?"

The girl didn't answer. Gave no indication that she even heard.

Bruenor smiled. "The Mastren? No, I haven't forgotten." He rubbed the stump at his shoulder, losing his smile as his fingers felt the smoothness of the wound beneath his robe. "Oh, he'll pay dearly for this!" Then Bruenor laughed. "You, my dear, shall meet your death with ecstasy and agony. His shall be agony only. Watch!"

Ω

Corin's eyes followed the priest as he left the center of the platform to confer with his second, leaving Alethea alone with shaven-headed man who clutched a wolf skin to his chest.

Scant minutes had passed since he'd abandoned his concealment. After crawling down the gargoyle's throat he had slipped among a pair of stone carvings of feeding wolves and sprinted the remaining few feet to the back edge of the central platform. The sides of the platform were smooth, but contained enough small cracks to allow a cautious climber hand and footholds. While no expert, Corin managed to work his way up to where he could peer onto the platform. No one had spotted him yet, but that couldn't last. His fingers also strained to keep him from falling. Corin knew he would have to make his move soon.

Alone on the platform, the shaven-headed man edged closer to Alethea. One of his hands reached out and Corin made his decision. With one quick thrust, he pulled himself up onto the platform's surface. "Leave her alone!" He managed to keep his voice calm, yet commanding. He strode forward as though he owned the cavern.

"So, the coward prince appears," the man drawled. "You're just in time to watch my friends and I violate your girlfriend. Well, perhaps violate is too kind a word." A flash of dull silver betrayed a knife in the trader's hand. A plasteel knife.

"You don't know what you're in for," Corin said, taking a cautious step forward.

"Oh, but I do, I do," the man said. "I've missed my calling in life, you see. I was born to devour souls!"

Corin frowned and rubbed the scar on his wrist. "You still don't know what you're in for." Four more steps.

Laughter erupted behind him and Corin spun around. It was Bruenor. The one-armed priest had circled around from the top of the stairs to position himself behind him. The priest held a glare-beam.

"So, we meet again, fool! You don't really think I'd have begun the Pae-thn without you. You are the main course. Or have you come for my other arm now?"

Corin's head whipped back and forth between the shaven-headed man and the priest. Even if he called the Hest now, how could he fight them both at once?

"If he comes for me, Lathan," Bruenor called out, "kill the girl."

Lathan? Alethea's Lathan? Corin peered more closely at the trader who had sold his own men to the Skin-Runners.

"If he goes for you," the priest patted the glare-beam, "I'll take his arm off."

"Kill the girl!" Lathan sputtered. "I want her first. He's just one man, unarmed."

"Idiot! He's the Mastren. He bears the Hest! He was unarmed when he took my arm." Bruenor raised the glare-beam and rubbed the stump at his shoulder with its muzzle.

Incomprehension filled Lathan's face. "What the hell is a

Mastren?"

Bruenor's attention remained focused on Corin. "I'll have your arm, boy. We'll see what good the Hest does you lying across the floor. Then I'll feed you to the Beast. I know he wants you." The priest let out a demonic laugh.

Corin saw something flicker through the air, narrow and steel-bright. Bruenor's laughter rose to a howl as his fingers released the glare-beam and pulled his hand to his wounded chest. A knife clattered to the platform beside the fallen glare-beam.

From the edge of the platform rose an old man who casually walked over and stooped to retrieve the blade. He then kicked the powered weapon a distance away. "I always was good with a knife," he said.

"Minesh?" said Corin. "How did you find us?"

The manea grinned. "Came to check on your progress, boy. I take it you haven't your True-Friend yet?" He shook his head, making tsk-tsk noises.

$$\Omega$$

Minesh couldn't help but feel bemused as, despite the wounding of their high priest, the drummers never faltered. Neither did the dance of the wolves throughout the cavern. Legend was taking place on the central platform and the hundreds, perhaps a thousand, in the cavern were content to watch it play out rather than interfere.

"I killed you!" Lathan blurted from behind Corin. Minesh couldn't help but note a measure of awe in the trader's voice. "I filled your chest with the drug."

"Y-e-s," said Minesh, drawing out the word. "I owe you for that." Then in True-Speech, "Galin, you're still watching my back, I hope?"

"Have I ever failed you?"

"We won't go into that now." The manea started walking toward Corin, toward the trader.

Lathan snarled and pressed a plasteel knife against Alethea's throat. "I'll kill her!"

Minesh laughed. "I don't even know that girl." He saw Corin begin to speak, but even as the boy drew breath, Galin gave warning.

"Duck!"

Moving with a dexterity that surprised even himself, Minesh dove to the ground. A beam of white flashed where he had stood, then continued up to the ceiling where the singing of insects abruptly ceased. Pieces of gargoyle rained down beyond the platform. Grunts and cries disturbed the beating of drums, but elsewhere the Skin-Runners continued their vile dance.

Minesh regained his feet in an instant. "That was stupid." He stared darkly in the direction the beam had come from. "I could kill all of you with a thought. Just give me a reason." It was a bluff, but a good one. No more shots were fired.

When he turned back to Lathan, the trader was gone. Demons! He fixed his gaze on Bruenor instead. The priest managed to work up a sick smile. "A clever trick, old man. But a trick nonetheless."

From the corner of his eye, Minesh watched Corin run to Alethea and saw at her bonds with the hunting knife he had given him for his quest. At least he had found a good use for it. There seemed little reason for further delay.

"Summon your Beast, priest," he said. "Let's get this over with."

Bruenor's eyes narrowed and he sucked in air through gritted teeth. The Skin-Runner did not move, but held his one hand against the wound in his chest. Almost in the exact same spot as Minesh's own wound. Minesh grimaced. *How I would have enjoyed strangling that trader before beginning this.*

The drums continued drumming. The wolves performed their dance. A grave-faced Skin-Runner wordlessly slipped a bowl onto the edge of the platform. It stank of sagcryl. The man ducked back down the stairs.

Minesh shook his head. *Wolves. These truly are a pack. Hunting together, but making their leaders fight for dominance. That will make things easier. Not easy, but easier.*

Bruenor still had not moved. The priest's face was cold beneath the dry bones that covered his skull. His eyes stared at the bowl, but he made no move toward it.

A chill passed through the manea's spine. He must take the drug to summon the Demon. Why doesn't he move? If he doesn't act, his pack will act for him. First taking me out, and then him, selecting a new leader afterward. I'd rather fight one man than the entire pack. One man I can handle.

$$\Omega$$

Bruenor stared at the elixir. It's a trick. Why would he have me take the drug? It will make me stronger. Why have me summon the Demon? None can stand against the Demon!

He flicked a glance at the boy, the so-called Mastren, who stood by the Gorging Poles with the girl, an uncertain look on his face; afraid to leave the platform and let an old man fight for him.

This is my nemesis? I, the Ruler of Sindarin? With Herlen's weapons? With the strength of the Demon? This is what I am to fear? A boy, a girl, and an old man?

He glanced quickly about the cavern at the other platforms, at Arnor who had rejoined his pack to stand near the glare-beams and grav-sleds. All of them watched, not interfering, waiting to see what he would do.

Demon take that Arnor! He wanted my place all along!

Bruenor knew he could handle the old man. The boy and girl would be no challenge. The Hest would not be a problem once he was one with the Demon. He had been caught unawares at their previous encounter. There would be no surprise this day. This day he would succeed.

But it was Arnor's place to watch his back. To lend that sly blow that would ensure victory without Bruenor appearing weak. That blow would never come. He could read it in Arnor's eyes. Arnor wished him to fail. Then Arnor would step in, glare-beam in hand, and take control. Arnor would be the new High Priest. Until one of the others did the same to him.

Movement seized Bruenor's attention. He watched as the old man strolled insolently to the bowl, peered down into it, and curled his lips with disgust. With his knife he drew a line across his forearm, just below an old scar. Red liquid dribbled into the bowl. "I seem to recall," he said, "that you prefer blood in your wine."

Bruenor tightened his fist. "The offering is more than blood. It is hunger and it is pain. It is power and it is dominance. It is lust and it is death."

"My feelings exactly where wine is concerned," the old man said. He tore a strip of cloth from his worn vestments to staunch the wound. "Go ahead and summon your Demon. Let's get all this hunger and dominance whatnot over with. I've had a long and trying day." With that, the old man backed away.

Bruenor resisted the urge to strangle the old geezer right then and there. Even onehanded he could break the graybeard's scrawny neck. Something held him back and it was more than the old man's knife. Something else was going on here, a confrontation beyond what was immediately apparent; but he couldn't fathom what it was.

The drums continued to beat and the wolves to dance, but Bruenor could feel the restlessness growing among the Skin-Runners. They saw his inaction as weakness. Despite his misgivings, there was only one thing Bruenor could do. Very well. The old man wants the Demon. The Demon he shall have.

No one interfered as Bruenor strode toward the elixir with long, certain steps. He crouched to lift the bowl. The pungent stink of blood and sagcryl lent him strength. I'm weak, he told himself. The Demon will make me strong. Raising the bowl to his lips, he drank. Deep, deeper than he ever had.

The intensity of the drums surged ahead; the singing of the insects seemed to rise with it. Bruenor felt the drug rush through him, straining against his stumped shoulder. He grew dizzy. Fought against it. Overcame. There would be no collapsing in disgrace like that first night in Toroth. Not this night.

He glared at the other platforms. Blood had been spilt. The elixir was being shared, the Demon summoned. The Pae-thn had begun, the gathering of Demons. Bruenor felt the approach of frenzy, could hear the voices of the cavern. Packs of Skin-Runners ran with the drug, their howling filling his ears. The Demons were coming, the slaughter about to begin.

"You've lost," he growled at the old man, his voice low from the drug. Already he could feel the strength of the Demon rush into him.

"Come to me!" he groaned, raising his one arm in the air. His empty shoulder burned with acid, but he didn't care. The Demon was coming. "Arazmud! Come to me!"

The Mastren

Corin watched the exchange between Minesh and the Skin-Runner Priest with rising horror. What did Minesh think he was doing? Despite his barriers, Corin felt the pressure mounting. From all around him came wave after wave of vile emotion, though no one attacked him directly. Not yet.

He flicked his gaze from platform to platform. Innocent people bound to Gorging Poles were either dead or dying, their minds and bodies mere playthings for their tormentors. The priests, dressed in animal skins, eyes burning red with hate, blood lust, and cruelty, carved away at their victims with delicate strokes of their knives.

Madness! He knew where the pressure was coming from. Beside him, Alethea pulled herself tighter beneath his shoulder. It was the Skin-Runner grotto all over again. A hundred Skin-Runner grottos.

"I hope you're up for this."

The True-Spoken thought came unexpectedly, breaking through the mounting noise of the cavern. My True-Friend? Hope soared in Corin's breast and then died as he realized the Sender was Minesh, ten paces away and as powerful as ever.

"Me?" Corin sent back. "You're the one doing everything."

"Not everything, I hope," Minesh answered.

Then Corin heard the manea groan aloud. He looked and found Minesh slumped on the floor with Bruenor standing over him. The priest's eyes burned like blood and his face radiated hate. It was not a human face.

Minesh's thoughts flooded into Corin's mind. "Now, Corin. Kill him. You must do it now!"

The manea groaned again as Bruenor ripped the knife from his hands. The priest's blood-red eyes searched the old man's body as though trying to decide where to begin.

"Do something!" Alethea cried.

Corin's gaze searched the platform. Bruenor had dropped a glare-beam. Where was it?

Wracking sobs filled the air. Corin looked back to find Bruenor sawing at Minesh's shoulder. Blood already poured from the old man's chest, an old wound reopened. Corin's eyes widened to see the glow of the Hest attempting to rise from the manea's forearm.

Bruenor saw it too. Minesh screamed as the Demon within the priest smashed against his barriers. The manea was dead even before the knife buried itself in his heart.

Howling exploded throughout the cavern. Drumbeats rose to drown out the singing of the insects. Several white lines of glare-beams flashed; insects screamed and pieces of ceiling rained down onto the cavern floor.

Corin didn't turn to see. Instead he stared at the manea lying dead on the platform, and then up at the priest.

What stood there no longer resembled a man. Bruenor had grown taller and bulkier and now had two arms. Thick, oily hair had sprung out on his face and arms, and the flesh appeared to be rotting. The priest had lost his wolf's-head cap, but his jaw now resembled that of a wolf, long and full of sharp teeth. A thick, red tongue lolled between pointed incisors. The Beast's glaring red eyes met his.

Corin stepped back, once, twice, pulling Alethea with him. She stumbled and fell. He dragged her along.

"Corin. Use the Hest!"

"Minesh?" Corin's gaze swept back to the manea. The old man was surely dead.

"There's no time for that. Use the Hest! While the Beast is inside Bruenor, you can destroy it. Permanently."

Corin placed himself between Alethea and the Beast, and stood tall despite his fear. The Demon laughed, a deep, cold laugh that had nothing to do with humanity. Corin saw what it had done to Minesh, what it could do to him, but he had no choice. It was stand and fight or be killed while running away. Either way, he would be as dead as Minesh. But was Minesh truly dead?

"The Hest, Corin."

Breathing deep, Corin strengthened his barriers and summoned the Hest. It didn't come. Like Minesh, his wrist glowed like a dying coal. The pain was there, as excruciating as ever, but no blade.

The Beast howled at him with the sound of a thousand angry sten-bears. Corin saw the inhuman gleam in its eye, knew what was coming, and held his barriers firm. His thoughts raced. If Minesh fell so easily, what chance have I?

Then suddenly the Hest was there, its brilliant flame brighter than any glare-beam.

The Beast shrieked with rage and lunged left, then right, uncertain.

Corin looked down and saw that Alethea had grasped his wrist as she had when they cut through the crystal barrier. He grinned as Alethea rose to her feet to stand with him.

The Beast backed away to the edge of the platform, and it seemed to Corin that it would jump. Howls of contempt rose from the other platforms and it halted.

The other priests still appeared as men, obscene men with drug-reddened eyes, but their cries halted the Beast. When Corin looked from the corner of his eye, however, he saw images of Demons super-imposed on the priests.

The Beast spoke, its awkward jaws twisting to form a word that came out as a low, alien growl. "Mastren!" Then it spat and charged.

Corin felt the assault on his barriers before the Demon took its first step. Its strength was unbelievable.

"You can't keep it out." The sending was Minesh's. "Let it in, accept it, encompass it, and consume it. Then use the Hest to slay the Beast. It's the only way."

Minesh? How could it be? And what kind of advice was that? Was this a Demon trick?

"Have no fear," the manea said. "I am with you, now and forever, your True-Friend."

True-Friend? Corin dropped his barriers and a flood of evil engulfed him.

The Beast was so surprised by Corin dropping his barriers, that it stopped its charge and stood staring at him.

Hatred, lust, hunger, and a dozen unnamed emotions Corin never knew existed assaulted his senses, the shock so great that it shut down his nerves before registering on his face. Darkness and cold. And a stink he couldn't describe. Memories of Minesh's hutch joined with the attack. The night he had accepted the Hest. It had been the same then.

"Yes," the manea's voice was in his mind. "The Beast was there that night, hoping to take you before you were ready."

"Am I ready now?"

Minesh didn't answer. Instead he said, "The Beast is alien. Its hunger has nothing to do with Man. Its hatred is not your hatred Its lust not your lust. Its corruption not your corruption. Let it go."

Corin mentally turned to face the Beast's attack. Waves of dark emotion washed against his soul, pressing him backward. He picked a rising swell that looked like arrogance and tasted it. It had a strange texture, a coarse grain, nothing like the silk-smooth pride he had cultivated while growing up in his father's tower. He spat it out.

Next he chose hunger, a sensation he learned well his first few days in the wilderness. The beast's hunger had nothing to do with sustenance, the need for nourishment. He ignored it and latched onto the Demon's anger. It was incomprehensible to him.

Emotion by emotion, the beast's assault slid off Corin. He stepped forward, bringing Alethea with him.

A chorus echoed throughout the cavern. "Mastren. Mastren. He masters the Beast."

Doubt washed over the Demon's face. Then it turned its hungry gaze on Alethea.

"No!" Corin cried. The Hest dimmed as he thrust Alethea behind him, then brightened again as he advanced alone toward the Beast.

The Demon shrieked and leapt to the left. Corin followed it, lashing out with the Hest. The Beast dodged and came up behind him, swinging its hands like the claws of a sten-bear. Corin turned and ducked feeling the claws catch hold, then dove forward and down, leaving his sten-bear coat in the Beast's grasp. He slid onto his back, waving the Hest before him like a shield. The Beast threw the coat at him, hoping, perhaps, to encumber the blade; the Hest tore through the thick hide like paper.

Corin scrabbled back to his feet while the Beast shrieked and lunged with its long arms, coming within inches of Corin's face and chest. Corin refused to back away, but lashed out with the Hest. The Beast screamed in agony as the Blade connected. It stumbled to its knees, its right arm severed at the shoulder just like Corin had done to Bruenor. No blood flowed.

Corin had let Bruenor live after severing his arm. He would not make the same mistake twice. Drawing the Hest back behind his shoulder, he swept out with his arm. Light seared through flesh and the Beast's head rolled off its shoulders. The carcass stood for a moment, then collapsed to the platform floor. But Corin struck at it again and again. He wanted to be sure.

"Enough." It was Minesh. "The Beast is dead. Twice dead. And will trouble us no more."

The Hest faded as Corin looked up, the agony of the Shard fading with it. All about the cavern the wolves had ceased their dance. Many of them continued to chant. "Mastren. Mastren." Others lay on the floor weeping, some tearing at their own flesh.

On the platforms the priests appeared subdued. Many still had the aspect of Demons about them, a double image of man and beast. Corin assumed that the Demons could not leave until the drug wore off. Perhaps that is why the Beast had not left Bruenor, had not fled back beyond the Shroud.

Bruenor's pack was another story. They still held the glare-beams.

"Duck!"

Corin dove to the floor as Minesh's voice echoed in his

mind. A beam of brilliance flashed where Corin had stood. It struck one of the two Gorging Posts, blasting the stone to rubble.

"So that's how you did it."

"Never mind that now. This is going to be a little trickier than the Beast, though not nearly as important."

"What do I do?"

"You wait."

Corin blinked. "Wait? For what?"

"For Herlen to finish his part."

"My father? Here?"

"You always did underestimate that man. Well, I guess I have as well on occasion."

Alethea crawled over beside him as white flashes began crisscrossing the cavern like lightning, only with gravel for rain. The Skin-Runners resumed their wailing as glare-beams fired from grav-sleds carved into their numbers. Bruenor's men fired back with the weapons Lathan had brought them. Many of the weapons struck the walls and ceiling, sending broken rock in all directions. The destruction drew attention away from the central dais. Corin smiled at Alethea as she took his hand and squeezed.

"You were very brave," she said.

"Then why is my heart racing?"

"Probably," she said slowly, "because I'm holding your hand."

Corin laughed, was not able to keep from laughing, and Alethea laughed with him.

They watched as grav-sleds raced through the air, firing and drawing fire, pushing Bruenor's men and the other Skin-Runners toward one end of the cavern. Among the carved statues, the Toroth Guard advanced, cutting down unarmed Skin-Runners where they stood. Herlen's grav-sleds seemed to outnumber the armed Skin-Runners. It was only a matter of time. There really was nothing Corin could do, but wait.

"Kill me!"

Corin looked up. Lathan stood there, a wolf skin draped over his shoulders and his face a conflict of misery. One eye burned a deep, dark red from the drug. The other gleamed a cold, evil light.

"Kill me!" Lathan rasped again. "The Demon wants to take me. I-I can't fight it."

"Demon take you, then!" said Alethea. "I can't think of anyone more deserving."

The trader shrieked with despair and began pulling at his face, tearing away flesh with his fingers. A laughing Demon face super-imposed itself over his.

Then Alethea leapt in front of him and pulled the plasteel knife from the trader's belt. "For Ilsa," she cried, thrusting the blade deep into Lathan's chest.

The trader straightened, throwing back his bloody face as a soul-sundering, inhuman sound escaped his lips. The cry trailed off as Lathan sank to his knees. The Demon eye bled from where Lathan had clawed his face, raw flesh exposed beneath. His human eye saw her and widened. "Thank you," he rasped, his voice grating. "Thank you."

Alethea spat. Pulling the knife loose, she dragged its blade across the trader's throat. Because of the drug there was little blood, but death came just as surely. With a purposeful shove of her foot, she kicked Lathan's corpse to the floor. "It was the least I could do," she said.

Corin grabbed Alethea's arm and pulled her back down to him. Bruenor's men still had grav-sleds in the air. And though most of the battle had moved away, occasional glare-beam fire still came disturbingly close.

"I always wanted to do that," Alethea admitted, a single tear rolling down her cheek. "Ever since my uncle sold us to him. Somehow... it isn't as satisfying as I thought it would be."

"There is no satisfaction in killing," Corin whispered, startling himself by the admission. "The Beast taught me that."

A shadow loomed overhead, blocking the insect light. Corin glanced up to see a grav-sled descend to the platform. His father jumped off, glare-beam ready.

Corin helped Alethea to her feet and looked around. The battle was won. Here and there across the cavern a glare-beam winked its deadly light and a fleeing Skin-Runner fell. Grav-sleds sped away in search of others. Won, but not completely over.

Still holding Alethea's hand in his, Corin walked to where his father stood. Herlen gazed down at Minesh's crumpled body.

"No more evening cups, my friend," he whispered. "No more long debates."

"He still lives, father." Corin averted his eyes from the manea's corpse. "My True-Friend. It's Minesh."

Herlen's eyes widened. "Minesh? Your True-Friend?" Then he laughed. "There's no escaping him, that old rascal. One of the Elsan now, is he? He'll continue to plague our family for a hundred generations."

Corin's gaze fell to the glare-beam in his father's hand. "The vaults. You opened them?"

Herlen dropped his eyes. "I had to. The Skin-Runners ran free through Toroth. Through all the towns and villages. Dumas is dead. And Curthan. And... many others. We couldn't defend ourselves."

Corin nodded. "What about the Hunters?"

The King's face tightened. "Now you're talking like Minesh. It's just a legend. We can't be sure that the Hunters will find us. We can't even be sure they're still looking for us. It's been two thousand years!"

"Legend," Corin said. "Just like that glare-beam in your hand. And that grav-sled that brought you here. They've been sitting in the vaults those same two thousand years. All we ever knew of them was legend. Now they're here."

His father ducked his head. "You're right. I just keep hoping... I'm the one who opened the vaults, who released the technology. If the Hunters do come, I'm the one who is responsible." Then he glanced up, his face haggard. "I heard them. They called you the Mastren."

Corin turned to regard at the mangled body of the Beast that was once Bruenor.

Herlen followed his gaze, and then quickly looked away.

"They call me that because I killed a Demon."

His father shook his head. "There are no Demons. They've been dead longer than.... They're like the Elsan, gone and dead and come back to haunt us." Herlen looked at Corin directly, his eyes piercing. "The Beast. Arazmud. You've killed a dead Demon, son. A creature that died so long ago that we probably can't count the years."

"Twice dead, Minesh called it," Corin told him. "And will trouble us no more."

"I'm certain it won't," Herlen agreed. "This ought to make the Elsan happy. Arazmud has been their greatest enemy." He paused. "Will the Hunters truly come?" There was awe in his voice.

Corin groaned inwardly. "I'm still your son, father, nothing more. I don't know if the Hunters—"

"The Hunters come even now." It was Minesh. "Mastering the Beast will weigh in your favor, but it will not save you. It is the resemblance of Man's evil to that of the Beast that drives them. They hunted the Beast once. Removed it and its kind from the realm of the living. They will not see the Beast rise again, not in any form."

"Yes," Corin said, with more authority than he had ever used. "The Hunters are coming. We must make ready. And then we must welcome them."

Herlen's lips twisted, but he said nothing.

Change

Alethea sat on the central platform with her knees tucked up under her arms. Grav-sleds flitted about the cavern, hovering close to the insect-covered walls, like bees above flowers. Where they passed, broad beams of white light erased the orange-red glow, leaving blackness. They were destroying the insects. Corin had ordered it. It seemed a good idea.

No insects; no sagcryl. No drug; no Demons. That was a difficult idea to get her thoughts around. She had lived her entire life in fear of the drug and the Skin-Runners; it was difficult to imagine a life where they didn't exist.

And no more angel-flies. "They are linked to the insects," Corin had told her. How, exactly, she still wasn't sure. She had overheard Corin speaking with his father.

"If the insects survive, there will be angel-flies. Like those in the Singing Stones outside this mountain. We can track them back to their nests. Once the angel-flies are gone, we can be certain that the insects are gone as well."

Alethea let out a sigh. She would miss the rainbow wings and the rapturous song. Nothing would be the same again.

"Change." Corin had said. "The Hunters are coming. If we don't change, we are dead."

At least Ceric will be happy. Alethea remembered the Peace-Ruler's kind, bearded face. The Circle has been telling us all along that we need to change, to follow Arwyth's Path and actually be nice to each other.

But now that Corin was acting the prince, would his feelings for her change? Alethea watched as he argued with his father, still dressed in what was left of those shabby bear-skins of his. No, she didn't think he would change that way. She wouldn't let him.

Corin had his True-Friend now. Minesh. A dead man. She had watched the manea die just hours earlier. How was that possible?

"Everyone here is dead."

"Ilsa!" Alethea spoke aloud.

"Shhhh. It's our secret. If you want to keep that princeling in line, you'll need an edge."

"But... Ilsa? How?"

"I think Minesh had something to do with it. He pulls a fair bit of weight around here. I'm your True-Friend now."

"My True-Friend?"

"You do want me, don't you?" Ilsa sounded fearful.

"Of course I want you, don't be silly. But... what's it like beyond the Shroud? How can you talk to me?"

"Oh, Alethea. It's wonderful here. People are so kind. There's no one like Lathan. And everyone uses True-Speech without barriers. And there's no— Oh, but I shouldn't be telling you this. We have rules. It's like Arwyth's Path. That's why the Elsan didn't tell the Hunters where Sindarin is, even though they could have. Minesh says it's very important to keep the rules."

"I'm sure he's right," Alethea said, thinking, I'm sure he's very right. What power they could misuse!

"Maybe someday I'll be allowed to tell you what it's like," Ilsa said. "Oh, I have to go now."

"Ilsa? Ilsa?" But there was no answer. Alethea sighed. Ilsa.

Herlen stalked away toward a grav-sled and Corin turned to face her. He saw her happiness and returned it, a lopsided grin. He looked so tired. She supposed she looked no better.

"My father wants to mount the Beast's head in the Tower Hall as a trophy. What do you think?"

Alethea frowned at the Beast's dismembered body and felt nauseous. It still looked like a giant, hideous wolf; any remnant of the Skin-Runner priest was gone. "I think it's the worst decision he ever made."

Corin nodded. "I think you're right." He took the glare-beam his father had made him stick under the strip of sten-bear hide he used as a belt, and bathed the rotting corpse in pale, white light. The Beast's remains smoked and turned to ash. Then he set the weapon on the floor.

"My father can finish up here. You and I have business in Toroth."

"Oh?" Alethea took his offered hand and Corin pulled her to her feet.

He smiled at her. "How would you like to go for a grav-sled ride?"

Alethea nodded.

$$\Omega$$

Alethea watched as Corin buttoned up a fluffy white shirt with far too many frills. Bathed and rid of those smelly sten-bear skins, the Prince looked like a new man. He adjusted the shirt's sleeves and then grinned at her. "I need you by my side if I'm going to keep overstepping my father."

Alethea swallowed. "What? Me?"

A knock sounded at the door and a servant of some kind entered bearing an armload of dresses that she laid carefully across the end of Corin's wide bed. Dresses! Alethea had never worn a dress in her life. The servant curtsied to her and Corin and left.

The woman curtsied. To me!

"I like the silver one," Corin said. "But it's your choice. Any of them is appropriate for our meeting."

"You need me?" Alethea fingered the delicate cloth of the silver dress. Linen? Surely the material was too fine even for linen. How did they make it shine like silver? But the bulk of her attention remained focused on Corin's earlier words.

"I'm still only the prince," Corin said, "but my father will never do everything that needs doing if we are to have a chance. I'll need to force his hand. Your perspective will help."

"Mine?" Alethea still couldn't understand why.

Corin sat on the bed opposite the array of dresses. "The kings of Sindarin have always been surrounded by yes-men. Decisions are never right because they are the best course, but because the King made them. That has to end."

"Yes, but how can I help?"

"You're not a yes-man... yes-woman." Corin grinned. "You say what you think. You ask good questions. You offer good advice."

Alethea felt her cheeks redden.

"You'll tell my father when he's wrong. You'll tell me as well. Also, Ceric likes you. We may need to twist his arm a few times as well."

"So we're... partners then?"

"Yes. Exactly."

Alethea liked the idea. But what was Corin really proposing? Business? Pleasure? Or both? "The prince and the pauper?"

Corin shook his head. "The voice of the people. All of the people."

Business then. "What about us?"

"Us?"

"You asked me to be by your side. Is that just for fancy dress and twisting arms?"

Corin gave her a blank look. Then he stood and pulled

Alethea into the circle of his arms. His gray eyes searched hers. "No fancy dress needed when we're alone," he said. "If you'll have me."

Alethea answered him with a kiss. A deep kiss that seemed to go on forever.

$$\Omega$$

In the end Alethea chose the silver dress. She had to rescue it from the jumble of dresses that had fallen to the floor while she and Corin put the bed to other uses. After dressing, she spun around watching the bright silver swirl in a tall mirror set against one wall.

Her hair was still a bit dusty from the caverns. She suspected it would take more than one bath to get fully clean again.

"You look just as beautiful with or without bedraggled hair," Corin said. He stood behind her in the mirror, his own hair mussed and a line of dirt that had eluded his own earlier bath running behind one ear. "We've been through a lot. Everyone on Sindarin has. We should wear our smudges as a badge of honor."

Before leaving Corin's bed, Alethea had helped him formalize his ideas. They were good ones. At least she thought they were. Just a little rough around the edges, much like Corin himself.

As they made their way from the Tower to the Hall of Peace, Alethea noted odd looks from staff and soldiers. Most were directed at the Prince, now returned from his sojourn in the wilderness, but eyebrows were raised at her as well. Who was this young woman who garnered the Prince's smiles and touches?

The Hall of Peace was unchanged from her prior visit. All of the First Circle were present. The Skin-Runners had punched a few holes in their number, but soon full Circles would be established all over Sindarin, just as there now were Squares in every city and garrison. That was part of Corin's plan.

The mood in the Hall, however, was nothing like her previous visit. The Elders seemed somber, without hope.

Everyone's barriers were up and no musicians played. Most telling, the Elders spoke aloud rather than using True-Speech.

Alethea had seen some of the damage the Skin-Runners had wrought when she and Corin had entered the city riding a grav-sled. Ramshackle barricades. Broken homes. Few people in the streets. Few children. But she felt that was only part of the problem. The Elders knew they had arrived in a grav-sled, but did not speak of it or any of the other technology. Even news of the Skin-Runner defeat failed to move them. They didn't want to hear about glare-beams killing hundreds of men and women, even if the Skin-Runners were barely human.

"Do you truly intend to move the vaults to Stonepast?" Ceric asked when Corin paused to take a much needed breath. He had been describing his plan nonstop for several minutes.

Alethea squeezed his hand.

"I mean for the Dome of the Ancients to be empty," Corin said. "That is where we will greet the Hunters when they arrive. Instead of weapons, they will find the Dome occupied by the First Circle."

"But why Stonepast?" The Peace-Ruler's forehead pinched with worry. "Why empty the vaults at all? Herlen can reseal them."

Corin shook his head. "Think, Ceric. If we still have the glare-beams, the Hunters will slay us. If we have pikes, they will slay us. If one man lays his hand upon another, they will slay us. No. We shall fill Stonepast with all our tools of violence: glare-beams, swords, shields, anything that is not primarily a peaceful tool. Then we will collapse all the tunnels leading into it."

Ceric nodded, but his face remained creased with worry. "But will the Hunters not slay us still?"

"Perhaps not." Corin took another deep breath. "The Circle has held the answer all along. This place, the Hall of Peace, is the key. All of Sindarin must adopt its rules. You must teach us, Ceric. Teach us all to abandon our barriers. No one on Sindarin must hide himself from another. And when the Hunters come, we must open ourselves to them."

Ceric sighed and chewed his lip. "The heart of Man is a fertile field for evil, Corin. I fear what the Hunters will find."

"The Hunters," Alethea suggested, "will love a fertile field."

Corin nodded. "Man may be many things besides evil. I am the Mastren. I have mastered the Beast and I know what it is that the Hunters of Orion abhor. Believe me, they will welcome with open arms the Circle and all who follow Arwyth's Path."

Ceric still looked worried, as did the other Elders. "How soon?" the old man asked. "How soon before the Hunters get here?"

Corin shrugged. "You know the Elsan; they never give a straight answer."

The Elders still refused to smile. Ceric shook his head. "The Circle has never fared well in the past."

Corin leaned forward, speaking as earnestly as Alethea had ever heard him. "I know my father. And I know how the Square has given the Circle only lip service. Those days are over, Ceric. And the Skin-Runners have painfully chastised the people as well. I think you will find that most everyone is ready for Arwyth's teachings."

Ceric stood quietly for a moment. Then looked at Alethea then back at Corin. Then sudden tears welled up in the old man's eyes. His lips trembled, a wavering smile, and new hope spread across his wrinkled face, bursting into full bloom — Ceric's smile, the Peace-Ruler's famous eternal smile.

As though a floodgate had opened, the Circle Elders all smiled, joining with Ceric, grinning from ear to ear. Many of the Elders wept openly at the prospect of long-sought dreams at last coming true.

The Circle's thoughts converged together in True-Speech, a practice Alethea now learned they had abandoned since the Skin-Runner raids had begun. No one had wanted to share his or her sorrow. But now the Elders dropped their barriers and shared their overwhelming joy, their hope of better times, of being prepared for when the Hunters arrived.

Alethea and Corin joined with the Elders now. It was glorious!

"This is what Corin means!" Alethea shared in True-Speech. "With our hearts and minds joined together, the Hunters will lift us in their arms and weep!"

THE END

ABOUT THE AUTHOR

Randy McCharles is active in Calgary, Alberta's writing community with a focus on speculative fiction, usually of the wickedly humorous variety, with short stories and novellas available from Edge SF&F Publishing, House of Anansi, and Reality Skimming Press. He is the recipient of several Aurora Awards (Canada's most prestigious award for speculative fiction). In 2013, his short story Ghost-B-Gone Incorporated won the House of Anansi 7-day Ghost Story Contest. In addition to writing, Randy chairs the award-winning When Words Collide Festival for Readers and Writers. Visit Randy at: www.randymccharles.com